SECOND TIME AROUND

"Surely you can oblige me with one little kiss, considering the hell you've put me through."

Olivia's throat almost closed at the impact of his hard body against her soft one. His handsome face was a breath from her own, and although she knew if this happened she would pay dearly, she couldn't stop him. Command of her mind and body evaporated.

John-Michael touched his lips tightly against hers, then used his tongue to outline the frame of her lips. With a deep moan, he cocked his head and plunged into the deep, sweet recesses of her mouth. When he felt her responding, he deepened the kiss. When evidence of his passion was known by both, John-Michael lifted his head. "Olivia, I love you."

Olivia, shaking with desires long subdued, kept her eyes closed. Oh, how she wanted to believe that love conquered all—but she had a broken heart that proved otherwise.

SECOND TIME AROUND

Anna Larence

Pinnacle Books
Kensington Publishing Corp.
http://www.pinnaclebooks.com

PINNACLE BOOKS are published by

Kensington Publishing Corp.
850 Third Avenue
New York, NY 10022

First Printing: September, 1997
10 9 8 7 6 5 4 3 2 1

Printed in the United States of America

To the Fields family rooted in Slidell, Louisiana. This story of family love and togetherness is for you. I love you all and pray God continues to bless each one of you.

ACKNOWLEDGMENTS

For answering so many questions and for letting me pick your brains, thank you:

Dr. Charlotte Myles-Nixon, Ph.D.
Dr. Carol Doss, Ph.D.
The Tuskegee Chamber of Commerce
E. E. Lightsey, Texas farmer

One

The university issue, white utility van rolled to a smooth stop in front of the sprawling, multi-level farmhouse. None of the three passengers stirred immediately, preferring instead to study the surroundings which they would call home for the next three months. Beautiful green fields stretched as far as their vision allowed, and a profusion of early autumn flowers bloomed everywhere. The purple, green, red, and yellow plants served as a perfect mat and frame for the white painted wood house and outlying buildings. The wind sighed peacefully in the fruit trees which lined the gravel driveway and stretched out toward Highway 85. The whole scene spoke of luxurious calm and slow, satisfying living.

"Wow. This is some setup!" Micky Zelnick, the youngest member of the agricultural research team spoke first. His mouth hung open in astonishment, and his pale, pimply face was an exhibition of appreciation.

Dan Humphries, State of Alabama Department of Agriculture employee with the most tenure, spoke clearly despite the wad of tobacco in his left jaw. "Yeah. I don't know how I'm going to return to my small apartment in Huntsville after living here for . . ." His memory failed him, even after he snapped his fingers. He turned to Olivia Johnson, who sat quietly in the back of the van with the equipment. In a booming voice which matched his enormous belly, Dan asked, "Hey, boss. Just how long are we supposed to be here, anyway?"

"Three months," Olivia answered absently, quietly. Her

thoughts and memories had her cocooned in a daytime nightmare. *Three months and counting . . .* she thought reflectively. Unconsciously, Olivia wrung her hands and thought about the ironic hand life had dealt her. Three years ago at this very place—Johnson Farms, a 3,000 acre farm outside of Tuskegee, Alabama—her dream of obtaining a PhD had almost ended, and now the very real possibility of her garnering a PhD resided at this same farm. *Just stay focused, Olivia, and you'll be all right.* She tried to coach herself into a confident state of mind. *I'll just conduct my research experiment, maintain a professional relationship with the owners, and get the heck out as soon as the experiment is over.*

Olivia was pulled from her contemplative thoughts when she heard Dan's hearty laugh. Realizing the two guys had exited the van and congregated on the passenger side, she corralled the nervous flutters in her stomach and carefully stepped over the research equipment and out the back of the van. She rounded the corner of the vehicle in time to hear Dan explaining, ". . . and the lead researcher is—"

"Olivia." Technically, John-Michael Johnson whispered the name, but since the three men were standing relatively close, it was clearly heard. His toffee-colored face wore a look of relief.

Three pairs of brown eyes—varying in size and color—watched Olivia close the gap between them. Her worn cowboy boots crunched loudly on the gravel, and the sound seemed to reverberate through the peach trees.

Olivia reached the small group of men and, with her heart surely beating loudly enough to drown out the chirping of the birds, stretched out her hand. "John-Michael. How are you?" Their eyes met and held.

More out of curiosity than courtesy, John-Michael took her hand and tore his eyes from hers to look down at the small, brown hand enclosed in his. He reversed the positions of their connected hands and focused on a princess cut, multi-carated diamond surrounded by smaller, round diamonds on a silver-gold band.

Dan and Micky exchanged confused looks and then alternated their questioning eyes between Olivia and John-Michael, their host. They sensed something was not *quite* right.

Not having the experience or maturity to keep quiet like his counterpart, Micky asked, "You two already know each other?" His face was an open book of curiosity. "Olivia, I thought—"

Dan's not so gentle nudge sent a strong message to Micky to shut up. Micky did so.

John-Michael broke physical contact with Olivia and answered Micky's question. "Olivia's my wife . . . or at least, she's wearing my wedding ring." Turning eyes the color of sun-tea to his wife, he stated in a controlled voice, "Sorry I spoiled your secret."

She knew she should have been up front with Dan and Micky about her past life here; goodness knows she'd had plenty of occasions to do so in the past few weeks as they had made final preparations for the study. But, even with Dan's thinly veiled curiosity and Micky's outright observations, she refused to acknowledge John-Michael's statement right then. They deserved an explanation and she made a mental note to provide one at tomorrow morning's briefing, but it would be the Cliff Notes version.

Focusing on her greater mission, she said, "Thank you for allowing me to run my experiment here. I know this is a busy time of year on the farm, so we'll try not to get in your or your staff's way." Mentally, Olivia tacked on, *If I'd had my way, we wouldn't be here at all*. She was not happy that she'd had no choice of where her research study could be conducted. Chem-Co, the chemical company which had agreed to co-fund her study, and the State Department of Agriculture had been unyielding in their request to have the experiment conducted at Johnson Farms. As Dan and Micky's boss at the ag department had said, "If you want the funding and your PhD, you'll

do the study at Johnson Farms. The end." It had been a hard
pill to swallow, but she needed the funding. And, most importantly, she wanted her PhD. It was the only goal she had ever
set out to achieve, and after eighteen years of schooling, she
was not going to lay it aside.

"I would appreciate that." John-Michael turned to Dan and
Micky, rewarding them with the trademark John-Michael
smile: friendly, brilliant, and to Olivia, heartbreaking. "We're
in the middle of preparing the fields for the next crops. I do
a summer, winter, and spring crop here, so you'll see all kinds
of activity. Speaking of which . . ." He consulted his watch
and turned back to Olivia. "I've got business to attend to and
Mama is gone on vacation, so Lena will show you to your
rooms." John-Michael paused, his beautiful eyes guarded as
he added, "I had the old barn cleared. You can use it as your
lab. If you don't remember where it is, ask Lena." With that
said, John-Michael tipped his cowboy hat to all. His long, bow-
legged strides carried him two paces before he turned back
and added, "Congratulations on your studies, Olivia." Before
she could say thanks he had turned and was soon swallowed
up by the double front doors.

Dan turned to Olivia and held up a beefy finger. With a
wink and a mischievous smile, he wagged his finger and in a
singsong voice said, "You've been keeping something from
us, Boss."

Olivia smiled despite the fact that her insides were in a royal
tizzy. *Thank God for Dan,* she thought as she followed her
colleagues to the back of the van to help unload. In the relatively short time of their acquaintance, she already knew she
could count on Dan to lighten any mood, and count on the
young, sheltered Micky to pique her maternal instincts with
his open, innocent questions. Right now she was extremely
thankful for her companions. As they carefully separated personal suitcases from lab boxes and paraphernalia, their light
banter served as a balm for her shaky legs and racing heart.
John-Michael's presence and comments had unglued her more

than she cared to admit. *It's just those weeks of waiting and anticipating this reunion and his reaction,* she thought in a brush off effort.

She was not surprised to see that John-Michael had not changed physically. When they were living together as husband and wife, she used to tease him about his youthful looks and Michael Jordan body. Her comments still applied. Although thirty-five, he looked no older than his late twenties. A few more wrinkles did not subtract from his incredibly long, black lashes and friendly, brown eyes, but added a wise dimension to his thin, rugged face. A generous mouth and a strong, square chin and jaws punctuated the severity of his handsome face. John-Michael had always maintained a lean frame with not even an ounce of fat on his sculpted body. Olivia knew that his leanness was a result of the long hours of work and physical activity he put in on the farm that he loved. When she recognized leakage threatening the damned, suppressed memories, she forced herself to stop her current recollections. *Stay focused. Stay mindful of the reason you're here,* Olivia scolded herself. *Remember this is the man who almost stopped you from reaching your goal.*

A loud hoop and holler halted her thoughts. Angling her body so she could see around the back door of the van, she saw Lena Washington, longtime housekeeper and cook of Johnson Farms, flying down the front steps.

Lena's eyes quickly scanned the group and targeted on Olivia. Despite her sixty-something years and generous weight, she took the steps two at a time like a torpedo, and didn't stop until she had Olivia wrapped tightly in her arms. Tears of happiness mixed with words of welcome as she squeezed Olivia to her ample, grandmotherly bosom. After a gentle time of rocking, Olivia was partially released and Lena exclaimed, "It's so good you're back. We've missed you."

Until that moment, Olivia wasn't sure she'd made the right decision to accept Chem-Co's offer. However, surrounded by Lena, Dan, and Micky, and reinforced by her commitment to achieve the highest level of education possible, she knew she had. *Now I know I can handle whatever John-Michael or Roberta throw at me.*

"Girl, let me look at you." Lena leaned back, her large hands clasped vise-like onto Olivia's upper arms. Making a *tsk tsk* noise, she shook her head. "Whatever you've been eating these past three years ain't been good enough, 'cause you're too skinny, Chile."

Olivia could only laugh. During her five-year stay at Johnson Farms, Lena had always lamented her petite frame. No amount of Lena's Southern, homecooked meals had added a pound to Olivia's five-foot two-inch, one hundred twenty-five-pound frame. Then, as now, Olivia had just been too busy with school to let the food settle anywhere.

"Lena. It's so good to see you." Olivia threw her arms around the older lady's neck and kissed her ageless, honey-toned cheek. "I feel so guilty for not writing as frequently as I should have, but I did get all of your wonderful letters." A twinge of guilt passed through her as she realized that even though she had fallen out with Roberta, her mother-in-law, and John-Michael, she shouldn't have backed away from Lena. Lena had always been a comfort and support to her, even in the bad years.

Without any rancor in her tone, Lena remarked, "Honey, I know your studies keep you goin'. I just wonder if you've taken time to search your heart and mind." With a brief lift of her eyebrows and a knowing smile, Lena released Olivia and turned suddenly to the men standing patiently in the background. "Boys, ya'll gather up those bags. I'ma show you to your rooms and then ya'll come to the dining room for a meal that'll make you slap somebody."

Micky, skinny as a beanpole and ready for a good, home-cooked meal, asked responsibly, "What should we do with our equipment?"

"Oh, just leave them there. I'll have the boys take care of that. Come on now."

As the men retrieved their and Olivia's personal things Olivia made quick introductions, and in a short time they marched single file behind Lena into the grand house.

Being thoroughly impressed with the outside view, they expected nothing short of spectacular on the inside. They were not disappointed. Walnut hardwood floors gleamed to a polished sheen in the foyer. Reflected in the mirrored shine was an antique table on which sat a huge, fresh cut flower arrangement reflecting the colors of autumn. A sparkling crystal chandelier twinkled merrily at them from high above, and a wide sweeping staircase beckoned for them to come and explore heaven.

As Lena led Micky, then Dan, to their rooms, she briefly outlined the design and history of the house. Downstairs contained two living areas, two dining rooms, and a sun room which led to the flower and herb garden which separated the house from the outlying buildings. Roberta's bedroom was also downstairs, along with a guest room and several bathrooms. Four guest bedrooms, several matching bathrooms, the master bedroom suite, and an open sitting area formed a perfect U upstairs. "We'll have time for the grand tour later," Lena remarked as she swept through the upstairs area.

Lena performed as if "settling" visiting guests was a routine part of her job, but Olivia knew better. John-Michael was a very private man, and didn't allow a lot of company at Johnson Farms, which made her wonder again why he'd allow researchers on his precious fields. *Perhaps he's getting some sort of government subsidy by having the testing done here.* As soon as she thought it, Olivia discounted the idea. John-Michael had one of the largest farms in the state. The last thing he needed was a subsidy. *What then?* her mind persisted. *What's the connection between him, Chem-Co, and the ag department?* Olivia shook her head in surrender. No one at the ag department had answered her question, and Chem-Co was simply interested in getting their new soil conservation compound tested with the innovative procedure she had developed.

Which left John-Michael, and Olivia didn't want to know the answer enough to ask him. *As long as I get to complete my study, I shouldn't care.* But she did.

Olivia was last to be shepherded to a room, and she noticed that Lena stopped at the guest room closest to the master bedroom suite, where John-Michael no doubt continued to sleep.

Noticing Olivia's hesitation, Lena shrugged her shoulders and said plainly, "The other rooms are being aired out." She turned her back to Olivia and opened the door.

Olivia frowned, but decided to let the matter go. Lena had been kind to help them settle their things. She was determined to keep her term at the farm to a minimum and maintain a purely professional relationship, despite the fact that her husband would now sleep a few feet from her. As Olivia entered the navy and creme decorated room, absently biting her lip, she thought, *Just knowing John-Michael is next door will help me stay on track, maybe even help me finish the project early.* Olivia surveyed the room and quickly remembered why she had fallen in love with Johnson Farms. Everything—the cotton fields, pond, flower garden, work buildings, and house—could have been in a layout for *House Beautiful.* In addition to beautiful scenery, the air was clean and the environment was serene. With a contented sigh, she dropped her bags and walked to the padded seat at the window and leaned her head against a pane. In a memory-inspired voice, she said, "Oh, Lena. I'd forgotten about the beauty of this place." Just looking out over the landscape created the desire within Olivia to be near the earth, to let the soil run through her hands and revel in the fundamental peace that came from being so close to God's most perfect creation. The love of the earth, of watching life spring from it, was one interest she and John-Michael had shared. Regardless of the fights and disagreements, they had always derived pleasure from the goodness of the soil.

With a wistful yet slightly pained expression, Lena looked at the lovely young woman at the window. "It really is good you're back. Promise me we'll talk before you leave."

Olivia transferred her caressing eyes from the scene beyond the window to Lena. "Promise," she said softly, and held up two crossed fingers.

Lena closed the door behind her and Olivia returned her gaze to the panoramic scene spread before her like a picture postcard. Unwillingly, she felt her thoughts return to John-Michael as she wondered where he was in the midst of all the loveliness he called Johnson Farms—his inanimate mistress.

Downstairs in his study, John-Michael flipped through a photo album. He studied pictures in that white leather memory keeper of him and Olivia on their wedding day. Back then, eight years ago, the future had seemed so bright that they had been poised to conquer the world. Who would have thought that happiness was to be a fleeting thing; wrecked by the single-focused actions of two individuals? John-Michael closed the album and passed his fingers across his eyes. Leaning back in his leather chair, his tea-colored eyes focused in a dead stare, he mentally inventoried the lovely woman upstairs.

She's still as beautiful and sexy as the day I married her, he thought with appreciation. At age thirty, she'd maintained the same slender yet curvy figure she'd had when they married. She now wore her naturally curly hair close to her scalp in short, tight ringlets that framed her heartshaped face; the auburn coloring highlighted her soft, brown eyes and mocha skin coloring. Her most arresting feature was her mouth: full lips perfectly carved for kissing, flanked by a Dorothy Dandridge mole to the side and slightly above her upper lip. In short, she was perky, attractive, and she was his estranged wife.

John-Michael walked to the picture window facing the front drive. Several of his laborers were moving Olivia's equipment from the van to the old barn. He watched absently as they loaded her precious school equipment onto a dolly and cart. John-Michael's mind was on the surprise she had given him. *Despite the years of separation, she's still wearing my ring.*

His heart did a tap dance as he considered the implications of that. *There may be a greater chance than I thought to pull this off.* His smile deepened, and he barely stopped himself from hollering for joy.

John-Michael wanted Olivia. She was his wife, and he needed her by his side. His plan was to convince her to stay, but to pull that off he knew he needed to watch and read the facts correctly. He took it as a positive sign that she hadn't filed for a divorce during the past three years, but caution advised him not to hang his hat on that. It was possible that she had divorced him mentally and emotionally, and that was the thing that scared him the most. He just didn't know how willing she would be to resume their marriage. Earlier, in the driveway, she'd maintained an impassive face, giving not a clue to her thoughts or emotions. But, when he had privately observed the genuine, warm welcome exchanged between her and Lena, he knew Olivia hadn't turned into an ice queen. He was going to have to adopt a sedate, effective plan in order to discover her feelings about him before he could convince her to stay at Johnson Farms—permanently.

Sighing deeply, he turned away from the window and swept his Stetson up off the desk. Giving the album a passing look, he thought, *I'll take her wearing my ring as a sign of good luck. In the meantime, I still have a farm to run.*

Dinnertime at Johnson Farms, except for holidays when Roberta put on the ritz, was a casual, informal affair. Knowing this, Olivia tucked her coral knit shell into the waistband of her jeans, slipped a coral-colored belt through the loops, slid into similarly colored sandals, and headed downstairs to the living room. She had purposely delayed her attendance to avoid any one-on-one contact with John-Michael, so she wasn't surprised—when she lingered at the opening of the rectangular living room fashioned in hunter green, white, and rose—that all others were accounted for.

The men were so engrossed in conversation and their beers that they didn't notice her in the doorway. She was grateful. Although she'd had all afternoon to prep for John-Michael's presence at dinner, she treasured the few extra moments which allowed her to gather her nerve. Her eyes automatically fastened on John-Michael's lean, handsome figure. Even though he was partially hidden from her view, she knew he was wearing his customary jeans, cotton shirt, and cowboy boots. Their wedding day was the only time she had seen him in formal dress, and even then she'd had to seduce him in order to gain his agreement to wear the tuxedo. Their reunion this afternoon refreshed her memory of how sexy and manly he made the simplest of clothes look.

Perhaps it was telepathy, or maybe John-Michael sensed her presence, but Olivia found herself suddenly locked in a visual jail with John-Michael. A flash of awareness sizzled across the space separating them and, as if using a line and fishing pole, his seductive gaze seemed to pull her to him. Her body grew uncomfortably hot as his bold look traveled the outlines of her body and then returned to snare her yet again.

"Olivia, hey, it's about time you showed up. We're starved." Dan's hearty greeting broke the invisible line drawing the couple together.

With a start, Olivia blinked and turned her attention to Dan and Micky, who occupied plaid, green, and white easy chairs. Pasting on a cardboard cutout smile, Olivia crossed to the small congregation and stood by Dan's chair, smiling down at him. Olivia flipped her wrist to look at her watch. "You just ate—five hours ago. And, if I remember correctly, you had three helpings of Lena's fried chicken and potato salad, and two slices of cherry pie."

Dan leaned back in his chair and rubbed his big belly. With a friendly grin he said, "It's not my fault that woman can cook."

They all laughed at Dan's stock answer. The three colleagues had been working together for the past year, outlining duties and responsibilities for the experiment, preparing a list of and obtaining supplies and equipment, and reading and rereading textbooks, manuals, articles, in preparation for the job. In that time, they had shared a number of meals. Dan's appetite at every occasion had been healthy . . . and the subject of a number of comments.

After the laughter subsided, Micky reported, "Olivia, after lunch, while you were upstairs studying, Lena took me and Dan on a brief tour of the grounds and, more specifically, where we'll be working. We already took inventory of the equipment and organized the stuff, so we did a little work today."

Olivia sat down on the couch, aware that John-Michael had moved behind her toward the bar. "Oh, that's great, but you didn't have to. I was leaving that for tomorrow."

"Honestly," Dan remarked, "I tried to tell the boy you didn't expect anything for today, but he insisted. And, I'll tell you it was hard for me to concentrate. That pond out back and my fishing pole were calling my name."

"Thank you, guys. The work you did will save us some time this week." Olivia almost clapped happily. *If they keep this up, we'll be finished before the three months is up, which will suit me just fine.* With her female intuition, she tuned into John-Michael's whereabouts. She could have saved the effort. No sooner had she tuned in than he sat down on the couch, leaving a few inches between them. He placed her beer and glass on the green wrought iron and glass coffee table in front of her and leaned back into the cushions, balancing his own beer on his knee.

"Micky, I get the impression you're a workhorse," John-Michael casually remarked as his free arm slid along the back of the couch behind Olivia's shoulders and head.

Olivia stiffened imperceptibly when she felt the heat from his nearness saturate her consciousness. His nearness was a distraction she didn't need. *If only he wasn't so masculine and handsome—or my husband.* Olivia realized where her thoughts were taking her, and she snapped to attention. She had one goal and only one reason for being here: to conduct the experiment which would allow her to obtain her PhD.

Animatedly, Micky replied, "I just enjoy what I do, Sir."

"The name's John-Michael, and I'd appreciate it if you'd drop the sir. I know I've got a good ten years on you, but you don't have to remind me." John-Michael smiled in his special, heartwarming way, convincing the young man he meant what he said.

"Thank you, S—" Micky stopped himself.

Dan piped in. "One thing you can say, his parents raised him right. In this world today, it's rare for young folks to show any type of respect for their elders."

His voice dripping with pride, Micky said, "I owe it to my dad. He's my inspiration and role model."

John-Michael uncrossed his knee and turned so that he partially faced Olivia. "So, how did you three get together?" Although he threw the question out to the group, his eyes were focused on Olivia.

Deferring to their leader, Dan and Micky took swigs of their beer while Olivia explained. "My study involves a new soil conservation compound, sort of like a vitamin for the earth, that a major chemical company called Chem-Co invented. I'll also be trying out a new testing procedure I developed. I went to Chem-Co and asked if I could study the effects of their new product, and they agreed that my study would serve two purposes—they could have their product pre-tested for less than the usual price tag, and—with the experiment being "supervised" by the university and the state ag department—they would have an impressive stamp of approval, hopefully, when the time comes to officially file their product. If my new procedure proves to be more efficient, but with the same level of validation as the current process, many companies in Alabama will experience a decrease in the time it takes to get a product approved by the ag department and FDA. They'll be able to get their products to market sooner. And, of course, farmers will rest more comfortably, knowing they're using a safe product that will enhance their soil." Olivia didn't realize until she paused to take a breath that she had gone off on a tangent. Her research project was her life, and her excitement about it shone in her sparkling eyes and smiling face.

Embarrassed that she'd exposed so much of her feelings to John-Michael, she transferred her gaze to her glass and continued in a slower voice. "I'm sorry. I haven't answered your question, have I?"

In a deep, seductive voice, John-Michael encouraged her. "That's all right. Go on." He thought he would never tire of watching her, especially when she was excited. He was reminded that stroking her in her erogenous places evoked the same animated response.

The tone of his voice forced her to cut to the chase. It raised images she didn't want to remember. "Um . . . well . . . surprisingly, Chem-Co said yes. However, to avoid conflict of interest, I couldn't use their employees, so I went to the ag department and asked for their help. They're lending me Dan and Micky, who are experts in the current testing process used by the ag department. Luckily for me, the ag department also came up with an organization of private donors which agreed to co-fund my study along with Chem-Co. We've been together for quite some time now."

"I see." With another question on the tip of his tongue to spur her on, John-Michael was interrupted by Lena's entrance to announce dinner.

Dan and Olivia, for different reasons, happily jumped up and made a quick trek to the dining room, with an eager Micky behind them. A less enthusiastic John-Michael trailed behind, cursing Lena's timing. He felt cheated about the short amount of time he'd been able to share with Olivia thus far. *That's okay,* he consoled himself, *I've got three months to be with her, and convince her to give our marriage another try.*

Just inside the dining room door, Olivia stopped short. Lena had outdone herself. Olivia walked closer and sniffed appreciatively, closing her eyes to savor the aromas. Smothered pork chops, fried catfish, greens, yams, okra and tomatoes, sweet corn on the cob, cabbage, cornbread, and homemade rolls. Olivia opened her eyes and saw Lena bring in a freshly baked peach cobbler.

Olivia could not contain herself. A smile as wide as the Nile River and eyes brighter than the sun in the middle of summer reflected her joy. Impulsively, she hugged Lena, who stood in her usual stance, hands clasped under her bosom. Kissing her smooth, brown skin which was almost devoid of wrinkles, Olivia said, "Oh, Lena. You cooked all my favorites. Thank you."

Lena simply smiled and handed her a plate. "Welcome home, Olivia."

"I swear I've died and gone to heaven," Dan murmured hungrily. His eyes were as big as the yams. He took the plate Lena offered him and stepped behind Olivia.

Micky didn't need an engraved invitation. He fell in behind Dan. They had discovered that Micky, too, could hold his own at a table. "John-Michael, gosh, if I were you I'd feel like a king, what with the large expanse of farm land you own, the beautiful green meadows, the pond, and your gorgeous home. Why, you have everything!"

Not quite, John-Michael thought, his light eyes focused on Olivia. He smiled at Micky just the same and fixed his plate.

Lena slipped out of the room and the eating began in earnest. John-Michael, at the head of the dining table which had been in his family since Reconstruction, kept the conversation light and entertaining. He was the perfect host, telling them stories of life on the farm and general goings-on in the nearby town of Tuskegee, and he even shared history related to Tuskegee University, one of the nation's oldest historically black universities. The atmosphere in the large room was relaxed and enjoyable, and Olivia concentrated hard on trying to exude the same feelings, but occasionally when she made eye contact with John-Michael, or when accidental physical contact happened, she could feel her insides twist and dip in reaction. She was relieved when the last morsel of peach cobbler was consumed. She was ready to escape John-Michael's substantial presence.

"I'm sure Lena has set up a tray of after dinner drinks in the living room. Please join me," John-Michael enjoined his guests, his eyes burning especially bright in Olivia's direction.

Standing to gain a small advantage point, Olivia remarked as casually as possible, "I'm very tired. It's been a long day, and tomorrow will be even busier. Thanks for the offer, but I'll pass." She *was* tired, but more than anything she needed distance from John-Michael.

"Fine. Then I guess I'll see you some time tomorrow." John-Michael tipped his head as his wife said goodnight to her colleagues and disappeared through the kitchen door.

While the three men retreated to the living room, Olivia bid goodnight to Lena and quietly headed to her room.

Back in her paisley and stripe-decorated room, she showered and donned a long, white eyelet gown and robe. Settling in her bed with a research book the size of a New York City phone book, she looked at the bedside clock and was surprised to see it was half-past nine. Her body screamed that it should have been later. *God, what a day!* she thought tiredly.

Ever since she had learned with finality that she would be returning to Johnson Farms, she hadn't slept well. The unpleasant memories from the past had crowded her mind. She had wrestled at night, wondering what type of welcome she would receive. What would John-Michael say or do? What did John-Michael think about the study being done on his property, especially since her schooling was one of the things that had led to the bust up of their marriage? How did he feel knowing he was, in essence, helping her with the very thing that had separated them? Given that, why had he agreed to let the study happen on his property? And would he try another reconciliation, even though she had unequivocally turned down all of his previous reconciliation attempts? The questions had flown rampant in her head, causing the already muddy waters to dirty more, and preventing her from sleeping.

On the day of their arrival, the dreaded reunion had been anticlimactic. John-Michael had been formal and cordial. And she had found out from Lena that she would have a month's reprieve before Roberta returned from vacation. Olivia had mumbled a quick prayer of thanks upon hearing that news. Toward the end of her tenure at the farm, Roberta had made her life uncomfortable. Roberta's extended vacation would give Olivia plenty of time to make tremendous progress on her study and manage a professional relationship with Roberta's son.

Dousing her troubling thoughts, Olivia opened her book and tried to concentrate on the carefully typeset words. It took her reading one paragraph four times before she realized her concentration level was shot. Thoughts, memories of the past and present, swirled in her head, making one monumental distraction and provoking a restless, nervous energy.

Throwing back the covers, she climbed out of the sleigh bed and sat crosslegged on the windowseat looking over the bountiful landscape. *Micky's right,* Olivia thought with a fond smile on her face. *The Johnson holdings are extensive and beautiful enough to make people think they're in a private kingdom. Lord knows at one time I thought I was in heaven living here.* Familiarizing herself with the acreage below her again, Olivia felt the tightly wrapped coil within her beginning to unwind as the beauty of the countryside at night beckoned to her. Recalling some very pleasant memories, Olivia felt an urge, a desire to walk the grounds. In the happier days of their marriage, she and John-Michael used to end the day by taking a stroll around the property or through the flower garden. Acting on that memory and feeling safe that the men were probably still downstairs spinning tales, she pulled the gown over her head and pulled on her dinner clothes. Deciding to ramble through the garden barefoot, she ran down the back stairs to escape detection and exited the house through the back door near the kitchen.

The smell of the freshly cut lawn, flowers, and soil mixed to create an aroma that made her stop just feet from the door and inhale deeply. The night air ruffled her curls and seemed to wash away by magic the nervousness which had occupied her body for the past months. She opened her arms to let the breeze flow through and around her, and leaned her head back to stare at the black sky punctuated by a billion white stars. Aromatic scents from the herb and flower garden teased her nostrils. With a feeling of new birth flowing through her, Olivia heeded the call of the garden which she and John-Michael had designed in the early days of marriage. The garden, half an acre from the house, covered an acre of land and was designed like a boxed, sideways S. Domestic and exotic herbs, jasmine, peach and red roses, and a wild assortment of hothouse flowers called to her, imploring her to let them ease her troubles. Mature pine trees, seven-foot high trellises with clinging vines, and imported African stoneware vases as large as tractor tires and as small as a water bucket completed the assemblage. In the middle of the garden was a working well, and several white, scrolled, wrought iron benches with matching tables. The flower garden had always been her testimonial altar, and even now, with her three-year absence, she felt the healing power steal over her, promising peace and strength. And if there was ever a time that she needed some fortitude, it was now . . . and for the next several months.

Stopping at the well, she scanned the clearing, which was large enough for several simultaneous games of croquet. With a satisfied smile, she took another deep breath of the clean, country air and felt her anxieties disappear. She stepped gently onto the wood planks surrounding the shaft of the well and leaned down, staring unseeing into the bottomless, black pit.

"I wouldn't lean too far over the edge. It's in need of some repairs." John-Michael spoke quietly from the shadows.

Olivia jumped, startled out of her peace, and swiftly turned around to face the direction of his voice. One hand clutched her slim neck; the other settled at her stomach. "John-Michael, you scared me." The sparse mercury lights did not fully extend to where he sat. She squinted to discern his outline and form.

"I'm sorry." The red glare at the end of John-Michael's cigarette flared as he inhaled. "I only meant to warn you."

Olivia's innocent eyes followed the red glare to the ground, where seconds later it was extinguished altogether. "What are you doing here?" A little teed off that he had spoiled her cleansing act, and suffering from some residual fear, Olivia spoke in a voice higher than usual, and tight.

"I live here," John-Michael stated calmly. "But I bet I can guess what you're doing." John-Michael's shadow grew into living flesh as it disassociated itself from the darkness in the corner of the clearing. With slow easy strides, he walked toward her. Although he still had on the same clothes from dinner, he'd untucked and unbuttoned his shirt and, like her, had discarded covering for his feet.

John-Michael reached her. With her standing on the planks, he was still inches taller. "You came to hug and kiss me good night, like you did Lena."

The clutch hold she'd assumed earlier tightened as she stammered. "I . . . I just . . . I needed some fresh air. I . . ." Although she fought like hell to ignore his suggestive undertones and his fresh, male scent mixed with the heady aromas from the garden, she lost the battle. Physical awareness flashed through her like an electric shock.

"You know, Olivia, when you pulled up to the house this afternoon I thought I would feel anger and bitterness toward you. But when you stepped around the corner of that van, looking as fetching as a new spring hat, every antagonistic thought I'd ever had fled. All I wanted to do was to haul you into my arms, kiss the living daylights out of you, and never let you go." John-Michael closed in on her, blocking her with his body. He left her with one direction—down the well. "But then, from my previous attempts to reconcile our lives, you know that I love you, that I'll always love you, don't you?"

His nearness was starting a stampede in her blood, and she

was helpless to stop it. Her body had acquired a will of its own. Without any prompting from her, memories of John-Michael's strong, lean body poised over her during lovemaking flashed through her troubled mind. "John-Michael, please. We've been through this before."

"Then let's go through it one more time. Why won't you come home?" he pleaded, fighting for his future.

"John-Michael. We both know that it takes more than love to keep a marriage together. It's fruitless to rehash all this. All I want is to complete my study," Olivia said, appealing to his sensible side.

A moment of silence prevailed while Olivia watched John-Michael's face change from open appeal to closed book. "All right, Olivia. For now, I'll be satisfied with a kiss." Without waiting for her agreement, his hand crept around her waist, drawing her to him. "Surely you can oblige me with one little kiss, considering the hell you've put me through."

Olivia's throat almost closed at the impact of his hard body against her soft one. His handsome face was a breath from her own and, although she knew if this happened she would pay dearly, she couldn't stop him. Command of her mind and body evaporated.

John-Michael touched his lips lightly against hers, then used his tongue to outline the frame of her lips. With a deep moan, he cocked his head and plunged into the deep, sweet recesses of her mouth. When he felt her responding, he deepened the kiss. The small space that had separated their bodies was eliminated. Another moan escaped, from which of them, they didn't know. When evidence of his passion was known by both, John-Michael lifted his head. "Olivia, I love you."

Olivia, shaking with desires long subdued, kept her eyes closed. Oh how, she wanted to believe that love conquered all—but she had a broken heart that proved otherwise.

With no verbal response from her, John-Michael continued his assault. His hands moved freely over her flat stomach and caressed her breasts while his mouth planted sensual kisses along her jaw, chin, on her eyelids, and returned to reclaim her mouth. A warning flashed through her head that she should stop John-Michael, but her body refused to obey. What they were doing felt so right that she could only melt at his touch and sigh in surrender.

It was John-Michael who brought them back to reality. With Olivia reeling from his ministrations, he backed away, setting her gently away from him. "Thanks for the kiss, and think about what I said." He kissed the tip of her nose and walked away. "Good night, Olivia."

The dark shadows swallowed him, leaving Olivia alone in the darkness. Wrapping her arms around her middle, she felt exposed and lonely. After several deep breaths, Olivia walked to the bench John-Michael had previously occupied. *Oh, God what a mess. Why did I allow that to happen?*

A well of emotions kept her from answering that question. She had to remind herself she was there to fulfill her PhD requirements. Now, John-Michael had upped the stakes. The task of remaining on track had become more difficult. *It would be foolish to start up with him again,* she warned herself. The past had proved neither she nor their marriage had been a priority in his life. He'd made it clear during their brief time together that the farm was his main priority, followed closely by his mother's needs. *I will stick to my original agenda! I will leave this farm in three months . . . if not sooner!*

Her fingers massaged her throbbing, swollen lips. She trembled at the thought that he still had the power to wreck her physically; his kisses still left her weak and vulnerable. "No more kisses, no more touching . . . no more." She pounded her fist in her open hand.

Running her fingers through her curls, Olivia slowly returned to the house to her bedroom. After safely reaching her room, she switched her jeans for her nightgown, refusing to think about the immediate past. After several hours of tossing and turning, fluffing and re-fluffing the pillow, though, she resigned from the sleep game. The little peace she'd been able to recover in the garden had fled with the potent kisses John-Michael had extracted from her. Rising for a second time that night, she dressed and went out to work in the old barn.

Two

Olivia rummaged through the foam and newspaper shavings in the open equipment box. While her fingers searched for any remaining research paraphernalia, her mind continued to run an instant replay of the brief, private interlude she'd shared with John-Michael. No matter how many times she forced herself to think of other subjects, her mind always returned to John-Michael's touches, kisses, and words of love. *He still has the power to arouse me with very little effort,* she thought. *I've got to stay focused. I can't let John-Michael's attentions sway my course.*

The door to the old barn opened and Olivia tensed. She straightened and turned front and center as Dan and Micky entered their temporary work environment. A sigh of relief whispered through her lips.

"Yo, Olivia, we missed you at breakfast," Dan boomed as he walked to the stainless steel table and snagged a stool with his cowboy boot.

Watching him tug on his belt buckle, Olivia was reminded yet again that, if not for his curly, black hair, and copper skin coloring, he could pass as a body double for Carl, the father figure on *Family Matters;* his heart was just as genuine and gentle as Carl's, too.

"Good morning, guys." Olivia's smile was as perky as a cheerleader's although the dark circles under her eyes tarnished her genuine attitude. The previous night, she had worked well past midnight before physical exhaustion claimed her, shutting down her mind and allowing her to sleep for a few hours. She'd risen before the sun and had been back in the barn by 6:00 A.M. "I just finished doing a double check on the inventory and supplies. I really appreciate the work you did yesterday. It helped a lot."

"Does that mean we can knock off early this Friday afternoon so me and Little John can go fishin'?" Dan's friendly pat on his partner's back almost sent Micky sprawling across the barn.

"We'll see," Olivia hedged. She really did appreciate the prep work, but after her encounter with John-Michael, she wanted to get this experiment over with as soon as possible.

Micky rubbed his stomach. "You should have been at breakfast. It was grand."

Her thoughts of John-Michael had affected Olivia like a severe thunderstorm affects a picnic. She was reminded that she needed to share some of her past with her colleagues. *Now is as good a time as any.*

"Speaking of John-Michael—before we get started, I feel as if I owe you guys an explanation about that little surprise I pulled on you yesterday."

"Only if you want to, Olivia. You don't owe us anything but the opportunity to test this new procedure and work in the field. All else is none of our business." Dan's words truly stemmed from his heart.

"Thanks, Dan, I really appreciate that. But, there's really not a lot to tell." Olivia shrugged her thin shoulders and launched into a greatly edited version of the past. "It's true. John-Michael and I are married, have been since June of eighty-six."

Olivia pulled up a seat and hitched a foot on one of the four rungs on the stool. "You know I've lived in Huntsville for the last three years, so obviously we've been separated for that long. We were young, made some mistakes, learned a lot from the experience, but for the most part we've lived our lives as individuals. That's it. If you have any questions, shoot,

because after this, I'm not planning to talk about it any more."
Olivia waited, trying to retain a calm exterior. Her gut was
twisting and churning as if it were playing Twister, in anticipation of the probing questions that might follow.

"Your relationship with your husband won't impact this
study, will it?" Micky asked with eyes wide and innocent. His
young face was one big question mark.

"One has no bearing on the other." Olivia shifted in her
seat, the garden scene rolled out like a red carpet in her mind.
She wondered if she had just told a lie. "John-Michael gra-
ciously allowed the ag department to use his farm for this
study, and I'm thankful. This is a professional study that's cost-
ing quite a bit of money. I'm confident it will be a success."
Olivia smiled and proudly proclaimed, "How can it not be,
when three sharp minds are involved?"

"Here, here." Dan saluted. "I think enough time's been had
on this subject. I say we get to work. I'm dying to get to those
fields."

The threesome turned earnestly to the reason for their being
in Tuskegee. They got busy, setting up the lab and marking
the test and control fields. When John-Michael had mentioned
the old barn as the base for the study, Olivia had cringed.
When she had lived at Johnson Farms, the barn had been used
as a storage house for farm implements that were in need of
repairs or outdated, and several old trucks greatly in need of
paint and engine parts. She had hoped for a cleaner, more
sterile environment. The surprise had been hers when she entered the structure last night. It had had a complete makeover.

Over the passing years, the outside of the two-story wood
building had been painted the same ultra white as the house.
The old pull-up door had been replaced with a sliding door,
and small windows had been added to each side of the barn.
Inside, artificial tube lighting and pale yellow painted walls
had been added to make the interior almost as bright as the
sun. Instead of the old pull-down ladder that had been in use
previously, a five-foot wide staircase led to the loft upstairs.

The hay, grass, and dirt floors had been replaced with the same walnut hardwood flooring as used in the main house. A stainless steel deep double sink stood in one corner at the back of the building, and a private toilet and shower occupied a good amount of space near it. For use for their study, five six-foot stainless steel tables had been shipped in, and they stood end to end across the bottom floor with a smattering of matching stainless steel stools.

She was delighted after she had completed her inspection of the renovated barn. It would be more than adequate for their needs. The only thing that had disturbed her was the upstairs loft. She had discovered it last night during her preview of the building. John-Michael had started implementing one of his lifelong dreams, tracing his mother's family's roots. He had turned the upstairs area into a mini-library. Several wood tables held large reference books, a microfiche machine with a box of film, tablets of paper, aged pictures of his ancestors, and black and white shots of the growth of the farm from forty acres to a little under three thousand. He had laminated newspaper clippings, flowchart paper, a smattering of office supplies, and the black leather Johnson family bible was turned to the appropriate page on one of the scarred wooden oak tables. There was a small sofa, an Ozarka water dispenser, and even a computer setup for on-line research. A three panel room divider hid a full size iron bed which was as old as the barn. When Olivia had stumbled upon his tribute to the past, she had been tempted to sit and review his work. Because she loved and was well educated in research methods, and because John-Michael had always expressed an intense interest in his past, they had naturally drifted into geneology. It had become another of their shared interests.

In the good days of their marriage, as they sat side by side in his study reading census records, telephone books, newspaper announcements, and various other materials, John-Michael had always said he wanted to help his children—the children she had not been able to give him—to know and understand their legacy by leaving them a historical account of their past; a visual and documented monument to their forefathers. In the back of her mind, Olivia had always suspected it went deeper than that for John-Michael. She had always felt it had something to do with his own absent father, but whenever she had mentioned her thought to John-Michael, he had always played it off. That same nagging feeling had struck her as she had descended the stairs last night, and, while she had been working, disturbing thoughts circulated through her mind as if through a revolving door. John-Michael was serious enough about tracing his roots. Was he still planning to have children? Was he dating someone seriously, even though last night he had professed to love her? Could he love one woman and be married to another? Would he ask for a divorce, if that was the case? These thoughts had whirled relentlessly through her mind, making her redo lots of work. She had been grateful when physical exhaustion had claimed her body and mind.

After a couple of hours of labeling, arranging and joking around, the group was interrupted. John-Michael entered the lab, bearing a fresh carafe of coffee. His light eyes scanned the group, lighting on Olivia, who was bent over a box with her back to him. The sight was attractive, and more tempting than John-Michael cared to admit.

"Lena thought you all might like some more coffee." John-Michael set the container on the steel table. He placed the platter in his other hand, next to the carafe. Lifting the cloth napkin, he revealed pastries and biscuits.

At the sound of his voice Olivia did her darndest to straighten as quickly as possible. When she turned to face her husband, she was struck again by his handsome being—from the top of his head to the tips of his boots, he was manly, attractive, and too damn sexy for his—and her—own good. Her eyes on autopilot, she locked in on his lips, those full lips that had given great pleasure to her last night—a sinful pleasure that she must never experience again. Her reprimand didn't stop an intense sexual need from ripping through her small body, causing her to almost drop the glass vial in her hand.

"Good morning, Olivia. We missed you at breakfast." John-Michael's beautiful eyes scanned the various shapes and sizes of dishes, vials, test tubes, burners, plastic bottles—with colored and clear liquids in them—and opened, disgorged boxes. It looked like unpacking time at any household, except that household goods had been replaced with scientific instruments.

"I was up early . . . working. I told Lena on my way out that I was skipping breakfast." Olivia followed John-Michael's gaze, imagining what he was seeing. The place was in a shambles, but by the end of the day it would look like a mini-lab.

"I see." John-Michael ambled closer to the tables and picked up a few items, inspecting them as if they were part of a new crop. "Do you have everything you need?"

"I think we're okay for now. I'll know better at the end of the day when we have things better organized."

John-Michael turned light, piercing eyes to her, "You'll tell me if you need anything, right?"

Meeting his eyes, acknowledging the gauntlet he threw down, she wasn't altogether sure he was talking about her PhD needs. "Sure." Olivia's eyes did a quick search of the table contents. "Um . . . as a matter of fact, there's more paperwork the university would like you to sign, but I can't seem to locate it right now." Olivia picked up a few sheets of crumpled newspaper and moved a few small implements on the nearest table, but found no forms.

"Come see me when you find them." John-Michael turned to leave but stopped at the door. "Lunch will be ready at high noon, and Olivia, if you have a few minutes after lunch I'd like to talk to you, anyway."

"Okay." Olivia's heart sank. *He wants to talk about last night, I just know it.* Olivia returned to the search that John-Michael had interrupted, her mind going a mile a minute and her heart beating even faster. *If he thinks I'm going to fall back into his arms again he's in for disappointment. I'm just here to conduct this study so I can get my Ph.D.* Throughout the rest of the morning she continued her mental litany; reaffirming her number one goal. With the help of Dan and Micky's friendly teasing and the consuming work, she managed to stay focused on the lab setup. However, snatches of thoughts centering on John-Michael, their pending conversation, and the geneology room he was creating upstairs wavered in and out of her consciousness.

It had always been very important to John-Michael to have children and to ensure that his offsprings understood and appreciated their history. Sadly, Olivia thought, *The only thing missing now is the children.* That thought led to the miscarriages they had suffered, the arguments that quickly followed the final miscarriage, and Roberta's condemning statements of her. A bubble of bitterness welled within her, and when the tears threatened to flow she retreated to the private bathroom.

Dan and Micky went on blindly with their work, totally ignorant of the emotional upheaval racking their leader.

Upstairs will be a constant reminder of what could have been. I've got to be strong in order to make it through the next three months with that reminder literally hanging over my head. Olivia blew her nose, wiped her eyes and, taking a deep breath, rejoined the men at work. *Just concentrate on the task at hand, Olivia. After a few months you can go back to Huntsville and forget this place: this monument to the Johnsons—past, present, and future.* Even as she thought it, she wondered if she was fooling herself. Would she ever be able to forget the pain, bitterness, and happiness she had experienced at Johnson Farms? Would she ever forget the man who at times had made her feel she was the most important person in his world, and at other times had forgotten she even existed? Honestly, she had to admit she wouldn't. She hadn't been able to bury the past in the three years she lived in Huntsville. She knew she wouldn't be able to in the future. The memories—good and bad, but mostly bad—were as fresh as an early morning spring daisy.

With all the hustle-bustle activity from setting up the lab, the morning flew by, and before they knew it lunchtime was upon them. Washing their hands and joking all the way into the house, they arrived in the dining room at the same time as John-Michael.

"How did it go this morning?"

"Fine. Fine." Dan took a seat next to their host. He took a deep whiff of the delicious aromas emanating from the kitchen.

Olivia took the seat farthest from John-Michael, leaving the three men grouped in a semicircle.

Dan continued, "By tomorrow, we should begin testing. Isn't that right, Olivia?"

"Yes, as long as everything goes as planned. We still have to review the testing plan and methodology, and mark the test and control fields."

Olivia took a long drink of iced tea, wishing she could wash away the painful memories as easily as she washed away her thirst. Sitting in front of her husband, watching him entertain, she could almost feel the pull he had on her. Although her commitment to her goal had become a constant in her mind, her body and heart would not let her forget the obvious: John-Michael hadn't changed. He still exuded the same characteristics that had attracted her to him when they had dated. He was friendly yet guarded and private in his affairs, public in his concern for others. A man with old-fashioned values and morals, he still believed in opening doors and taking off his hat in the presence of a lady. Even though he was the wealthiest man in the county, he was one of the most humble men she had ever met. He never used his extensive power to ride herd over any type of business deal; he was nothing but fair, and always willing to lend a hand to a neighbor or local business. *So, if he's all that, Olivia, why did you leave him?* a mocking dark angel prompted. Without hesitation, she recalled that meeting her emotional needs had not been as important to him as meeting the needs of his mother, or those of the farm. She and their marriage had always rated a distant third.

Olivia was called from her trip down memory lane by the

entrance of Lena, who was carrying a big pot of red beans and sausage. Going back into the kitchen, she returned moments later with rice and cornbread.

"Good afternoon, Olivia. I'm only going to tell you *once* that breakfast is the most important meal of the day," Lena scolded. She *humphed,* then sashayed into the kitchen.

Olivia smiled in spite of the chastisement. She knew Lena's no-nonsense words and delivery meant she cared. If she didn't, she wouldn't have said a thing.

"I guess she told *you,* huh?" Micky half-teased, not really sure if Lena's scowling face was fact or fiction.

Through the open connecting door, they heard Lena *humph* again. Although everyone smiled, no one felt brave enough to laugh aloud.

John-Michael, grinning mischievously, said, "If you don't follow Lena's orders, I'll have to hold you down while she forcefeeds you." The men laughed, and even Olivia couldn't resist a smile at the image John-Michael painted. She wouldn't put anything past the two of them. Her smile faded when the rewind of her past played the last scene of him holding her down. It had been a lazy Sunday afternoon, one in which neither she nor John-Michael had anything to do. They had walked aimlessly in the garden, holding hands. At the clearing in the middle, a playful game of wrestling had ensued. John-Michael had easily pinned her and her punishment for losing had been to massage John-Michael's sore back. The massage had led to caressing, caressing to kissing, kissing to lovemaking.

Battening down the need to run to her work for refuge from the spirit of the past, Olivia returned to the present with a start. Glancing up from her plate, she realized all eyes were on her. "I'm sorry. I . . . did someone ask me something? I was thinking about the lab work." She crossed her fingers so that no one would see through her lie.

"I asked if you enjoyed your teaching job at the university." John-Michael put down his spoon and leaned back in his chair.

His eyes narrowed imperceptibly, but Olivia recognized his look as his "sizing up" posture.

"I . . . uh . . ." Olivia cleared her throat and tried again. "I'm not really teaching. I'm a staff assistant. I tutor, grade papers and tests, assist with research projects for the professors . . . you know, stuff like that." Olivia prattled on until she recovered from the emotional memory. "I also spend quite a bit of time running back and forth between the ag department and the university. We have a number of joint projects we're working on and well, it . . . it's rewarding work. I've learned a lot."

"How long have you been a staff assistant?" John-Michael knew the answer to the question. He was seeking verification . . . and he wanted to hear her sweet, melodic voice caress him . . . and he itched to see the animation that roused her when she talked about her work. He remembered a time when he used to incite that same excitement in her.

Since that last damaging fight that had sent her packing, he'd tracked her movements. He knew she'd spent some time at her parents' home in Meridian, Mississippi, and then transferred all her school records from Tuskegee University to Alabama A & M University to start her doctoral work. He'd continued to keep tabs on her, praying and waiting for the day they could repair the past.

"Just a year. I wasn't able to work previously because of the demanding course work. Since I've been in the dissertation stage, I find that I can handle a job and course work and my study project." Olivia was growing very uncomfortable. She didn't want to catch her husband up on what she'd done since she left the farm. She just wanted to eat and get back to work. She frantically searched for a topic to swing the spotlight away from her. A delicate chime, signalling that someone was at the front door, saved her.

Within moments, Lena shepherded Walter Sawyer into the dining room. The gruff, grayhaired accountant headed straight for John-Michael, nodding his head in Dan and Micky's direction.

"Walter, good afternoon. You're running a little late, I see." John-Michael stood and extended a hand toward his long-term associate.

"Yep. I got sidetracked, and now I'm trying to get back on track." Walter's ash-brown face split into a friendly smile and his eyebrows, which resembled caterpillars, arched dramatically.

"Well, have a seat. Let me introduce—"

"Olivia?" Walter's keen, dark eyes lit on her. "Olivia. My goodness, Girl, when did you get back?" He walked toward her, chuckling, with arms stretched out as wide as the Tennessee River.

Olivia walked into the friendly embrace, delighted to see him again. "Hello, Walter. How are you?"

"Look at you. Looking all pretty." Walter held her back, surveying her from head to toe.

Olivia giggled, remembering that the Sawyers were as friendly as they come. "Thank you, Walter. How's the family?"

"Wonderful. Just wonderful. My son's graduating from Morehouse this spring, and he'll be sitting for the CPA exam. And I don't mind telling you that once he passes that test, I'm turning the business over to him. Me and Martha are ready to take that trip around the world. You know we've been talking about that ever since we got married."

"That's good news. I wish John well with the test."

"Thank you, Dear." Walter's attention switched gears as easily as a race car driver in a qualifying race. "Enough about me and mine. What about you? What'cha been up to? When'd you get back?"

Olivia motioned for him to take a seat, buying her time to come up with a good answer to his questions. She hedged, growing hot under the collar. This was one angle she hadn't considered—the townspeople and the talk her arrival would generate. It would be natural for them to think she and John-

Michael had reconciled, and that she was back for good. Obviously, John-Michael hadn't shared news of her return with Walter, and knowing John-Michael's penchant for privacy, she wasn't surprised. However, the cat was out of the bag now, and she could have kicked herself. Although Walter was the best accountant in the state, he belonged to the "Coffee Club"—a group of mostly retired farmers and local businessmen who started off their day every morning, except on the sabbath, at the Tuskegee Grille with a cup of the owner's Jo-Jo, steaming, black, put-hair-on-your-chest coffee. There, they talked shop and speculated on the private lives of the residents. Now that Walter knew she was back, one might as well say the whole town knew.

Olivia wanted to groan but smiled instead and answered as vaguely as possible. "School and more school." Turning the spotlight from her, she added, "As a matter of fact, let me introduce you to two of my colleagues." Olivia launched into brief introductions.

John-Michael's gentle interruption saved her from having to answer any more of Walter's embarrassing questions. To Dan and Micky, he explained, "Walter is a Thursday staple here at the farm. We always eat lunch, then lock ourselves away from the rest of the world for the afternoon while he does the books." The displeasure of having to be present at the regular meetings seeped through John-Michael's words. It was a necessary evil he had to stomach.

Even so, Olivia knew John-Michael had a great deal of respect for Walter. He was the only one except the household members who knew the exact value of the Johnson's holdings, and even though people knew the Johnsons had plenty of money, exact numbers had never been bantered about—thanks to Walter's discretion.

"That's right. The Sawyers have been doing the books and taxes for the Johnsons for a long time. I remember my first meeting with your great-grandfather after my father turned the business over to me." Walter leaned back in his chair and tucked a hand into his waistband. Olivia knew she was safe. When Walter assumed that posture, he could talk all afternoon. "Boy . . . he was tough to hold down." Walter laughed and shook his head. "He didn't like to spend any time indoors, and especially not with no numbers and figures. If he wasn't out on the land, planting, harvesting, or just plain relaxing at the fishing pond with a cigarette, surveying his property, he could get mighty cranky. He was a farmer through and through—just like you, John-Michael. Now, your grandfather—Madison—he was different. He understood that bookkeeping was a vital part of the business. He didn't mind spending the time indoors, especially as he started to age. Why, I remember . . ."

Olivia risked a glance at John-Michael and met his penetrating look head on. He winked sexily at her.

In the midst of taking a drink, Olivia dropped the glass, spilling liquid on her camp shirt and the lace heirloom tablecloth. "Oh, I'm sorry." Flustered, she dabbed at the spill.

"Are you okay, my Dear?" Walter asked, concern lining his voice.

"Oh, I'm fine," Olivia lied. That one small wink had turned her insides to jelly. "Excuse me." Following Lena's path into the kitchen, Olivia retrieved a dish towel and then returned to mop the spill. Walter had already resumed the storytelling she had interrupted, but a sixth sense told her John-Michael was observing her every move. "Excuse me again, Gentlemen, I'm going back to work."

Not waiting for a response, Olivia headed for the stairs and hightailed it to her room. As she changed shirts, she recited her personal litany. *I am here for only one reason, and that reason is to complete my project study. Nothing more, nothing less.* Still, she couldn't stop her hands from shaking long enough to button her shirt. What should have taken seconds, took minutes. *Damn him,* she thought raggedly, *I am NOT going to let his sex appeal get in the way of me obtaining a PhD. I've worked too hard.*

Forcing herself to leave the security of her room, she took the back stairs and headed for the barn. With forced concentration, she thought about the answers she needed to prepare for the townspeople. *I could kick myself for not thinking about this earlier.* In the hustle-bustle of preparing for the study and her preoccupation with the reaction of the Johnson household, she had given little thought to the town's and neighbor's perceptions of her return. Before she made her first trip to town, she needed to have some *safe* answers ready to pull from her back pocket for their well-intentioned but nosey questions.

With a deep sigh, Olivia sat on a stool and framed her pretty face with her hands, elbows on the table. She was still in that position, deep in thought, when Dan and Micky returned to the new-old barn.

"Hey, Boss. What's so interesting on that back wall?"

Dan's hearty voice pulled her from her thoughts. "Hi, you guys." Olivia twisted in her seat and turned on a hundred watt smile for their benefit. "I was just thinking about the study, just making sure that we covered everything."

Micky spoke confidently. "With all the checking and re-checking we did before we left Huntsville and since being here, I'd lay my life on the line that there's not a thing we've left out or haven't considered. You're very thorough, Olivia."

Yeah, right. So why did I forget about a town full of people?

Still smiling outwardly, Olivia agreed with Micky. "You're right. But, you know what a worrywart I am."

Scooting off the stool, Olivia missed the observant look that crossed Dan's face.

The afternoon flew by and by five P.M. their work area looked like a typical science lab, with Bunsen burners, test tubes, microscopes, a multitude of glass slides, and books.

The threesome stood back and surveyed their major feat. A thrill of anticipation and excitement coursed through Olivia's body. It had taken years, but now she stood on the brink of achieving the one thing that had always sustained her—achieving her PhD.

"It looks real good," Micky remarked with a big, boyish grin on his face.

"Amen," Dan answered with great exaggeration. "The hard part is over. Now comes the fun." He rubbed his hands in anticipation.

Olivia turned to her co-workers and said, "Well, we've worked hard today. What say we call it a day and start fresh tomorrow?"

"Works for me."

Micky agreed. "Me, too."

The men gathered the few remaining boxes and stored them in the back of the barn. As they gathered their notebooks, their questioning gazes sought Olivia. "Hey—" Dan yelled, "you coming?"

"No, go on. I just want to make sure everything's on course for tomorrow. I'll see you at dinner."

"Suit yourself," Dan called on his way out the door.

Before they shut the door completely, Olivia could hear Dan and Micky discussing whether to take a swim or stroll on the grounds before dinner. She smiled and opened her notebook.

Thirty minutes later she was still reading, trying to contain her growing excitement about the experiment, when the door opened. Assuming it was Dan or Micky, she asked without looking up from her book, "Back so soon?"

"Yes, but not soon enough."

Olivia swung around and almost fell off the stool. John-Michael's powerful physique was silhouetted in the receding afternoon sunshine which streamed through the windows. Her heart jumped in her throat as a vivid image of last night's garden scene sprang forward in her mind. She didn't want a repeat performance of last night. Sensing the direction of her thoughts, John-Michael stopped a few feet from her and surveyed the orderly, sterile lab.

"Looks like you've got your work cut out for you."

"Yeah. My major professor said I really picked a toughie. He asked me several times if I wanted to change my topic."

A stainless steel table separated them. Olivia was thankful, because even with the space between them she could still feel the invisible power exuding from John-Michael's body, calling to her like a siren. She had thought she would be strong enough to handle John-Michael and the past, but this was only day two and she was already feeling flashes of heat when he was around. She blamed it on her celibate years and the fact that—although she'd had only one lover, John-Michael—his lovemaking had made her glow from head to toe, had made her forget her own name, had made the bad times seem like heaven.

John-Michael eased his long body onto a stool. One hand dangled between his legs, the other rested on his denim-clad thigh. "Listen, I really didn't come in here to talk about your project. I want to talk about last night."

Olivia stiffened and her heart dropped even farther. The litany for her return to achieve her Ph.D. raced through her mind. She was not going to be derailed. She would meet her goal, even though John-Michael *had* saved her butt at lunch.

"I didn't plan to kiss you. I care for you a great deal, and I miss you more than you will ever know. My feelings, those feelings just took control last night and I couldn't stop myself from kissing or touching or holding you. It was damn pleasant, but it won't happen again unless you want it to."

John-Michael stood to leave. "I want you to think about the future. We've been in limbo for the past three years. At some point when you're here, think about the past, so we can discuss the future. I know your main concern is getting the study completed. However, it's really important to me that I know where you stand regarding us. We can't spend the rest of our lives hanging in limbo. I mean, think about it—what if you meet some man you want to marry, yet you're still married to me? Think how awkward that would be."

John-Michael was right, of course, but she couldn't comprehend a thorough review and discussion about their multitude of problems in the past. The gate slammed shut behind that thought. She wondered briefly if John-Michael had had affairs in the past three years, and if he was ready to settle down again with some other woman. It was an uncomfortable thought which produced an unpleasant feeling.

When he left, Olivia's heart was still thundering in her petite body.

It seemed like the longest walk John-Michael had ever taken, and all he did was cover the ground from the old barn to his room, to freshen up for dinner. His body kept telling him to turn around and go back to Olivia, to kiss and make love to her until she cried *Uncle,* but after last night, he knew he couldn't. Olivia was scared of him—no not him physically, but of how the past could still inflict harm on her in the future, because of the butchering job they had done to a young relationship. He was determined more than ever to get her to stay home permanently. They had been so young when they married, and their outlook on marriage and its responsibilities had been youthfully innocent. In the ensuing years since she left him, he'd had a lot of time to think about life, their marriage, his love for her, and how to correct the future. His thinking had led him to realize he hadn't been totally fair to Olivia.

When Madison his grandfather died, and he accepted sole responsibility for the continued success of the farm, it was important to him to ensure its success. Johnson Farms had been in his family since slavery times and with each succeeding generation, except for the brief time it was managed by his father, it had grown and prospered. With the passing of his grandfather, the weight of making the farm successful to recoup the negative effect his father's mismanagement had had on the farm had burdened him. His father had proved to be a slovenly farm owner. He'd been more interested in taking the money and spending it on women, booze, and a good time. John-Michael, the son, was determined to make the farm a success, to the exclusion of his young wife and to the inclusion of his mother. He now realized how Olivia must have felt— third wheel, left out, with him blindly egging the situation on. Added to that was the fact he'd never understood her search for education, more and more education. He had finished college with pretty decent grades, but that was where it stopped for him and he was quite okay with that. He'd been eager to learn all he could about the farm from his granddad, and school was an interference. At the time, he just didn't understand her driving need to seek a masters. When she started talking about a Ph.D., he'd reached his limit, especially since he was providing her with a lifestyle many women would love to have. She didn't need to work. Lena took care of all the household things, and Roberta took care of their social lives. She had everything a woman could ask for. At the time he didn't understand but as his preacher said, "Just keep living and understanding will come." It did, and he was ashamed to realize he'd been the biggest contributor to their break up. He had travelled many miles to her parents' home to convince her to come home and try it again. She'd refused. He'd tried several more times after that, in person and in letters, trying to convince her he'd changed, that he understood her now and he wanted to work out their problems and begin building for the future. His attempts at reconciliation had always been met with a brick wall, but he was determined to make it work now that he had a second opportunity.

Last night had taught him, though, that he needed to take a different approach. He needed to back off, give her time to adjust and get her study going, ease his way back into her heart and life. With three months of convincing, he felt he could do it. He just needed to take it slow and easy, not pressure her. Three months. Ninety-two days. He hoped it was enough time to make her want to stay with him for eternity.

Three

John-Michael parked his navy blue, two ton pickup in the gravel drive between the old barn and the house. As he swung his lean body out of the truck, his gaze wandered to the barn, where there was a fifty-fifty chance Olivia might be working. This was her second week at the farm, and day five of his plan to stay out of her way to give her some adjustment time; time to erase the negative memories so that he could convince her to stay at the farm permanently. *Five days of pure hell,* he mentally bemoaned.

It had been obvious from her standoffish reaction to him during her first few days back at the farm that she was not going to be an easy convert, but he had been encouraged by her passionate response to his kisses in the garden on her first night back. So, he'd begun relaxing his initial, dedicated host duties by skipping meals and navigating around their work schedule to reduce the number of personal contacts. Every once in a while, to remind Olivia he still existed, he would join them for the evening meal or check in on them at their work site. He looked forward to those visits, as they allowed him an opportunity to feast on her beauty and fantasize about their reunion.

Enough of this hoping and wishing, John-Michael prodded himself, *it's time to step up this plan. She has to decide to stay here before she finds out I had a hand in her returning to Johnson Farms.*

Poking his head through the entrance door of the old barn,

he was greeted with silence. The hands of his watch indicated it was too early for lunch. Closing the heavy door, he turned toward the fields. With longlegged, slightly bowed strides, he quickly covered the acreage from the barn to the section of the fields they had partitioned off for their experiment. As he neared their work site, he faltered, then stopped to gawk. Olivia, in khaki shorts and a plain, V-neck white cotton tee, was bent over from the waist with a pile of dirt in one hand and a magnifying glass in the other. His physical reaction to her was immediate and powerful. The fly of his jeans bulged, and his heart thumped hard in affirmation of his affection and desire for her.

"Damn, she looks good." His thirsty gaze consumed every part of her. He could have spent the afternoon in that spot just admiring the woman to whom he had given his heart. Hers was a natural, healthy beauty that required no assistance from Fashion Fair—a look many women would have killed for—yet Olivia had never seemed to appreciate it.

"Hey, John-Michael . . . hiya." Micky's tenor voice shook John-Michael free from the physical and mental spot he had rooted himself in.

With a friendly wave of acknowledgment, John-Michael moved forward. *Pull it together, man. You've got bigger plans than ogling her.*

Tucking his feelings away, he created a blank yet friendly facial mask. He needed what he was preparing to offer to be framed as nothing but host courtesy. He didn't want Olivia to feel he was singling her out, even though secretly he had plans to do so.

With deliberate steps he approached the group of researchers, who were involved in analyzing the soil's composition and applying the chemical compound invented by Chem-Co. Every farmer in the world wanted fertile soil year round, and Chem-Co hoped to get rich from their compound, which promised just that, and . . . Olivia hoped to walk away with a Ph.D. in research methods.

John-Michael had his own hopes and dreams, and they involved not riches or education but a happy family life with the full unit intact—a mother, a father, and children—*that* was the context of his innermost dreams.

"How's it going?" he threw out to the group. Earlier in the day he had been cussing the hot August sun, but now he gave praise. Olivia's full breasts were prominently outlined by the damp T-shirt clinging to her shining skin. His mouth watered as he absorbed the sight. Dropping down on his haunches to hide his obvious approval, he scooped up a handful of dirt.

In unison, three voices greeted him.

"The study is coming along well," Olivia responded. "We had a couple of start-up problems, but with our three smart minds we were able to conquer those. Now we're trucking right along." Olivia let the soil in her hand sift downward to rest at her feet. Not having seen him for two days, she was instantly aware of his attractive features and hard, muscular body. The cliché *Absence makes the heart grow fonder* came to mind. Taken aback at the unwelcome notion, she immediately ditched the thought, and with a shortness of breath not brought on by physical exertion she added "Actually, we were just talking about how the study seems to be directing itself now."

"Good. I'm sure some of that has to do with the orderly work environment y'all have created. I peeked inside the barn on the way out here. It looks a lot different from the first week."

"Yeah, it didn't take long to get it organized," Dan, who sat on his haunches, agreed. He slapped Olivia—lightly, in deference to her size—on the back of her calf and guffawed. "And, with this young taskmaster at the lead, it was operational in record time."

"I hope what we did at the barn is okay. I assure you all of our equipment is portable, and you have our word we won't damage a thing."

"Oh, the barn is the least of my worries." John-Michael fixed Olivia with a direct look and let temptation direct his eyes downward to luxuriate in her curves. "I only sought y'all out because I want to invite y'all to be my guests at the Founders' Day Celebration this weekend in town."

"Hey, that sounds great." Micky just barely stopped himself from jumping up and down like a kid at Christmas. His eyes shining bright like tiger-eye marbles, he turned to John-Michael. "I've never been to a Founders' Day Celebration. What goes on?"

"Founders' Day is an annual event in these parts. It's a two day celebration recognizing the men and women—past and present—who made Tuskegee into the fine city it is today. We always have a parade Saturday morning, and in the afternoon there'll be contests, food, carnival rides, and loads of family activities. Sunday church service starts at eleven, and then there'll be dinner on the grounds. I think y'all will enjoy it."

"Cool! This is going to be neat."

Dan stood upright and joined Micky's enthusiastic response. "This *will* be fun. Tuskegee has such a prominent place in African-American history. We'll get more insight hearing historical accounts from the townspeople, who have firsthand knowledge."

Olivia screwed up her face. She was torn. She didn't want to put a damper on her colleagues' excitement, especially that of Micky, who had become her protege, but she also didn't want to spend any more time in Tuskegee or at Johnson Farms than she had to. Right now, with John-Michael within touching distance, she was having trouble concentrating. Images of their happy times together kept encroaching on the present, making it difficult to stay focused. She had to—no, *needed* to—keep her distance from him so she could return to her life in Huntsville with no new scars. "Uh, there's just one little problem. We agreed to spend some time in the fields this Saturday morning."

It was hard for Olivia to look at Micky. Her own eyes dropped to the ground as she twirled the stem of the magnifying glass in her hands. She knew she was making the right decision for the study, so why did she feel like a world class loser?

Dan turned imploring eyes to Olivia. "We could always make up the time later."

Stay longer, my foot, she thought. Already pleasant memories of past Founders' Day Celebrations were circulating in her mind, shaking the foundation of her commitment to maintaining an emotional detachment. The most jolting memory that surfaced was of the first Founders' Day she had attended, for it also marked the occasion of her meeting John-Michael for the first time. She had been a junior at Tuskegee and her roommate at the dorm had tricked Olivia into a double blind date. The foursome had met at the parade, and for her and John-Michael it had been instant connectivity. That date had turned into many more, and a year later they had married.

A bittersweet smile played around Olivia's firm, full lips. Founders' Day Celebrations held a special place in her heart, but it would be too painful. *No, I have to stick to the original plan to work seven days a week. It will help to keep me focused, and possibly get results sooner so we can put the wraps on this study in a shorter time frame. Then I can escape to Huntsville, away from the tall, slim farmer with a captivating smile.*

With mixed feelings, Olivia verbalized her answer. "Sorry guys, it's not in the plan. Before we left Huntsville, we agreed to work weekends. Besides, we have to test the soil every day, three times a day. I'm sorry."

John-Michael offered a remedy. "Lena will be here and, if you tell her what to do, she'll confidently follow your orders." He knew he was butting in, but he wanted his wife at the annual celebration with him. For him it represented the first blow at demolishing her wall of resistance.

Dan jumped in quickly before Olivia could voice the negative reply he saw forming on her face. Diplomatically, he offered, "I know we agreed to work weekends, but we also said we'd have some fun so we wouldn't get edgy. It's the second week and we've got a great start. Even *you* just said earlier things are going well. So, I think now is the time for some of that fun we talked about in Huntsville."

Olivia felt like a parent who had walked into an age-old child trap—using her own words against her. She hated it, but Dan was right. As uncomfortable as she felt with the prospect of spending the entire weekend in John-Michael's company, even with hundreds of people around, Olivia didn't have one excuse left. Sighing, she lifted her hands in defeat, "Okay, okay. I know when I'm outnumbered. We'll go to the celebration. But we still have to maintain our schedule, which means we need to collect samples in the morning, afternoon, and evening."

"Deal," Micky agreed, grinning like the cat that ate the mouse. "I'll even volunteer to be the evening checker. How's that?"

"Okay by me," Dan quickly answered, locking Micky into the agreement. "I'll take the afternoon."

"That leaves me with the morning."

Olivia turned to John-Michael. With a strained smile showing on her chocolate-colored face, she asked, "What time should we be ready Saturday morning?"

"How about right after breakfast?" John-Michael smiled that dazzling smile that made any female within a fifty-mile radius swoon.

"Fine. After breakfast," Olivia agreed. Now that his business was over, she was anxious for him to leave. "Is there anything else?"

"No, Ma'am." Still smiling, John-Michael tipped his hat and turned to the south in the direction of the house, leaving the mixed bag of researchers to their work. With his back to the group, he allowed himself a few moments to gloat. "So far so good," he whispered. Like Micky, he had barely kept himself in check, but when he was safely from their view, he whooped—loudly.

* * *

Despite the weatherman's threat of rain on Saturday morning John-Michael, Dan, and Micky, like a crowd at the Vatican awaiting the appearance of the Pope, eagerly waited by the idling van while Olivia finished recording the morning's observations.

"Here she comes!" Micky hollered and jumped into the back of the van. Dan claimed the front passenger seat.

"Sorry, I'm late." Olivia panted, trying to recapture her breath from the short jog from the barn to the van. "Some of the results looked a little odd, so I had to do a double check."

John-Michael tipped his head in acknowledgment, trying not to notice how her breasts heaved from the action of pumping air into her lungs. It was a useless exercise in control. He stared until the sight of Olivia climbing into the van took precedence. The vision of the wonderfully enticing way her derriére shaped those faded Levi's was more tempting than ice cold lemonade on a hot summer day. Pushing his hat back on the crown of his head, he slammed the door shut and whistled low under his breath. "It's gonna be one heavenly day," he whispered.

"Did everything check out okay?" Dan asked as John-Michael eased into the driver's seat.

"Yeeesss, but . . ." Olivia dragged the words out, concern lining her face. "You know how sometimes you get a nagging feeling that you're missing or forgetting something?"

Micky asked jokingly, "Olivia, did anyone ever tell you you're a worrywart?"

Olivia playfully stuck her tongue out at the youngster. *Something's weird, but I can't put my finger on it,* she thought. With a sigh and a shrug, she settled back into the uncomfortable backseat. *It'll come to me later, I'm sure.* With work tucked away in one corner of her mind, her attention was drawn to the masterful way John-Michael handled the temperamental old van. *Just like he used to handle me in the early days of our marriage—patiently and thoughtfully.* The thought was there before she could censor it. *Good heavens. The sun must be really getting to me.* An inner voice prompted the truth. It wasn't the sun causing her awareness of John-Michael, but the pleasant memories of their first date. She'd thought back in Huntsville that she'd be able to handle these three months with professional detachment. It was only week two and she was already wondering if he was dating someone, if that was the reason he hadn't been around much after the first few days.

Shaking her head to rid herself of the unwanted thoughts, she stared out of the window at the lush, green landscape and resurrected her goal. *My Ph.D. and future are at stake. I can set aside my history with John-Michael. I can ignore those old conflicting feelings. I'll just have to concentrate harder, that's all. Cowardly,* she added, *but, as security, I'm glad Dan and Micky are around to put as much space as possible between us.*

John-Michael's narrative about The George Washington Carver Museum caught her attention, pulling her away from her thoughts. She listened intently as he rattled off points of interest and local history.

By the time they arrived at the main square in downtown Tuskegee, the sun was just starting to wake up the west coast. Parking space was already at a premium, but John-Michael used his position as Grand Marshal to maneuver the van into a safe though tight spot near the assemblage of horses, twirlers, bands, gathering VIPs, and vintage cars.

"This space will allow you easy access to come and go so you can finish your testing for the day." John-Michael switched off the motor and climbed out of the front.

With a couple of creaks and groans from her and the old van, Olivia exited the van and was soon assaulted by the smells of a parade—horse droppings, diesel gas, popcorn, pink cotton candy.

"Let's hurry and find good seats." Micky grabbed Olivia's arm and started pulling her in the direction where the other parade watchers were gathering.

"Okay, Micky, but we've got to wait for Dan." Olivia caught

Micky's arm before he dashed into the sea of colorful uniforms. "He's locking up the van. He'll be through in a sec."

John-Michael had explained on the drive in that as Grand Marshal for the parade, he was required to ride in one of the vintage cars with Miss Cotton. As they waited at the back of the van for Dan, Olivia watched as a tall, slinky brown-skinned beauty sidled up to John-Michael with a smile that should have stopped the world from revolving. She was surprised when a stab of jealousy cut through her. She would have laughed at the woman's obvious approval of her escort, except that the green-eyed monster frightened her more than she cared to admit.

Dan joined them in time to hear John-Michael throw final words of instruction over his back. "In case you don't remember, Olivia, the best seats are in front of the county courthouse. I'll meet up with ya'll later at the Alumni Bowl."

John-Michael attached his hand to Miss Cotton's back and they vanished in the mass of confusion before Olivia could identify the sickening feeling in the pit of her stomach as disappointment. Disappointment that John-Michael had so casually dismissed her. *Silly,* her inner voice mocked, *that's what you want. Remember the you-can-ignore-him-and-your-feelings pep talk we had minutes ago?* She knew her inner voice was right, but it still didn't make her feel any better. She had the distinct impression that despite her objections she was wavering under her husband's spell.

With a sour grapes expression lining her face, she motioned for Dan and Micky to follow her to the courthouse. They followed her unmarked maze without question.

In the past Olivia had always enjoyed Founders' Day, and soon the excitement of the day crept into her bones; she found herself starting to relax. Even though she was nervous about seeing some of the people who knew she was Mrs. John-Michael Johnson, that nervousness abated after she ran into a few old acquaintances. It appeared the Coffee Club had indeed spread the word that she was back, and working on the farm in some type of school capacity. The people she ran into were thoughtful enough not to ask any probing questions. Rather, they simply welcomed her back to Tuskegee and received Dan and Micky with warm smiles and open hearts. For a few minutes, she was even successful in pushing thoughts of John-Michael to the back of her mind.

Claiming ground seats front and center, the threesome stretched their legs in front of them and read their programs while they waited for the start of the parade. Within minutes of the official starting time, the streets in downtown Tuskegee were filled with watchers. At the appointed time, a cheer rose from the forward crowd as the Grand Marshal's car was spotted. The parade inched through several crooked miles, with the spotlight being a circle around the municipal complex, where the judge's table was set up along with a raised platform for public office holders and other dignitaries.

A Valentine-heart-red '69 convertible 'vette loomed into view, and even if she had been wearing a patch over one eye with the other eye half-closed, Olivia would have recognized the handsome man sitting in the backseat of the car with Miss Cotton. She had to admit that John-Michael looked gorgeous—a sight any woman would appreciate waking up to. He had upped his customary attire, opting for heavily starched jeans and a yoked cowboy shirt with pearl studs for buttons. Sitting next to Miss Cotton, who was clothed in a silk, ivory-colored, fitted dress with a side slit up to yonder, they looked like the perfect couple—the successful farmer with a supportive, beautiful wife.

That green-eyed devil made its presence known again.

"She's a beauty, isn't she?" Micky asked in awe.

"Yes, she is." Dan whistled under his breath. "If I were a farmer, I wouldn't mind taking her home to help me raise some cotton." Dan clapped and whistled loudly in Olivia's ear as the 'vette with its important guests traveled slowly by them.

"I was talking about the car."

"I was talking 'bout the girl."

"You would."

Despite the inner battle she fought to control, Olivia laughed and somehow caught John-Michael's eye. It was almost as if her laugh had been picked up by the gentle breeze and carried straight to his car. His light brown eyes caught her darker ones and a message of desire and awareness passed between them, causing Olivia to think—for a split second—that the universe belonged to just the two of them.

"How about that *car?*" Micky's question to Dan pulled Olivia from the secret, silent world hidden in John-Michael's beautiful eyes. His car continued the slow ride down the street; eye contact was lost; the universe opened up for the rest of the world.

"Well, it's okay, but—" Dan and Micky became engaged in a detailed discussion about the best car ever to hit the American roads. Olivia didn't even attempt to join in the conversation, but settled back to enjoy the rest of the parade.

The parade ended after a couple of hours, and as agreed the co-workers headed over to the football field to meet up with John-Michael. His services were still needed as a judge for the band and drill team competition, and as they jostled for seats near the fifty yard line, Olivia decided that that suited her just fine. She would enjoy the entertainment much better without his presence.

As the first college band belted the opening notes of their performance, Olivia thought about the changing times. True, she'd never been in a band, but several of her siblings had, and they had never performed like today's high school and college bands. It amazed Olivia that the kids could play their instruments and simultaneously perform a sexy, high-energy dance step. Olivia didn't envy John-Michael's having to choose the best band. She knew they would all perform beautifully and with the skill and precision of a Swiss watch.

"Must be a pleasant thought," John-Michael cooed in her ear.

"John-Michael! What are you doing here? I thought you

were judging." Hands that had been clapping stilled and landed softly on her chest, near her heart. The feel of his warm breath on her ear and the heat from his magnificent body enveloped her in a lazy, hazy mist. Oh, it would be so easy to let her imagination wander down forbidden paths . . . paths teeming with memories of their marriage in the good days when lazy Sunday afternoons in bed, pillow fights in and out of bed, and midnight snacks at two A.M. followed by thirst quenching love-making were as common as the flu in winter. *Banish those thoughts,* her inner voice exclaimed, *where's your commitment to your goal?*

"I got a reprieve when the parade officials realized I didn't know a thing about formation, showmanship, interpretation, and presentation," John-Michael said, ticking off the categories from the judges' ballot with his fingers. "Hi, guys. How'd you enjoy the parade?"

Micky gave him the thumbs up, and Dan issued a hearty hello. Both quickly but politely turned their attention back to the field while shuffling over to make room for John-Michael. Neither had seen a band contest of this scope before. They didn't want to miss a thing.

"Looks like they've found a new sport." John-Michael claimed the newly formed seat next to Olivia. The tight space brought their legs and hips into full contact.

Olivia had to make herself concentrate on John-Michael's words and not the heat emanating from his body. "Oh, yes, I'd say they're in heaven right about now."

"Are you comfortable?"

Olivia mumbled she was fine and then forced herself to concentrate on the action on the field.

"I'm glad y'all came. I know getting a Ph.D. is very important to you. It really means a lot to me that you gave up some study time to share this day." John-Michael studied her profile, sending a silent message, daring her to turn and look at him, to respond to him.

Olivia darted a glance in his direction and managed a small

smile. "Thank you for asking us. I don't think I've had the opportunity to thank you officially for your hospitality. I know it's not easy for you and Lena, having to put up with three extra people."

"Believe me, it's no trouble." John-Michael wanted to tell her having her in his life again was as far from trouble as heaven was from earth. He wanted to ask her if the significance of today's event registered for her, and if it had softened her stance toward him. Instead, he kept his mouth closed and his thoughts to himself. *One day soon, I'll share my thoughts and dreams with her.* For now, sitting next to her, and inhaling her country girl freshness put a permanent smile on his face and made his heart turn flips.

"As you said, this study is very important to me, but even more to farmers all over the country. Just think about the significance of never having seasonal down time ever again. There'll be an increased chance for farmers to make a better living for their families. There'll be plenty of food to feed the homeless. The possibilities are endless." The excitement of her work made her eyes twinkle like diamonds. Momentarily, Olivia forgot she was sitting next to the man who had made her last few years in Tuskegee miserable. She forgot about the ocean of tears she had shed at his and his mother's hand.

In a flash, though, staring deep into John-Michael's sun tea-colored eyes, she remembered. The pain, the disappointments, the agony, returned, causing her to snuff out her enthusiasm and hush her commentary. Casting her eyes back to the field, she turned from John-Michael and said in a more subdued tone, "Sorry. I get carried away when I think about the potential benefits of Chem-Co's compound."

"I can understand your excitement. I hope some day soon we can sit down and talk about your work in more detail." And John-Michael knew just how soon he was talking about. Assuming everything went well today, he expected to be on first base at the conclusion of the weekend, with his foot out to steal toward second.

Olivia offered a weak smile in response and gave the bands her complete attention. She didn't want to talk to him anymore. In the last few moments, she had exposed a side of her she had learned to conceal during her last few years at Johnson Farms. It would be dangerous to let John-Michael see again just how important it was to get her Ph.D. He hadn't appreciated her need years ago, and she would only be setting herself up for more disappointment if she thought he would understand now. Suddenly she was angry at herself for still having feelings and desires for her husband. She wanted the day over with . . . now.

Sensing her withdrawal, John-Michael leaned forward and put his elbows on his well-defined thighs. "Micky, I saw you studying those cars in the parade. Do you have an interest in vintage cars?"

"It was that obvious, huh?" A crooked smile showed on Micky's pale face. "At my eighth birthday party my dad gave me my first model kit as a present. I'll never forget. It was a sixty four Chevy. Dad and I had a great time putting it together. Now I have over a hundred car and plane models in my apartment in Huntsville, most of them put together by me and Dad. It gives us both pleasure, plus it allows us to spend quality time together."

"It sounds like you and your dad have a really close relationship."

Because she was sitting so close to John-Michael, Olivia could feel an imperceptible change come over him. His voice inflection didn't change, his facial expression didn't alter, but somehow Olivia felt a transfiguration happen.

"We do." A shadow crossed Micky's young face. "I just wish he wasn't so sick. He has cancer, and the doctors aren't giving him much longer to live."

"I'm sorry to hear that. Please let me know if there's anything I can do." Even if Micky thought John-Michael was offering his help out of politeness, Olivia knew he wasn't. She had seen John-Michael on many occasions buy medicines, pay for ambulance rides, and in one case pay a hospital bill for neighbors. She had no doubt that if Micky asked for anything, John-Michael would try his best to fill the request. It was one of the things she loved about John-Michael. He willingly shared his resources.

Oh, my God! It had taken Olivia a few seconds to realize she had referred to her love for John-Michael in the present. She stopped just short of moaning out loud. *I don't love him. I used to, but not anymore.* The angel on her shoulder challenged her. *Is that true, Olivia? Have your feelings for John-Michael disappeared?* Taking a deep breath, Olivia thought, *It doesn't matter. I just want to complete my study and hurry back to Huntsville.*

"What about your dad? Did you two share a hobby, or was the farm your mutual interest?" Shaking his sadness, Micky turned a bright, inquisitive face toward his host.

"I don't know my father. He left Johnson Farms before I turned one." John-Michael was a mass of pain internally. Externally, he was calm. He couldn't show Micky how his innocent question pained him, nor how envious he was of the young boy's relationship with his dad.

"Oh, wow. I'm sorry to hear that. So you never knew . . ."

From her vantage place, Olivia saw John-Michael clasp his hands together tightly. That minute, casual action made her realize the change she had detected in him was due to his father—the taboo subject John-Michael had always avoided. Unknowingly, Micky had stepped into a minefield.

Olivia gasped as if a splinter had settled into the soft flesh of a finger.

"Olivia, are you okay?"

"Yes, um, excuse me, Micky." She turned to her husband. "John-Michael, I'm really thirsty. Do you mind going to the concession stand and getting me a bottled water?"

John-Michael was on his feet before she had finished her request.

"Can I get anyone else something?" At their negative responses, John-Michael was gone.

Olivia let a sigh escape. This time, they had sidestepped any mines, but what about the future? What if Micky was determined to learn about John-Michael's history with his absent father?

Olivia recalled a time when she had made a similar mistake. Years ago, she and John-Michael had been reviewing the wedding invitation list for the seemingly thousandth time when she realized his father's name was missing. Olivia had asked John-Michael about his father, and he had gruffly responded, "Don't worry about him." Determined to have the fairy tale wedding with all parents in attendance, Olivia had challenged John-Michael, and he had finally silenced her by telling her his father was missing, that they had lost contact with him. Unbeknownst to Olivia, it had pained John-Michael to admit this.

It had hurt Olivia to learn that detail about her fiancé's father. Then, and now she felt as if a bucket of cold ice water had been thrown in her face, waking her to the fact that John-Michael had, after that point, avoided the subject. He didn't mind talking about his mother or grandfather or the children he would one day have, but no one in the Johnson household dared to mention the name John-Michael Taylor.

People standing and clapping their praises for an exiting band raised her from her reverie. She had been staring at the field, but if someone had put a gun to her head and told her to name just one song the band had played, she would have been a dead woman. Her mind had stubbornly refused to part with John-Michael's negative reaction to the subject of his father. *No wonder Roberta is so protective of John-Michael.* Olivia placed her chin in the palm of one hand and shut out the world. Her thoughts were focused solely on her husband . . . and the protective feelings his not so obvious pain raised in her.

John-Michael returned a short while later and Olivia could

immediately detect that he was in control. During the next few performances, the men carried on a lively, "safe" conversation. Luckily, John-Michael didn't direct any more personal remarks her way, and the subject of fathers didn't resurface. The three men seemed to enjoy conducting their conversation without her input. Olivia was thankful, for she needed the time to collect herself and review her newfound understanding.

After a few more bands razzled and dazzled them, John-Michael suggested, "I don't know about you folks, but my stomach is pretty angry at me right now. How about we cut loose and find some food? This competition will be going on all day. We could always come back."

Micky quickly agreed, and Dan simply stood up and headed down the aisle in response.

In her haste to keep up with Dan and Micky, Olivia stumbled.

"Be careful," John-Michael said as he caught her small hand in his large, calloused one, preventing her from tumbling head over heels down the cement aisle. "I can't lose you now."

Looking into his lean, rugged face, Olivia tried to understand the meaning of his words. His blank mask didn't allow comprehension. Deciding to downplay the incident, she whispered her thanks and moved on. She was calming down emotionally until she felt his guiding hand on the small of her back. The control she had managed to collect scattered with the wind. Memories surged forth—memories of their first date nine years ago when they had held hands and John-Michael had kissed the stuffing out of her after a particularly gruesome carnival ride, when later that evening they had danced with the stars as their canopy. She had known after that night that her heart was in jeopardy, and now she knew she was still in trouble. As clear as a mild summer night, Olivia knew she still cared for John-Michael. With her stomach in knots, she moved mechanically in front of her husband, wishing that circumstances had been different for them, wondering how they had managed to mangle such a sweet, wild, innocent love.

A few blocks beyond the parade route were several red and white tents with a smorgasbord of food being served—barbequed chicken, hamburgers, hot dogs, brisket, sausage and shrimp, potato salad, greens, beans, cold drinks, and plenty of home-cooked desserts, including homemade peach ice cream. The dining area consisted of long trestle tables with wooden slat chairs.

Ahead of them, Olivia could see Dan and Micky. They were halfway through the line, smacking their lips. By the time John-Michael and Olivia made it through the line, there was not an empty seat at their table. Olivia groaned internally and headed for a nearby empty table. Trailing behind Olivia, John-Michael smiled all the way, enjoying her back view.

"Is this okay?" she asked an on-cloud-nine John-Michael.

"Works for me," he returned, struggling hard to maintain his excitement. This was the perfect setup, one he couldn't have orchestrated better if he had had nine months to plan it. Placing his plate next to hers, he pulled out Olivia's chair. After getting her settled, he went to fetch drinks.

In the short time he was gone, Olivia prayed she would have the strength to make it through the meal. It shocked her that she was still so attuned, physically and mentally, to John-Michael. It was natural for any woman to be attracted to him physically because he was so hard, so tall and so handsome, but mentally, emotionally, he had put her through the wringer, and she would be a fool to fall for his charms again. *Now's the time to practice that litany,* Olivia reminded herself. *I'm only here to complete my study for my Ph.D. I will not let emotions get in the way of achieving my lifelong goal.* When John-Michael returned, Olivia felt no more in control than a passenger in an airplane with an unconscious pilot quickly speeding toward earth. She knew she was in deep, neck-high trouble.

"Ms. Wimbley, over there, told me to tell you hi." John-Michael carefully placed a glass of tea by her plate.

"Oh." Olivia looked in the direction John-Michael was

pointing and smiled. Indeed, the ninety-plus-year-old woman was waving a spatula at them. "She looks great."

"She's in excellent health. Her mind is just as sharp as ever, and the only aid she uses is eyeglasses. Otherwise, she has all her original parts."

"John-Michael. That's no way to talk about your girlfriend." Olivia remembered Ms. Wimbley had told them at their wedding reception: "He may be your husband, but he'll always be my boyfriend." They had laughed with the old woman. She had always been a dear friend to them—one who minded her own business.

"Trust me, she would say the same thing."

"It's amazing. I thought people would treat me as if I had the plague, but everyone's been kind. I was nervous for nothing about coming here today," Olivia openly admitted.

"I don't know why you would have thought that. It's not as if you ran away with all the money from the bank." *You just broke my heart, was all,* John-Michael mentally finished. A subscription to a higher goal kept him from saying it.

Olivia was silent for a few minutes, toying with a question she wanted to ask him. If she had assurances that she could steer the conversation, she wouldn't hesitate to ask it. Unfortunately, with John-Michael there was no control. Curiosity got the best of her. Putting down her fork, she wiped her mouth and asked, "What did you tell them, John-Michael? Even though I didn't spend a lot of time in town, I'm sure my absence came up now and then, didn't it?"

"Yeah, it did, every so often. My answer was always the same. I told them you were away at school."

Olivia digested his comments. He had told their friends and associates the truth, and as she knew he would, he'd kept their differences private. Still, she wondered what John-Michael's true feelings were. True, he'd told her he loved her, but he hadn't spoken a word of reconciliation or talked about changing his priorities to accommodate her needs.

"How were the last few years of school? Were they as tough

as you imagined they would be?" John-Michael searched her face, interested in her answer. Had she missed him? Had she thought of him each and every night, as he had her?

"Even tougher." Olivia launched into an exposé about the doctorate program at Alabama A & M. After a while, when she realized she'd been dominating the conversation and John-Michael had an odd look on his face, she stopped. "What's wrong?"

"I was just thinking. I've missed out on something that's very important to you. I wish I'd been this astute earlier. Maybe things could have turned out differently."

Shock registered on Olivia's face.

John-Michael chuckled. "Don't look so surprised. I mean, I heard you say time and time again how important obtaining your degrees was, but I guess I never really *listened* to you. It's strange. I'm just now realizing how much you *need* that Ph.D."

Olivia protested, afraid that John-Michael would realize just how close to the truth he was. "It's not that I need it. It's just all I ever wanted." When she thought about how that must sound to him, she added quietly, "Almost all I've ever wanted." She honestly admitted to herself that at one point she wanted to be his loving wife.

"Olivia, are you sure you're being honest with yourself? You *need* that Ph.D." After a slight pause, John-Michael added speculatively, almost as if talking to himself, "I wonder if you know *why* you need it, and if you know you can have that same need filled by other means."

Anger, stemming from John-Michael's bull's-eye hit, came on as suddenly as a mosquito's bite. It flared bright and hot in Olivia. "John-Michael, may I remind you that *I'm* the expert on what Olivia wants or needs. Not you! You didn't pay enough attention to me when I lived with you to know how I feel or what I need."

"Whoa, there. I'm not trying to put a scorpion down your

back. It's just that I had a revelation, and I wonder if you've examined—"

"I don't need you to—" Olivia was interrupted by the appearance of Miss Cotton. Reining in her anger, Olivia pressed her lips tight, crossed her arms across her chest, and started bouncing her knee under the wooden table.

"Hi, John-Michael. I've been looking for you." Miss Cotton had exchanged her sophisticated attire for casual clothes consisting of skintight, faded jeans, a low-cut, curve-hugging, cotton T-shirt, and sandals. When she leaned over, more than just a hint of her cleavage was exposed.

"Hi, Sylvia. Let me introduce you to my wife." Both Olivia and Miss Cotton gasped . . . at different octaves. John-Michael continued, ignoring their identical responses. "Olivia, this is Sylvia McCarthy. Sylvia, Olivia Johnson."

"Why, John-Michael, I didn't know you were married," Sylvia said in an offended tone. She totally ignored Olivia's outstretched hand.

"There's a lot you don't know about me." John-Michael continued chewing on the thick, honey-coated rib.

"Well . . ." Sylvia finally accepted Olivia's hand and scanned Olivia from head to waist, the extent of her vision. "You've got yourself a fine man." Sylvia straightened and puffed her thick reddish-brown hair. Her eyes lighted on the twinkling diamonds on Olivia's finger. "Beautiful ring, Honey." She walked off, moving her hips suggestively, before Olivia could comment.

"Whew." John-Michael wiped his mouth and hands. "I'm glad you were here for me to finally, I hope, get her off my back."

"I would think any man would be glad to date her," Olivia remarked caustically.

"Oh, she's attractive all right, and once she settles down she'll make a hell of a wife." John-Michael threw one arm along the back of her chair and stared directly into his wife's face. "Personally, I tend to like my women with a little less curves and a whole lot more brains."

Olivia was tempted to ask how many women that had encompassed since she'd left. On second thought, she decided she didn't know if she could handle his answer. Besides, her co-workers, replete and happy, were approaching with determined strides.

"I ate too much, so the kid here has decided he's going to go back to the farm and do the testing." Dan hooked a thumb in the waistband of his jeans.

"Dan, is that really fair?" Olivia asked with a stern look. "Does this mean Micky's going to go back both times? We agreed we'd all chip in and do our part."

"Oh, please, Olivia. It's okay with me. The drive will help settle my stomach for the sack races and egg toss later. Besides, I don't want to get in the way of love."

Dan, a confirmed bachelor, quickly corrected him. "Try lust, kid. I'm going to go find Miss Cotton. I saw her over here a few minutes ago. Where'd she go?"

John-Michael pointed in a general direction and Dan lumbered off.

"Where are the keys?" Micky held out his hand to John-Michael, who quickly dug them out of his britches and tossed them.

"I'm finished eating. I can come with you, Micky. After all this *is* my study." Olivia saw this as a perfect opportunity to take a breather from John-Michael. He was causing her to re-think things, and she didn't want to do that. Her thoughts, wishes, and desires were compartmentalized, and she wanted to keep it that way. Around John-Michael, that was becoming impossible.

Micky was already walking away, twirling the keys on his finger. Turning to face her, he walked backward and replied, "That's okay. You enjoy the afternoon, and I'll catch up to you guys in a few hours."

Olivia sat staring at the half-eaten plate of food in front of her. She had no interest in eating, and Lord knew she had no interest in picking up where she and John-Michael had left off. She just sat there, waiting for inspiration.

"If you're through picking at your food, we can go ride a few rides. I remember you like the rides which test a person's mortality."

John-Michael knew the right thing to say to pull her out of her self-imposed shell. She did like carnival rides—the wilder and more dangerous, the better.

She was hooked. "Okay."

They spent the next few hours walking, riding the swirling, bumpy rides and playing the rigged carnival games. John-Michael surprised her by winning a poster of Michael Jackson's *Thriller*. At another stall he won several glass ashtrays by tossing dimes and since nobody except him smoked—occasionally, and always outdoors—he gave the cheap glass dishes to a little kid who was getting frustrated. John-Michael didn't fare as well at the dart game. After a twenty dollar loss, he gave up.

Laughing, Olivia teased him. "I would think by now you'd have mastered all these games."

"Actually, this is my first time attending this celebration in a long time. I quit coming after you left."

The teasing smile dropped from her face. Just as she had adopted a carefree attitude, he'd reminded her of reality. She was thankful, since she'd almost let herself slip into the happy past when they had been each other's balms.

"You know, I bet Micky's back. Maybe we should go to the field where the games are being played and see if we can find him."

John-Michael let her run from him, since he had so thoroughly enjoyed having her to himself for a while. He followed her to the games field, and shortly after arriving they spied Micky in a three-legged race with Dan. On the sidelines, Miss Cotton cheered them on to victory.

The three researchers, John-Michael, and Miss Cotton spent the rest of the day playing or watching the games, enjoying various bands and storytellers, and eating all the desserts their stomachs could handle. Finally, with the sun long since set and the moon shining brilliantly, Olivia found herself yawning.

Noting her sleepy appearance, John-Michael called an end to the fun and loaded a worn out Olivia and Micky, whose stomach ached into the van for the hour-long trip home. Miss Cotton happily agreed to drop Dan off.

Olivia was asleep before they hit Highway 85, and woke only when she felt John-Michael's hands on her arms.

"I'm not asleep," she protested with one eye open, "I can walk."

"Tomorrow you can walk. Tonight, I'm carrying you in."

John-Michael decided Olivia must be more tired and sleepy than even she realized, for the fight he expected didn't come. With a soft groan, she cuddled in his arms, and he swore he'd found heaven on earth. The hard part, of course, was putting her down in her own room and leaving her to sleep there alone. *There'll be time for sharing beds later,* he thought.

Even so, the fly of his jeans bulged when he laid her on the bed.

"Olivia, do you want me to take your clothes off?" John-Michael whispered in her ear.

Olivia's deep brown eyes popped open and she struggled to sit up on her elbows. "I'll manage from here." She spoke around a yawn. "Thank you."

"Goodnight, then." John-Michael couldn't resist planting a kiss on her cheek. It was a pleasant act, but a poor substitute for joining her in bed.

As soon as the door closed behind him, Olivia hurriedly undressed and crawled under the sheets. She touched the spot where John-Michael had kissed her and, with her fingers rooted to that spot, rolled onto her stomach and fell asleep.

Next door in the master bedroom suite, a barefoot and bare-chested John-Michael stared out of the window, watching Micky walk to the fields. He was proud of the young man, who was so obviously dedicated to the project. John-Michael made a mental note to check into Micky's father's condition. It was the least he could do, considering the young man seemed so committed to Olivia's success.

Olivia. Just thinking her name was enough to conjure up an image of his beautiful wife. He wondered if she still snored . . . and if she still favored sleeping on her stomach with her legs thrown every which way. A slight smile curved his lips when memories from the past crowded his mind, blocking out the dark, starry night and the rest of the world. Turning from his window, he sat in a chair in the corner of the crescent-shaped room to run a mental movie of happy images from the past and to fantasize about the happy reunion he hoped to experience soon.

Four

Olivia stepped onto the back porch, guiding the screen door shut with a booted foot. It was five o'clock in the morning and the stillness and darkness of this southern September Monday draped her like a shawl. Inhaling the virgin air deeply, Olivia walked softly to the top of the stairs and leaned her petite body against one of the white columns that surrounded the old house.

"Just me and nature," she breathed. A slight smile curved her full lips.

The things she most adored—pre-dawn mornings and nature—lay silent before her, making her heartbeat strong and steady. The urge to run to the fields to finger the plants and soil that sustained life ran deep within her, but she forfeited the feeling in favor of simply closing her eyes and deeply enjoying the Alabama countryside.

"Oh, how I miss this place," Olivia sighed, thinking of the many times in the past that she had stood in that same spot, sipping a hot coffee, waiting for the rest of the world to join her. *If only things had been different. I could still be here nurturing this place and my husband.*

Truth shot through her without warning. Straightening to her full five-foot-two inches, Olivia confessed to the morning sky, "I still have feelings for John-Michael, and I would love to reclaim Johnson Farms as my home." She expelled a deep breath, symbolically releasing that dream.

"Who you talking to, Sugar?" Lena, clothed in a pastel chenille bathrobe, walked onto the porch.

Olivia turned sharply. "Lena. Good morning." Relief colored her words. "I hope I didn't wake you with my ramblings."

"Oh, I needed to get up. John-Michael plans to get an earlier start than usual today, and you know how he is about starting *each and every day* with a good breakfast."

"Yes, I remember." Olivia smiled with the older woman. That had often been a source of contention between them. Olivia had to be reminded to eat, and John-Michael was a three meals a day plus midnight snack person.

"I see you're still an early riser." Lena sank down to sit on the top step of the porch. She held a Laurel Burch coffee mug between hands hardened by cooking and cleaning.

"Yes. After thirty years of it, I don't think I could change even if I wanted to. Besides, it's something about this clean country air that makes you eager to get up to greet the day."

"Yes, Ma'am . . . there's nothing like country living." Lena patted the wood seat beside her; Olivia took it. "How you can stand to live in the city, I don't know. Don't you miss it here?" Lena turned an inquisitive, searching face to Olivia. Three years ago, she had let a bad thing happen which led to the dissolution of the young couple's marriage. Olivia's return, no matter how it was orchestrated, had given Lena a chance to correct a wrong.

"I've been thinking that same thing since my return. In Huntsville, the people are nice and the city has a relaxed pace, but it's nothing like here. The sky isn't as blue, the grass isn't as green, and the brooks and streams aren't as clear." A sad shadow crossed Olivia's brown face. "I do miss it here but—" The words trailed off into silence as the past blocked her vocal cords.

Lena finished the young woman's sentence. "But the memories are too bad?"

With a crooked smile and a shrug of one shoulder, Olivia agreed. "Something like that."

"You and John-Michael shared a pure love. It's possible to relive it without the problems from the past, if you keep an open mind and an open heart." Lena placed a motherly arm around Olivia's shoulder and gave her a gentle squeeze.

Laying her head on Lena's strong shoulder, Olivia whispered, "Thanks, Lena, but really my focus is on my Ph.D. That's all I want or need."

"You telling me you don't need love?"

Olivia's mind flitted to her childhood, where love had been present in the form of providing the basics. Her sisters and brothers, the ten of them, knew her parents loved them because they provided for them. Mr. and Mrs. Foster made sure there was food, housing, medical care, clothes—usually hand-me-downs or purchased from Goodwill—and a minimal high school education. There had been little devoted attention from her parents to each individual child. So intent were her parents—working four jobs between the two of them—on providing externally that they hadn't had time to school the children in the internal needs that would help them grow into well-balanced adults.

Had it not been for the nurturing hand of her first grade teacher, Dr. Hill, Olivia could have developed into a cold machine of a woman like her younger sister, Dora, or a selfish, uncaring person like her oldest brother, Thomas.

Dr. Hill, who had the distinction of being one of the first African-American women in the state of Alabama to earn a Ph.D., preferred to expend her knowledge in the classroom. She had recognized Olivia's sharp, eager mind, and without children of her own, had 'adopted' Olivia. Although Dr. Hill passed away in Olivia's freshman year of college, she had already passed on a love for education to the younger woman and her house, which was filled with fond memories the two of them had created. A hollowness had resided within Olivia from that year on until she met and fell in love with John-Michael.

About Lena's question—"did she need love?"—she thought reflectively. Very important people in her life had provided her with love, but with the exception of one—Dr. Hill—it had been an obligating love.

So that Lena could see her response, Olivia shook her head negatively. No, she didn't want the dutiful, third place love that John-Michael offered. She wanted—had wanted, she corrected herself—his love and attention freely given.

"You don't need a place to call home and actually feel it in your heart?"

Olivia tried not to think about Dr. Hill's small, white wooden house, which had become her second home. She tried not to think about the warmth and comfortable, secure feelings enclosed in that house; the same feelings she had felt with John-Michael in their early years together.

Olivia lifted her head from its resting place and shook her head again.

"You don't need the comfort of a man's arms after a full day at school?"

Again, the same action answered Lena's question.

Lena's wise brown eyes misted in regret. "If the love you had for John-Michael is gone, then it was never really love."

Olivia didn't shake her head this time, didn't meet Lena's eyes, just stared in the direction of the garden. After several seconds passed with only the crickets filling the silence, Olivia stood. "I'm comfortable with my life in Huntsville."

"Sugar, being comfortable and being happy are two different things."

Olivia used the toe of her boot to dislodge a small pebble. Stooping, she picked it up and rolled it between her hands.

Lena knew that Olivia's silence meant she was thinking—really hard. She needed to make her point while she had a piece of Olivia's mind.

"When I lost my Andrew in that railroad accident, heaviest on my mind was the times we wasted arguing and fighting when we could have been loving, and I ain't just talking about the physical loving—"

"I got up earlier than normal to get caught up from the

weekend. We had a great time, but I need to make my way to the barn now."

Lena stood and spoke as if Olivia hadn't said a thing. "It's sad when two people—especially young people—love each other but won't allow themselves to be together." Lena turned and headed for the back door. With her hand on the handle, she spoke wistfully. "Olivia, don't be like me, regretting that I didn't use my time wisely. Most people only get one turn at real love, the love God intended for us to have." Before the door swallowed her from view, she resigned from the conversation—for the time being—and resumed her housekeeping role. "I'll bring you breakfast in a few minutes. You need to eat." The screen door slammed shut behind her.

Lena likened the door action to Olivia's heart and mind—both were closed tightly. Opening the refrigerator door, she withdrew fixings for breakfast. "It's going to take more than talk to bring that girl around," Lena muttered to herself. "John-Michael better do something and quick if he plans to keep her here after all her studying is through." In the middle of slicing sausage, an idea occurred to Lena. *Of course I could help the situation along.* There was one thing she could do, but she didn't know if she could pull it off, with her primitive schooling. Still, the idea had lots of merit.

Safely in the barn, away from Lena's unsettling words and compassionate eyes, Olivia sat in her usual seat at the worktable, weighted down by Lena's comments. Although Lena had made her extremely uncomfortable, she couldn't be angry with her friend. She knew it was love and concern that drove Lena's actions; she was thankful Lena still cared. Olivia shook her head, dismissing Lena's words. "Lena just doesn't understand what an impossible situation John-Michael and I are in. It doesn't matter that I still have some feelings, some attraction for him . . . what we had is not recoverable."

Olivia clicked on the computer, determined to put Lena's

comments and her gnawing feelings for her husband out of her mind. With convincing bravado, Olivia thought, *I'm here to do a job. I'm on the periphery of achieving my goal and I'm not going to let John-Michael, Lena, Roberta, or anyone else stop me. They tried once. It won't happen again.*

Drawing the record books toward her, she began to review the observations recorded over the weekend. It was way too early in the experiment to expect a miracle. The study she designed, which was approved by her doctoral committee, would take a year to actually conduct. However, her actual time on Johnson Farms would be in three month spurts with phase one encompassing August, September, and October. With little growth activity going on in the winter, they would retire to Huntsville during that time and she would have the computer lab begin the initial compilation process. The written presentation and more studying would also resume for her; Dan and Micky would return to work at the state ag department until it was time to reconvene.

Looking at the small desk calendar near her elbow, she quickly counted seven more weeks to go before she could retreat to Huntsville to lick her emotional wounds—with certainty she knew she would have some, and she could feel them budding—from round one.

Months ago, emotionally sheltered in Huntsville, Olivia hadn't given a thought to any involvement with the Johnson clan. She had assumed they would leave her alone, and she them. Now, she knew she had been too simplistic in her assumptions. The bittersweet memories which she had carefully sealed away had real life people attached to them, and she could no more ignore them than she could ignore her education goal.

"Curses to the state ag department, Chem-Co, and my committee for making this farm the be-all end-all location for my study." Silently, she added *And curses to John-Michael for still being so damned goodlooking and . . .*—she searched her mind for the most appropriate word—*hard.* She hadn't been able to

deny the warming of her skin when over the weekend, due to
the various sporting events at the carnival, their bodies had
collided. Even now, she felt herself warming at the remem-
brances, especially when her mind skipped to Sunday morning.

Vague wispy memories of being carried upstairs in John-
Michael's work-toughened arms followed her from sleep. The
shyness she had experienced as a virgin on their wedding night
resurfaced Sunday morning. She knew she was being silly.
John-Michael had seen her naked plenty of times—in the past.
These were different times, though. They hadn't been together
physically in over three years and it had generated a new sense
of modesty in her.

After delaying as long as possible, Olivia had joined the
men at the breakfast table. Wishing a good morning to the
crowd in general, she'd covertly peeked at John-Michael, who
appeared to be his usual cool, self-contained self. A scant nod
in greeting was the only acknowledgment she'd received from
him, and he'd maintained that same polite yet distant treatment
throughout church service and dinner on the ground. After returning to the farm from an eventful Sunday, John-Michael
had shut himself into his at-home office. Olivia had left Dan
and Micky in the family room watching *60 Minutes* and she
had walked the garden until duty in the form of a textbook
called to her.

A crick in her back caused her to glance at her Timex. Thirty
minutes had passed and she had yet to crack open a notebook
or finish logging into the computer. "So much for trying to
get caught up," she mumbled. *Thank you, John-Michael, for
the interruptions in my life . . . again.*

Stretching and yawning, she hopped off the stool and walked
to the kitchenette, where she started a pot of coffee. Leaning
against the sink, she casually eyed the barn, nodding her approval of the changes John-Michael had made. She remembered how she had always been after him to "do something"
with the old barn, especially after the new barn had been con-
structed. She would not have guessed he would take it this far.

Their research work had made them completely intimate with the downstairs rooms.

Her curiosity about the work he was doing upstairs spurred her to refill her coffee cup and head for the stairs.

Because it was so cavernous, the lights from downstairs didn't begin to touch the upstairs room. At the top of the stairwell, Olivia blindly searched until her hand happened upon the wall switch. Fluorescent lights crinkled on.

Olivia's eyes brightened like those of a child at a McDonald's playland. She advanced toward the table, speaking as she walked. "I wonder how long he's been researching his past?"

She pulled the flow chart paper to her and scanned it briefly. Next, she flipped open the Holy Bible to the page where marriages, deaths, and births were recorded. Finally, she held up one slip of microfiche film to the light and saw that it contained information on the U.S. Census.

Reeled in like a trout on a line, the devout researcher in Olivia stepped forward, eclipsing her conscious being. The chair made little noise against the highly polished, slatted wood floor as she pulled it from beneath the table and sat down to review his work. Slowly, methodically, she noted each limb on the flow chart. Some had names written in, others were blank. The "tree" started taking on meaning when she spied the limb where John-Michael's grandfather's name—Madison Johnson—appeared. She noted the single offspring—Roberta Marie Johnson—John-Michael's grandparents had produced, but pulled up short when she saw the empty limb adjoining Roberta's.

A frown marred Olivia's soft features. *Why is that not completed? John-Michael's father's name should be listed, even if he's no longer in the picture.* Unthinkingly, she picked up a pencil and started writing in the appropriate information.

"What are you doing?" John-Michael's authoritative voice filled the quiet space.

Olivia gasped and swung around in her chair. A mixture of fright and awareness made her eyes grow larger and brighter. The pencil she had been using fell from her hands and rolled to a stop at John-Michael's work boots. A flush crept up her neck to the roots of her hair. She felt as guilty as a child who had used her Sunday School money to buy candy at the corner store.

John-Michael picked up the pencil, and in two, long-legged strides reached the table. Looking down at her handiwork, he brushed her with a deep, cutting glance and then erased what she had written in. In a flash, as he did so, she wondered just how deeply his father's absence had impacted John-Michael. Factoring in his reaction to Micky's seemingly innocent question Saturday at the ball field, it seemed highly probable that here was an area that needed in-depth research.

"Is he still living?" Olivia asked boldly, risking further wrath.

John-Michael threw the pencil on the table. "I don't know."

His icy stare intimidated her but she bravely stood her ground, spurred on by the overwhelming hint of some past history involving his father.

Taking a deep breath, she assertively explained, "Well, whether he is or isn't, in order for this document to be accurate and complete his name should be included—right here." Her shaky finger pointed at the spot where remnants of pink rubber eraser rested.

John-Michael snatched the flow chart paper and walked to a file cabinet in the room. "I appreciate your advice, *Doctor Johnson,* but I didn't ask for your help." Opening the cabinet, he stuffed the paper in. "This is *my* family's business. Stay out of it."

Olivia should have let his last comment go, but indignation bested better judgment. With hand on hip and finger pointing at the file cabinet, she remarked, "According to *that,* I *am* family."

John-Michael walked stealthily toward her. His face, tightly composed, reflected his displeasure with her high-handedness. He said harshly, "It's nothing to do with you. Leave it be." He headed for the stairs. He had to get out of there, away from the ghost of his father. *If she knew John-Michael Taylor like I know the man, she wouldn't question my motives.* But, even in the midst of his anger, John-Michael recognized that she still had the power to elicit a stronger emotion—love. The thought propelled him toward the stairs.

Olivia stared at her husband, then started after him. Catching up with him at the top of the stairs, she grabbed his arm, determined to get her point across. "But, John-Michael, if *my* name is on there as your wife and I don't live here, then surely Roberta's husband . . . *your* father—"

John-Michael whirled completely around, bringing them face-to-face. Gripping her shoulders he pushed her gently, pinning her to the wall. With his face positioned within inches of hers, she could clearly see the pain in his light brown eyes. "You're playing with fire, Olivia. Just drop it."

"I only want to help," she replied meekly. Lost was the fiery determination that had caused her to charge him. This close to him, she could think of nothing more than how she had contributed to his pain, and how she could erase it from existence.

"Here's how you can help." His lips captured hers before she could draw breath. His hand anchored her jaw and chin, allowing him greater freedom to draw from her what he needed. Right now he needed her nurturing, her love.

The desperation and hardness of the initial kiss transformed into a softer kiss until John-Michael finally had what he needed. He withdrew fractionally, and frantically searched her face. Closed eyes, shallow breathing, and parted lips welcomed him. He used his tongue to outline the shape of her lips before darting it in and out of her mouth. Brief, moist kisses were planted along her cheeks, chin and sides of her mouth and eyelids, preceding an in-depth exploration of the inside of her mouth. When her arms circled his waist, drawing them closer, a moan escaped John-Michael and the fire which smoldered in his belly spread to his lower extremities and then upward to ignite his heart. The tension which had assailed his body earlier dissipated, allowing him to absorb her softness.

John-Michael could have easily taken her to the bed and made love to her with no regrets, but a warning bell sounded in his head as soon as the thought formed. Forcing himself to disentangle them, he recited the hands-off policy to himself, focusing on the grand plan to keep her at Johnson Farms permanently. *Stick to the plan and you'll have the rest of your life to love her.*

His ragged breathing mixed with her softer gasps, to fill the stairwell. Both pairs of brown eyes locked together, conveying need, desire, and want. John-Michael, throbbing from head to toe, broke the connection. "Lena sent you breakfast. It's downstairs, where you should be at all times." He turned and was at the bottom of the stairs before Olivia could push herself away from the wall.

John-Michael reached the door as Dan and Micky's loud, playful teasing announced their arrival. Holding the door open for them to enter, John-Michael greeted them, "Mornin', fellows. Get enough to eat?"

Dan smiled and rubbed his Hoss Cartwright belly. "You betcha. I think I may have to kidnap Lena and take her back to Huntsville with me."

Good-humoredly, John-Michael threatened, "You do that, and you'll never be welcome here again."

"Say, John-Michael," Micky interrupted the laughter, turning an earnest face to his host. "Lena mentioned The Black Rodeo'll be here this weekend. She says you always go. Are you this time?"

"Yes. As a matter of fact, I'm on my way to town." He cocked his head in Olivia's direction. "If you clear it with your boss I'll pick up tickets for you."

Two heads swiveled toward Olivia, who stood hesitantly by the bottom stair. She'd had difficulty following the conversation, intent instead on trying to corral her ignited passions. She was glad she'd selected jeans to wear for work today. The shorts she often donned would have displayed her shaky legs as she walked past the clustered men and toward their worktable.

Even though she wanted to refuse—spending a weekend with John-Michael after he had awakened her passions and feelings would be a damn fool thing to do—Olivia knew it would be easier to give in. Besides, she couldn't use the study as an excuse, since the past arrangement had worked fine. She could allow the men time together.

"It's fine with me." Olivia ducked her head, pulling one of the notebooks close to her. "Don't bother getting me a ticket. I need to study for my orals."

"All right!" Micky hooked a fist in the air. "This is the best research location I've ever worked on."

Olivia couldn't stop the small smile from skimming her face in response to Micky's reaction. Sometimes it was hard to believe he was in his mid-twenties, and not a teenager.

Dan was the one who latched onto her last comment. "Tired of our company already? You know we're all joined at the hip." Turning to John-Michael, he commanded, "Get her a ticket, too."

Before Olivia could sputter a protest, John-Michael tipped his hat to all and was gone.

Outside, with the azure sky and the see-through clouds, John-Michael could finally release the breath he'd been holding. There was never any doubt that Olivia could move him to feeling an intense range of emotions, spanning from anger to love, with a heavy dose of ardor. He just hadn't been prepared this morning to deal with the full gamut.

"And it all started with that so-called father of mine," John-Michael mumbled as he climbed into his work truck. Even now, safely away from the lineage chart that she had begun to boldly write *his* name on, he was still irked.

"He wasn't even man enough to give me his own last name," John-Michael said angrily to the gearshift.

With one simple act, Olivia had reminded him why he

needed her back home permanently. He loved and needed her, but he also had to disprove his father's genes. Driving down the blacktop, two-lane farm road headed toward Tuskegee, John-Michael fought hard not to suffocate in the past. But it wasn't long before he was reliving the night that he had learned to hate his father; the night he took on the burden his father had refused to.

One evening in June twenty-eight years ago, a young John-Michael had run into the main house at Johnson Farms, holding two handmade Father's Day cards high in the air. Excitedly, he had danced around Roberta while she had *ooohed* and *aaahed* over his amateurish art work. When she had asked John-Michael why he had made two gifts, the impressionable boy had answered with childish sweetness, "One for Grandpa and one for my daddy." It had taken Roberta several seconds to rebound from that statement, only to be doubled over by John-Michael's next question. "Can we go give it to my daddy?" Even with quick talking, Roberta had not been able to sway him from wanting to give the gift to his father. Roberta realized the time had come for John-Michael to know the real story about his father.

With tension and pain lining her face, she had explained that John-Michael Taylor had been hired by her father to be the foreman for the farm. His handsome, lean looks had sent Roberta's heart into overdrive, and after nine months of courting they had married. According to Roberta, it took another nine months for her to accept reality: the man she loved was a lazy, no-account user who had married her for the riches of Johnson Farms. She had also discovered she was pregnant. By the time John-Michael junior was born, the marriage was a wash. Roberta reported that the elder John-Michael had refused to manage the farm, had girlfriends too numerous to count, and had finally left one day with a large sum of money, giving not a second thought to the days-old son or the bro-kenhearted woman he had left behind.

John-Michael remembered the hurt and disappointment that flooded his small body that night. He remembered how his mother had cried long into the night, and how it had frightened him. That day was the birth of his hatred for his father.

That same night after his grandfather had tucked him into bed, he made a vow that he would be a much better man than his father, that he would disprove his father's genes by never breaking his mother's heart or deserting his children or wife. Additionally, he would love the farm as much as his father had detested it.

John-Michael snapped back to the present to find he had a death grip on the steering wheel. With a hearty blow of his fist to the dashboard, he turned his thoughts to his twenty-eight year old promise. Except for his relationship with his mother and his care for the farm, he had failed. He had lost Olivia, and the children they should have had. Thank God the arrangements for Olivia's return to Johnson Farms had worked out. Now that he had her here again, he was determined to meet the other commitment he'd made. Otherwise, he would be no better than his father broaking sacred vows and destroying souls.

Five

A Mercedes Benz sedan purred quietly in front of the main house on Saturday evening. John-Michael had decided to drive his guests to The Black Rodeo in comfort and style.

"Hey, hey, hey," Dan remarked appreciatively as he led Micky and Olivia down the front steps, "this is some car."

John-Michael stood in the open door on the driver's side. He took a final drag on a cigarette, flicked it out of his fingers, then stomped it out. "I thought I'd give you all a break from riding in bumpy trucks and vans. Besides, Mother's got a couple more weeks of vacation. It's not good to have her car sit up without some use."

John-Michael slid under the steering wheel while Dan opened the front passenger car door for Olivia. Olivia started to protest, to tell Dan she preferred to sit in back with Micky, then decided it wouldn't be worth the ruckus. A small voice inside her head taunted, *You're afraid.* With a frown, she acknowledged the truth of that mocking voice. She was afraid that sitting so close to John-Michael she would be tempted to touch him, reach out to him, to ease the internal battle she knew he *had* to be fighting, too.

For the past four days she'd only had brief glimpses of him around the farm. His appearances at meals had been scarce, and during the few times he had shared a meal with them, he'd seemed preoccupied. Olivia had a feeling his absences and preoccupation were related to the conversation about his father. It, and the smoldering, punishing kiss that made her shiver every time she thought about it, had been distractions for her, as well. She'd had to face the fact that she was tied to John-Michael spiritually and emotionally. Neither her commitment to obtaining her Ph.D. nor her estranged relationship with him could refute that. That knowledge had caused her to lose many hours of sleep during the past week.

A sidelong glance at John-Michael revealed his determination to get them to the coliseum safely. He was focused on the roads, the descending night, and the weather. The rain that had threatened last weekend's activities had wakened them this morning with a ferocious roar.

As it had this past week, her mind returned to her most prominent concern of late—John-Michael's unhealthy, submerged feelings about his father, and the work he was doing on his family tree. His adamant refusal to talk on Monday should have squashed any further thoughts she might have had about both John-Michaels. Instead, it had acted like lighter fluid to a match—her interest had intensified, and not only because it represented a research opportunity. *I lived with the man for five years. I can't believe I never noticed how deeply his father bothers him,* Olivia thought desperately. Sneaking another glance at the handsome, brown-skinned man sitting on her left, she thought she detected a tenseness that had made a home on the hard planes and hollows of his rugged, lean face. *How do I get him to open up and discuss it logically, scientifically?* Unable to come up with an answer, Olivia sighed, deeply and evenly, and scrunched down in her seat. She acknowledged that in the meantime the blasted argument lay like smog between them, blinding their path of discovery and understanding.

"Why the sigh?" John-Michael's deep voice floated through the enclosed space and landed softly around her. It was the first time he had spoken directly to her since Monday.

Olivia honestly replied, "I was just thinking about how to solve a particular problem."

"Did you run into a hitch with your study?" As much as

he wanted to look at his lovely wife he dared not, for fear he wouldn't be able to *stop* looking at her. He'd denied himself the pleasure of spending hardly any time with her this week. Not because he harbored anger against her for snooping into past, unpleasant business, but because that dynamic kiss had made his pilot light burn out of control; his desire and need for her had multiplied beyond measure. She was his hope for a lifetime of happiness, the one person who could eliminate his feelings of inadequacy, and yet she was so out of reach.

"You could say that," Olivia vaguely responded. Her mind also wrestled with the fact that her husband's problem was vying for first place with her Ph.D. study to take up permanent residence in her inner thoughts and actions. *Even though I want to help John-Michael with his problem, I have to be careful that I don't forget my main reason for being here in the first place. I will finish this phase of the study. I will get my Ph.D.*

John-Michael moved his free hand to cover one of hers, which lay on the seat of the luxury car. With a light squeeze he offered, "I know I don't have the advanced formal schooling you have, but if there's anything I can do to help, you'll let me know, right?"

His compassionate touch and kind words sent firecrackers of desire exploding throughout her body. She could feel herself heating at her core, and the explosive feel of his hand lightly rubbing her skin made it difficult to keep her breathing steady. Olivia turned her head. Their eyes met and the sincerity reflected within their depths caused a new rush of soft feelings. Words stuck in her throat, so she bobbed her head and croaked, "Sure."

The devoted look shared between the former lovers encased them in a world which promised hope. In their eyes they could see the *possibility* of forgiveness and reconciliation.

"Are we almost there?" Micky's tenor voice interrupted the affectionate interlude between husband and wife. With his whiny voice resembling that of a three-year-old child on a long trip with his parents, he asked again, "Is it much further?"

John-Michael transferred his eyes from Olivia's to glance briefly in Micky's direction. "A few more miles—not far." After a slight pause, he asked, "Are you excited?"

"Shoot, yes! I've never been to The Black Rodeo before."

Dan's booming voice filled the car, causing Olivia to think seriously about covering her ears with the heels of her hands. "If you've been to any kind of rodeo then you've been to a Black rodeo. There's no difference except the cowboys are better, and the musical guests have less twang in their voices." Dan laughed uproariously. It was obvious he got his kicks from teasing the younger man.

Olivia craned her neck to gauge Micky's reaction. She knew he was more sensitive than he let on. She could have saved the effort; Micky wasn't fazed by Dan's harassment. The boy-man lightly punched Dan on his thigh. Rolling her eyes heavenward, Olivia turned back around to face front. She noticed that even John-Michael was smiling. Speaking under her breath she quipped, "Men will be boys."

"Yeah, well, I'll bet a white rodeo has something a black rodeo will never have," Micky said, rebounding.

"Oh, you think so?"

"I know so." The duel was on!

"And *what,* pray tell, is that?" The sarcasm in Dan's voice was thicker than lumpy gravy.

"Kathy Mattea! That girl's a looker!"

Dan opened his mouth, only to close it. His eyebrows drew together and a bulky finger scratched a spot high on his head. "Hmmm," he hummed. Several seconds ticked by while Dan pondered the validity of Micky's statement. Finally, a loud, "Okay," broke the silence, accompanied by an affirming nod. "She does look good, and you're right, she'll probably never do a black rodeo, but . . ." Dan held up a beefy finger and smiled broadly, ". . . we got Gladys, and when that woman belts out a song she makes me want to give her my *whole* paycheck."

"Gladys Knight?" Micky questioned, his voice escalating to a higher note.

"Hell, yes, Gladys Knight! What other Gladys do you know that can make a man's bones melt with just one note?"

Micky thought about it momentarily, then gave up, "Just forget it."

In the front seat, John-Michael laughed heartily; Olivia tolerantly shook her head.

The rest of the ride continued in the same vein. Dan kidded Micky unmercifully and Micky hung in there like a champ, with John-Michael and Olivia contributing a few occasional chuckles.

They arrived at the arena with the car clock showing ten minutes before starting time.

"I'll drop you guys off at the entrance gates, then meet you at our seats." John-Michael fished in his jacket for three of the tickets, handed them to Olivia, and then reached across her to open her door.

The gentle brush of his arm across her breasts left Olivia stumbling out of the foreign car. Her body was instantly warmed from head to toe despite the harsh rains falling. *Calm down, Olivia. There was nothing sexual in his action.* Taking a deep breath, she ducked under the umbrella Micky held, and together they dashed through the gates and out of the temper tantrum Mother Nature was throwing.

Inside the enclosed coliseum, a teenage boy the color of an old penny showed them to their seats. They were fortunate enough to have box seats. Micky and Olivia took the front seats and Dan took a seat behind Micky.

Micky exclaimed, "Wow, box seats! I can reach out my hand and almost touch the cowboys." To prove his point, he stretched over the railing.

"Micky, don't!" Dan grabbed the back of Micky's corduroy jacket. In a harsh, out of character voice, he said, "I wouldn't do that, Micky. These *are* excellent seats, but if you're not careful you can fall over the rail and straight into the action."

Micky pulled back from the edge of the railing and regained his seat. Good-humoredly, he remarked, "Why Dan, I didn't know you cared so much."

Dan folded his arms to sit on top of his round belly and *humphed.* "Oh, hush. The show's about to start."

In concert with Dan's comment the lights dimmed, and primary-colored spotlights began rotating crazily on the dirt floor of the arena. While the announcer made his way through a long list of sponsors, Olivia scanned the darkened interior for John-Michael's silhouette. *What's taking him so long? He should be here by now.* Olivia turned front and center, determined to put her husband out of her mind and focus on the announcer's jubilant voice. Just as the announcer started introducing the rodeo participants, including horses and bulls, the short hairs on Olivia's nape told her John-Michael had arrived. Indeed, she heard the groan of the cushioned seat as he sat. Seconds later, with her peripheral vision, she saw a long leg stretch out into the aisle. The muscled, denim-covered leg was positioned close to her shoulder—so close she could caress his calf just by slightly shifting her arm.

Frantically searching for a diversion from the intimate thought, she latched onto Dan and John-Michael's conversation.

"Rodeos have sure changed from when I was a little boy," Dan remarked as the laser lights resumed their merry dance.

"How so?" John-Michael asked.

The thunderous voice of the announcer interrupted Dan's response. "Ladies and gentlemen, I present for your enjoyment, Frankie Beverly and Maze."

The crowd went wild, standing on their feet, clapping and shouting, drowning out the insistent *pat-pat-pat* of the rain on the roof of the arena. Dan bellowed to be heard. "Back in those days, we didn't have world renowned entertainers open-

ing up for a rodeo." Dan nodded his head and cheesed grandly.
"I sure like these days better."

The familiar opening notes of *Happy Feelings* caused a
greater uproar from the crowd, and acted as a cattle prod for
Olivia. In a flash, she remembered that Frankie Beverly and
Maze was one of John-Michael's favorite groups. Turning with
a smile on her face, she yelled, "Did you know Maze was
performing?"

"Not until I bought the tickets." John-Michael's pleasure
was evident on his face. "I stopped this short—" John-Michael
indicated a wisp of a length with his index finger and thumb—
"of hugging the young lady in line behind me when I saw the
opening act."

Seeing the joy on his face Olivia wondered, not for the first
time, how they had managed to kill the happy times they had
experienced in their first few years of marriage.

She recalled one particular time, an example of John-
Michael's thoughtfulness and love. . . .

She'd had a difficult test which she had spent weeks studying for. On the day of the test, a Friday, John-Michael had
been waiting by the door for her when she had arrived home.
In lieu of words, he had grabbed her hand and led her to the
truck, which had already been packed with a food basket and
suitcases. He had remained mute in response to her questions
until they hit the outskirts of Atlanta. Then he'd explained they
were going to have a relaxing, stress-free weekend in the city.
On the agenda for the weekend's activities, in addition to lazing
around the hotel room, had been a Frankie Beverly and Maze
concert. That had been her first time seeing them in concert,
his fourth. It had been a great weekend, one she would never
forget. Shifting from the past to the present, Olivia turned
around before her sadness and regret showed.

By the time Frankie Beverly and Maze ended their mini-
concert, the crowd was raring for the type of good entertainment that only a rodeo can provide. As the popular band left
the arena in an oversized, flatbed trailer, the announcer kicked

off the rodeo events over loud catcalls, piercing whistles and screams of pleasure.

The foursome settled back in their ringside seats to thoroughly enjoy the life-threatening activities—bull riding, steer roping and wrestling, barrel racing, and other events. Halfway through the line-up of events, the announcer called all brave souls interested in the greased pig contest to sign up at the announcer's booth. Micky, bitten by the rodeo bug, rose from his seat.

"Where do you think you're going?" Dan asked in his Father Knows Best tone.

"I'm gonna get me one of those pigs."

"Where you gonna raise a pig? You live in an apartment . . . in the city, for goodness sake!"

Motherly concern was evident on Olivia's face and in her voice. "But, Micky, you can be hurt. It's not as thrilling as it sounds."

"This is the closest I'm going to get to being in a rodeo. I'm going for it. Excuse me." Micky hopped over Olivia into the aisle. "And as for raising it, well . . ." Micky gave it a second of contemplation. "I can have it shipped home and have Dad raise it on our farm in Oklahoma. Yeah—" he said, his excitement building, "it'll be a great pet for him. You know, take his mind off his cancer and stuff."

"Micky, think about what you're doing." Olivia stood and, using her fingers as a counter, started to recite several reasons why Micky shouldn't pursue his idea. It was wasted effort. Micky was bounding up the steps to the sign-up post before she got to reason number one.

Dan got up. Mumbling something under his breath about foolhardy behavior, he trailed Micky.

Olivia turned beseeching eyes to John-Michael, begging for his assistance.

In response to her silent plea, John-Michael stated matter-of-factly, "Olivia, he's young. Young men will sometimes do dumb things." Shrugging his broad shoulders, he finished,

"You can't shelter him from the experiences that will develop him into a grown man."

With a frown puckering her brow, Olivia argued with his reasoning. "But lessons can be taught verbally. All of life's lessons don't have to be learned the hard way."

Accompanied by a derisive grunt, John-Michael remarked, "I know. I wish I had listened to you about separate living quarters for Mother. Maybe then we'd still be together."

As soon as the words were out, John-Michael regretted them. He wanted to ease his way back into his wife's good heart, not by force, not by intimidation, and certainly not by bringing up the subject of most of their horrific arguments. He had planned to focus only on the positives, to make her remember the good times and the love, but in less than a week he had succeeded in arguing with her about his family tree and reviving their disagreements concerning Roberta.

Olivia stood as still as a giant oak in the winter. Scenes from the past whizzed by her like stock cars on a fast track. There had been many arguments toward the tail end of their married life. The one which stood out far and above the others had pitted her against Roberta, and John-Michael had selected Roberta as the winner. She, Olivia, had been the one to pack her love and go.

"Olivia . . ." John-Michael reached for her hand, grasped it, and cocooned it in his large hands. He had sensed her withdrawal and knew she was thinking about their prior tribulations. He had to prevent her from thinking about the past . . . get her to concentrate on the future and understand he was a changed man. Desperation lined his voice. "I've had plenty of time to think about the mistakes I made concerning us. I don't want to get into it here—" John-Michael's light brown eyes scanned the area, indicating the full house at the arena. "Maybe we can talk later at the house."

His last statement brought her out of her reverie. A shake of her head cleared the memories, vaulting them into the darkness of her memory bank. "No, John-Michael. We can't." With more power and conviction than she felt, Olivia pulled her hand out of his and squared her shoulders. "I'm only here to perform a study." To let him know she was dead serious about her last comment, she added, "You might as well know that Johnson Farms was not my locale of choice. If I'd had my way, I would be doing my research at another farm."

John-Michael already knew that. That was why he had dumped thousands of dollars into the Alabama A & M at Huntsville's Agriculture Department, and called in many markers at the state agriculture department to make sure her study was conducted at his farm. All of his actions, unknown to her, were done so he could have a second chance with his one love.

Olivia spun around and reclaimed her seat. Crossing her arms across her bosom, she made it perfectly clear that the conversation was over. *Stupid, Olivia! That was just plain stupid. How could you have let yourself start feeling for him again?* Anger at herself and at the pain that she still felt when she thought about the love she had fought for and lost wound its way through her body. *Roberta and the farm will always be numbers one and two with him. He only needed me to bear his children. Well, he can just forget it. For the next two months, I'm here to finish my study. I don't give a hoot about his relationship with his father, and I don't care about him.*

John-Michael sat up straight. He knew he should have shared more of his thoughts, decisions, and expectations with her before they got married. As he had told Olivia earlier, boys do make dumb decisions on the road to manhood. As a young man he thought it would be a simple matter to balance the needs of his wife, mother, and farm. As a man, he now knew it was not simple. Added to that balancing act was the magnanimous chore of fighting the gene pool battle. It was never far from his conscious mind that he needed to prove he was not John-Michael Taylor reincarnate.

As a child he had hated it when his mother had told him, "You're just like your father." Every time she lost her temper, every time he had been irresponsible or made a mistake, she had likened him to his father. When those hurtful words erupted from her mouth, he had cringed and sworn to do a better job of maintaining watch on himself, to ensure that nothing he did ever reminded anyone that he was his father's son.

Damned if I give up now. Too much is at stake. Leaning over, he positioned his lips close to her ear. "You don't know the whole story, Olivia. You owe it to yourself to at least understand the background to some of our problems." Following his heart's direction, John-Michael shifted his head from the side of her face to plant a soft, affectionate kiss on the top of her head. Savoring the feel of her curly hair, he closed his eyes and rubbed his face lightly in it, while his hands gently massaged the tight muscles in her neck and shoulders. He waited for her response.

Her response came, invisible to him. The deep bass of his voice thundered through her chest, making her remember their long ago early morning lovemaking sessions when the only sounds were his masculine *oohs* and her feminine *aahs*. Now, with every gentle, soothing caress from his hands and lips, she felt herself blossoming, opening to him like a flower to the sun. The touch of his lips to her hair heated her blood, causing a paroxysm in her erotic zone. Her response to his gentle plea and caresses made a mockery of her earlier thoughts. She realized that for the past three years she had been living a lie. She had left Johnson Farms thinking she was ambivalent toward him, that she could politely pack away her feelings and love for him in a cedar chest, to collect moths and dust and be forgotten. A few weeks on his farm had opened the chest of lies—she did love John-Michael. Only he possessed her heart.

The sound of a man loudly clearing his throat pulled them from their cocoon.

Dan said, "The fool boy did it. You'll see him and a bunch of other cuckoos in the middle of the arena in a few minutes." He had the decency to ignore the lost look on Olivia's face and the crushed look on John-Michael's. He scooted past John-Michael and sat down hard. Huffing and puffing, he shook a white hankie from his pocket and wiped his brow. "Boy, that's some walk up and down those stairs." Chatting on amicably about the number of contestants for the greased pig contest, he thoughtfully afforded Olivia and John-Michael the chance to recover.

A siren sounding much like a stuck pig went off, echoing throughout the coliseum announcing to the world that time had arrived for the contest of luck. In single file, a group of approximately twenty participants hopped, skipped, marched, walked onto the packed dirt floor. A loud cheering went up to the rafters as the would-be pig raisers squared the marked area. Soon, a trailer backed to one side of the square, and several men coaxed ten, pink baby pigs tied together to the center of the square.

Simultaneously, a gun sounded the beginning of the contest and the men untied the pigs. Within seconds pigs and participants fell into mass chaos. Arms, legs, curly tails, and short, pink snouts became entangled, much like an ivy vine latching onto a tree root. The crowd laughed thunderously when someone thought he had a pig, only to have the slippery animal finagle its way out of his grip.

In the stand, Dan, John-Michael, and Olivia cheered Micky on. They started jumping up and down when they spied Micky on the ground with a pretty decent handle on a struggling pig. Just as the attendants were headed over to tie and claim the pig for Micky, though, the pig gave one final twist, accidentally kicking Micky in the head, and was free.

Micky grabbed his head and fell backward. At the same time that Micky hit the dirt, another recently escaped pig kicked him on the other side of his head, and several teenage boys trampled over Micky's still body in pursuit.

"Micky!" Olivia cried. Terror and fear had a stiff hold on her.

John-Michael was already out of his seat, over the wall, and into the ring, with Dan's lumbering body no more than two steps behind him. Fighting madly in the fray, John-Michael and Dan reached the young man as the Johnny-on-the-spot rodeo clowns lifted Micky and carried his lightweight body to a side entrance near a tunnel.

Olivia had followed her companions' trek, but seeing the emergency action of the clowns she had met them at the tunnel. Pushing her way to the gurney they had placed him on, she touched his shoulder. "Micky?"

His eyes batted open but closed again after a few tries.

"Micky?" she asked again. This time he gave no physical response to her cry. Fear was a weight sitting on her heart.

A short, squat white man in a white uniform bearing the insignia of the local emergency response unit spoke to Olivia. "Excuse us, Ma'am. We need to load him in the ambulance to transport him to County." With firm, polite handling, he moved Olivia to the side and strapped Micky in. Micky's companions followed close on the heels of the medical attendants as they quickly wheeled the gurney through the tunnel and outside to the waiting ambulance.

"Ma'am, you can ride in back," the same man said, and Olivia wasted no time heeding his command. Another medical attendant—and guilt—rode in the back of the ambulance with her. A series of "if onlys" began a mantra in her head as she prayed over the skinny, pale body.

Within ten minutes they were at the hospital, and Micky had been wheeled into an exam room. A floor nurse armed with a ton of papers on a clipboard escorted Olivia to a nearby waiting room. As soon as the nurse left, Olivia placed the insurance forms and patient information sheets to the side and began wrestling with her conscience. Fifteen minutes later, Dan and John-Michael joined Olivia in the waiting room. John-Michael, sensing her state of mind, hugged her close. Olivia submitted willingly.

"How's he?" Dan demanded, angry at himself for not being more stern with Micky. *I should have stressed the danger, been*

*more forceful with the boy. I know how unpredictable farm
animals can be, especially when they're young and scared.*

Olivia eased out of John-Michael's arms, thankful for the
strength they had given. Lifting her shoulders in an *I don't
know* gesture, she told them, "The doctor is in with him now.
They haven't reported on his condition." Wrapping her arms
around herself, she had to fight the desire to return to John-
Michael's arms for warmth and safety. She couldn't allow herself to become dependent on him to meet her needs. Oh, but,
how she wanted to return home to his arms! "It's only been
a few minutes. It may take a while for the exam to be completed."

John-Michael was battling his own guilt. He should have
made an attempt to stop the young man. He hadn't even tried.
He'd been too wrapped up in Olivia.

Dan sighed deeply. "Yeah. You're right." Scratching his
head, he stared at the floor. He spoke softly, something Olivia
had never heard him do. "I guess all we can do is wait." As
if that decision had truly been his, he selected a chair close
to the open doorway of the waiting room and sank low on his
spine, with his arms folded on top of his belly.

"I'll go find some coffee." John-Michael, a man of action,
hated slack time. Anything was better than sitting and waiting,
especially in this room where painful memories of their last time
at County waited to overtake him. He turned his back to the
room and to the past memories and went in search of coffee.

Olivia paced the floor from one end of the room to the
other. She, like Dan, studied the worn linoleum as if it were
the *New York Times* Sunday edition crossword puzzle.

In less time than it takes to clean a mess of greens, John-
Michael returned with three steaming cups of black coffee.
Yielding one to Dan, he asked, "Any word?"

Dan shook his head negatively. "Thanks."

Meeting his wife halfway in the room, he handed a second
cup to her. With silent will, he commanded her to meet his
gaze. He had to know if the memories were haunting her, as

well. When she mutely met his gaze, he saw that they did. The pain carved in her dark, brown eyes reflected his own. He reached out a hand, intending to caress her cheek, but she shied away from him. Turning her back to him, she walked to the window to stare out at the blackness. John-Michael sucked in his breath, sucked in the pain, and went to stand guard at the opening of the room.

They remained like that for an hour—Dan, posted near the door slumped in his seat; John-Michael leaning against the doorjamb, trying to occupy his mind with anything other than the past and present pain; Olivia at the window with her back to the men, encased in her own personal world.

Finally, with John-Michael on the verge of going to search for someone in charge, a light-skinned young doctor in his mid-thirties, bespectacled and sporting a 1970's Afro, entered. Dan, Olivia, and John-Michael pressed around him as if he were a celebrity.

"Doc?" Dan inquired quietly, almost too quietly.

"You're here with the young man from the rodeo?" At their nods, he resumed speaking. "It appears to be a minor concussion, similar to one caused by falling out of a tree or running smack dead into a brick wall. No major or permanent damage. He'll be fine, but just to be sure we're going to keep him under observation for twenty-four hours. Go on home. We'll call you if anything changes."

"You guys can go. I'll stay here and call if anything happens." To punctuate his offer, Dan reclaimed his hard seat on the beige plastic chair and picked up his Styrofoam coffee cup.

"I'm not leaving," Olivia said flatly.

The doctor wrapped a hand around the back of his neck and rubbed it as if magically rubbing away the long hours of emergency work. In a staid voice, he directed, "There's no reason for anyone to stay. Look, if it makes you feel any better you can—one at a time—talk to him just to assure yourselves he's in no danger. As I said, we only want to watch him for a short time, just to be sure."

With shrugs and head nods the three agreed to the doctor's compromise.

One by one they filtered in and out of Micky's room. Beside being bruised, swollen, and red, with tubes in his arms, Micky was himself. He'd even had the audacity to tell them he'd had fun trying to win a pig.

After the short visits, reassured by the sight of Micky, they somberly left the hospital, each person closed off behind a door marked *private*. The atmosphere in the car was funereal on the drive home.

Olivia, seated in the front seat with John-Michael, was wrapped up in thoughts of the past, for as hard as she tried she could not deflect the memories that the hospital visit had aroused.

The day she miscarried their last child had been a Saturday night, too.

Two days prior to the miscarriage she had argued with Roberta about the usual thing—her focus on school versus her wifely duties as spouse to a wealthy farmer. What had precipitated *that* argument was the regret Olivia had sent to the governor of Alabama. They had received an invitation to attend an opening session party at the governor's mansion at the state capitol. Roberta had found out about the regret and become infuriated with Olivia for declining the invitation without her or John-Michael's input. She had hatefully chastised Olivia. Olivia had ignored her mother-in-law and proceeded to open a schoolbook. That had inflamed Roberta, so much that she had hightailed it to John-Michael's study and complained to him about his wife.

John-Michael had sought Olivia out and asked her to explain what was going on. In her most factual voice, Olivia explained that she had a very important test coming up and could not waste time partying. She had also pointed out to him that he did not like "dressing up and politicking", so why bother? Diplomatically, John-Michael had agreed with Olivia's reasons, but he had gone on to explain that a farm bill involving state funds would be voted on this session and he needed the governor's support to ensure that the bill survived. He had asked Olivia to call and rescind the regret and register three for attendance. Olivia had done so, all the while growing more bitter with Roberta for running their lives and equally angry with John-Michael for allowing his mother to control them.

On the day and time they were due to leave for the party, Olivia had been missing. John-Michael had waited until the last possible second, but still no Olivia. With final instructions to Lena to have one of the men drive Olivia to Montgomery when she showed up, he and his mother had left.

John-Michael and Roberta had received word at the governor's party that Olivia was at County. They had practically flown to the hospital, where the doctor had explained that a fellow student had seen Olivia pass out in the library. The clinic on campus had done what they could, but eventually she had been transported to County. Olivia had miscarried, and the doctor attributed it to stress.

The three had returned home in the wee hours of a gray Sunday morning. Few words had been exchanged, and even fewer touches.

After that, the atmosphere at the house had become downright oppressive—not that it hadn't been a challenge before the miscarriage. This time, she and John-Michael became strangers; instead of turning to each other for comfort, they turned their backs to each other at night. Roberta had relegated Olivia to an ignore-it-and-it-will-go-away position, which had been fine with Olivia. Roberta had also started easing Olivia out of the decision making process in the running of John-Michael's home. Lena had been her only caregiver and friend—the only one who had listened to her regrets about that day.

Olivia imagined things would have gone on that way indefinitely if it hadn't been for the final, really big argument—several months later—which drove her away from John-Michael and Johnson Farms.

Replaying the situation now, Olivia knew she should have handled the situation differently, but then she'd been so angry with Roberta and John-Michael, so desirous of showing Roberta who was in control, that she had unwittingly taken it out on their unborn child by giving little attention to her physical needs—food, rest, vitamins, liquids, relaxation—and more attention to studying for her tests.

Even now, years later, tears burned in the back of her eyes, waiting for release. Refusing to give into the weakness until she was safely away in her own bedroom, Olivia turned her head to stare out of the window. Focusing on the millions of bright stars in the sky, she prayed that their two children, embryos on earth but surely full grown in heaven, played peacefully near the throne.

Six

John-Michael dropped Dan and Olivia off in front of the house, then drove slowly to the west side yard, to the five car garage. As the garage door lifted, revealing an empty spot next to his truck and the outside wall, his eyes automatically shifted to the car beyond his truck—a Christmas red '69 Mustang convertible. He had bought it for Olivia as a wedding gift. Now it sat as unused as their wedding vows. The car, the hospital visit, Olivia's return all converged to make the memories as real as if they were happening now.

Robotically, he parked Roberta's car, shut the engine down and sat still as a mummy as he relived the past. . . .

It had been a mild winter night. The sky was clear, the wind was absent, and the temperatures had been hovering around the forties. As he had requested, Lena had put together a snack tray, complete with a bottle of wine, while he had built a roaring fire in the stone fireplace. Christmas was just around the corner, and Olivia's semester was finally ending.

"I'll have Olivia see you soon as she gets in," Lena had promised as she backed out of the room.

Sitting in the study, waiting for Olivia to join him, John-Michael had contemplated the previous years. Things had not been going well for them for some time, and in fact had gotten worse since the last miscarriage, two months ago.

The chasm which had started with the first miscarriage in

their second year of marriage had taken on Grand Canyon proportions. Emotionally, Olivia had closed herself off to him, and they were acting more like roommates than husband and wife. To John-Michael, this meant he was proving as big a failure as a husband and father as his father had been. His failures had haunted his waking and sleeping thoughts, making him vulnerable to his mother's unsolicited comments. Something had to change. He would not be his father's son. The conversation he planned to have with his wife would hopefully cure him of that threat.

The study door opened and Olivia walked in.

"So how'd you do?" John-Michael had moved from behind his large cherrywood desk to sit on the burgundy leather sofa. He stretched his long legs out in front of him and positioned one arm along the back of the sofa.

Olivia wriggled out of her coat and moved to the fireplace to warm herself. "I think I did well on today's test. Thank God it was the last one." Turning her back to the fire, she had moved to sit on the sofa; a section separated them. "Of course, I'll know for sure in a few weeks when I get my grades in the mail."

"So what are you going to do with your time off?"

"Why?"

"Look, Olivia, you know I'm not terribly adept at expressing myself, but I want to ask you something."

Olivia nodded.

"Would you please take next semester off, so we can work on our marriage?" Unable to sit any longer, John-Michael got up and took long-legged strides around the room. "You know as well as I do that things are falling apart. We need some time to really work on our problems."

"Take a semester off? I'm just beginning my graduate studies."

"Are you telling me that your graduate studies are more important than our marriage?" John-Michael didn't want to hear the answer, but he could no longer afford to stick his head in the sand. His father's ghost was calling to him.

Olivia stood up to face her husband. "What I'm telling you, John-Michael, is I don't think my schooling is the problem."

"Awww, come on, Olivia . . ." John-Michael picked up a throw pillow and slammed it back onto the couch. "Don't start that again."

A sneer had accompanied Olivia's words. "What? The truth. You don't want to hear that your mother is interfering with our relationship, that you work harder at making this farm a success than you do at making our marriage work. I've asked you repeatedly to move your mother to a separate house, in town, and I've asked you to hire a foreman so we can have more time together." Mimicking John-Michael, Olivia continued. "Now's not the time to discuss this, Olivia. Be patient." Olivia's chest heaved; she struggled to breathe. "Well, I've *been* patient!"

In a dead-cold voice, John-Michael said, "And I've told you, Olivia, this is Mother's birthplace. I can't move her now . . . besides, I owe her. And, secondly, a good—no, make that an excellent—foreman is hard to find. You know no hired person will take care of my farm the way I do."

Stubbornly, Olivia had crossed her arms across her chest and issued a terse command. "Fine. When you move your mother out and hire a foreman, then I'll take off a semester. But, I'm not going to be the one making all the sacrifices."

John-Michael had stopped wearing out the rug and run a hand across his brow. This was not going as planned. They'd been down this path before, and had gotten nowhere. Frantically, he searched his mind for something that would make the ending different. In a calmer voice, he pleaded, "Olivia, I really want children. We know we're capable of producing, but as the doctors said you're too stressed to carry a child through the first trimester. It's happened twice now. I was just hoping if you took a semester off then maybe you could carry a child full term."

Olivia said sternly, "I have no doubt that the doctors are right. However, one thing the doctors don't know about is my living conditions. My stresses aren't only at school. They exist here, too, John-Michael. I'll gladly give you the child you so desperately want if you move your mother out of here and hire a foreman. There is no other way I will bring a child into this environment."

Anger was starting to percolate all over again. Roughly, he said, "You're starting to sound like a parrot, Olivia."

In an accusatory tone, Olivia had responded, "Maybe if you actually listened to me, John-Michael, I wouldn't have to keep repeating myself."

The frustration of the situation turned to fullblown anger; reasoning capabilities left with the onslaught of that anger. "I *am* listening, and what I'm hearing is a selfish, whiny woman who doesn't know when she's got it good."

"Got it good?" Olivia had advanced on him, meeting his anger with her own. "If living with Roberta is good, and living with a man I hardly ever see is good, then I sure as hell don't want the bad."

"You have a roof over your head. I pay for your schooling. I feed you, clothe you, provide for all your needs. I even bought you that car that carries you away from me. And, you have the nerve to stand here and complain."

"Yes, I do! Because life isn't about material possessions, John-Michael." Olivia couldn't stop her finger from pointing at his chest, despite the trembling that was starting to overtake her. "Yeah, you provide all those things, but where's the loyalty, the time reserved just for the two of us, the sympathetic ear, the respect? I haven't seen that side of you in years. It's almost as if you performed long enough to trap me and then, *wham,* you turned colors."

John-Michael's voice had escalated, his handsome face distorted in rage. "How can you stand there and tell me I've changed, when you're the one? If anyone here is acting, it's you."

Olivia walked to where she had laid her coat. Picking it up, she'd swung around. "I don't know what you're talking about."

He had matched her stride for stride. Barely an inch separated them. He bent from the waist, bringing their faces all the more closer. "Those miscarriages, Olivia, were they real or intentional?"

Stunned, Olivia had stepped back. Confusion lined her face. For the moment, her anger was forgotten. "What do you mean?"

"Mother thinks you purposely aborted those children. She thinks you hate the idea of having children before you finish your schooling. She thinks you somehow induced those miscarriages."

A lengthy silence filled the cozy room. Finally, Olivia had asked, "And what about you, John-Michael? Do you think I intentionally killed our children?"

"Getting your Ph.D. is overly important to you, Olivia. Overly important," John-Michael said softly, haltingly.

Olivia had sucked in her breath. "Good-bye, John-Michael."

Olivia had moved around him and headed for the door. Olivia didn't stop although John-Michael had called her name.

In the study, unaware of his wife's departure from the house, John-Michael had sat in his own pool of misery. After Olivia had left the study, he had started for the door a million times. *She's upset. I'm upset,* John-Michael had told himself, *it's best to let things cool before we finish the conversation.* He had walked back into the interior of the room, snagged a beer from the tray and popped the top, downing half the beer in one swallow. Full of self-derision, John-Michael had chided himself, *It didn't turn out as I had planned. All I wanted was for her to sit out a semester, have a baby. Everything would have worked out fine with a baby in the house.* John-Michael had banged his head against the mantel of the fireplace. *I know those miscarriages weren't intentional. God, what led me to say what I did? And then, to tell her what Mother thinks. Jeez, it's a wonder she didn't belt me.* He had berated himself for over an hour, paying little attention to the car pulling up outside, assuming it was Roberta coming home from Christmas shopping.

When he had calmed down sufficiently to think straight enough to try again, he headed for their bedroom. The room was empty. A full search of the house, the gardens, the outside buildings, every place imaginable, yielded no Olivia. With her car in the garage, he knew she couldn't have gone far. Two hours later, when she still hadn't shown up, he had passed from worried to frantic. Calls to her professors and study group resulted in no information. The only thing he knew to do next was to call his friend, the sheriff. Then had come the sickening task of walking the floor and tearing himself down.

The sheriff had finally called around three that morning to inform John-Michael that a cab driver had reported dropping Olivia off at the Greyhound station. The bus station manager, an associate of the Johnson family, had searched the receipts to determine that Olivia had traveled to Meridian, Mississippi. John-Michael had wasted no time throwing a few things into a bag and hitting the eastbound highway.

All the success he had had tracking her down had not carried over into the next step—getting Olivia to accept him. He had gone directly to Dr. Hill's house, but Olivia had refused to let him in. Involving her parents and the two sisters and one brother still living in Meridian in the matter helped to get him inside Dr. Hill's house, but after she let him in Olivia had stubbornly refused to accept his apology or go home with him. She had demanded time to think things through, and indicated she would call him. From the set look on her face, there was little else he could do but go home and wait for the steam from their argument to dissipate, for the cruel words to evaporate. He understood she needed time to let her anger trail into nothing.

With misgivings, he had left, returning to Johnson Farms. After forty-eight hours had passed with no word from Olivia, John-Michael had driven back to Meridian. He had returned

to Tuskegee alone. He had not been able to find Olivia anywhere in Meridian—not at the homes of her various family
members, and not at Dr. Hill's home. A week later, he had
found out that she had done some traveling and had ended up
in Huntsville. Knowing her new location, John-Michael had
visited her and tried desperately to convince her to return to
Johnson Farms. She had refused, and he had left, deciding to
give her more time to forgive him.

Days stretched into months, which stretched into years, and
although he had made numerous attempts to win her back during those years, she had shunned him and had refused to return
to Johnson Farms.

A pricking along his shoulders and neck brought him back
to the present. Forcing himself to breathe deeply to release the
tension which had settled there, he whispered, "Thank God I
knew her well enough to anticipate her Ph.D. project. I'm glad
things worked out with the state, Chem-Co, and the university.
Now, I can implement a study of my own." John-Michael refused to think about his father's ghost as he locked the garage
and made his way into the house.

He was up the stairs and at Olivia's bedroom door before
the crickets could start round two of their chorus. Lightly,
briefly, he rapped on her door, and—without waiting for a
welcoming command—entered her bedroom.

Olivia had wasted no time swapping her rodeo clothes for
a baby doll sleeper. She didn't care what anyone said, she *knew*
it was more exhausting to deal with emotional upheaval than
to do physical labor. She was totally washed out, what with
dealing with Micky's stunt and with John-Michael's admission
of fault concerning his mother, and then those damning memories at the hospital. God, but she was drained.

With the latest edition of *Essence* magazine in tow, she had
scrambled under the sheets and said a quick prayer for Micky's
safety. She had read two paragraphs of an article when the

knock sounded. Seconds later, John-Michael's head, then body, appeared.

The only light in the room stemmed from the table lamp by her bed, but she could see well enough to know John-Michael was gravely serious. In the soft glow from the lamp, their eyes caught and held. A nuclear blast could not have severed the contact.

Watching her husband approach with that solemn look on his face, Olivia thought immediately of Micky. "It's Micky?"

"No." John-Michael's voice was just as earnest as his facial expression.

He kept coming. Feasting on her beauty. Vowing to win her back.

Olivia continued to stare at him. With her initial fears relieved, she wondered what was on John-Michael's mind. Then, his expression changed from weighty consideration to desire. It was just a slight change, but she recognized it and responded to it. Her heart began a fast *rat-a-tat-tat,* causing her breathing to increase and her palms to become sweaty. Olivia realized that even her feminine core began vibrating in anticipation of what John-Michael was clearly signaling. Olivia was immobilized, caught in the headlights of John-Michael's light brown eyes.

The ticking of the small brass and crystal clock on her bedside table was the only sound in the room as John-Michael rounded the bed and stood over her; hands on hips, bow-legs spread apart. His gaze roamed over her delicate features. He noted with pleasure the flat mole set slightly above her upper lip. His eyes moved lower to the pulse beating quickly at her throat, and lower still to the small mounds silhouetted in the pastel fabric of her nightgown. Her hips and legs were shadowed under the folds of bedclothes, but he knew the perfect mold of them from his dreams. He could feel himself starting to harden from his intense perusal of her. Lifting his eyes before the hardening process was irreversible, he met her dark brown eyes. Wariness, anxiety, and something else he couldn't quite pinpoint—maybe desire, maybe hope—were reflected there. *Stick to the agenda, John-Michael. This is way too important to be led by your amorous desires.*

Letting his hands drop to his side, John-Michael spoke softly, matching the lighting in the room. "I'm sorry."

His eyes caressing her body had warmed her. Her breath was issuing way too quickly, and his simple words barely registered. Forcing herself to break the bond between them, she lowered her head. *Calm down, Olivia. Stop fantasizing about something you can't have.* She cleared her throat and pulled the Ms. Peabody glasses from the bridge of her nose. Laying them and the magazine to the side, she asked, "About?"

John-Michael looked down at her small hand laying on top of the covers. On her ring finger, his symbol of love sparkled brightly despite the darkened room. He moved to sit on the side of the bed and enclosed her hand in his. "So much." John-Michael ran his hand across his brow, overwhelmed by the many mistakes he had committed in the past. "I wasn't a good husband. You were right about so many things—my mother, the foreman, your right to be in control of the household, so many things. I can only apologize."

Olivia sat up straighter, drawn into the conversation by his words, his manner. Leaning forward, she asked, "What made you come to this understanding?"

"For the past three years I've had nothing but time to think. I can't tell you how many times I've replayed our first meeting, and how many times I've analyzed our arguments. I wasn't fair to you, Olivia." John-Michael released her hand and angled his body so he fully faced her, one leg hiked up on the bed, his clasped hands dangling between his legs. "I mentioned earlier at the rodeo that you didn't know everything. Well, you don't, but now you will." After a slight pause, John-Michael continued. "Ever since I was a little boy I've carried this great responsibility. I cherished it as some boys cherish a prized bicycle or an autographed baseball. I would take this responsibility off the shelf every day, polish it, and put it back. I've lived with it all my life, Olivia, I guess I don't know how to live without it."

"But, I don't understand what this has to do with us and the problems we encountered."

"The responsibility is this farm, and my mother. I grew up with the understanding that it would always be up to me to take care of both. And, I'm sure this logic would have gone unchallenged if you hadn't happened into the picture." John-Michael smiled, remembering the day they first met. "I think I fell in love with you that first day. You were so open, so pure, so sweet. I know for sure I fell in lust." John-Michael wiggled his eyebrows, and Olivia smiled. "I remember feeling this overwhelming need to protect you, to love you. Then, as time passed and we got to know each other, I knew you were tougher than you looked. You're a fighter, and as stubborn as hell." John-Michael flicked a finger against her nose. Olivia shook her head affirmatively. They both smiled. John-Michael sighed, growing serious. "Anyway, I don't know what other people call it, but I call it inflexibility. I just didn't know how to ease up on my old responsibilities to allow room for my new ones, i.e., my duties and requirements as a husband." A self-derisive chortle filled the air. "It's funny. I learned everything I needed to know about caring for this farm before I was twenty years old, but I didn't learn how to be a good husband until these past three years. Frightening thought, huh?"

"Yeah, it is," Olivia softly replied.

"I just wanted to apologize to you for my careless handling of our wedding vows, and I'm asking for your forgiveness."

Olivia didn't doubt his sincerity. She read it quite clearly in his eyes. But something was still nagging at her. "So if you've come to this realization, why haven't you hired a foreman? I still see you're working long hours."

"There's no reason for me not to work from sunrise to sunset. You aren't here." While the words settled into Olivia's brain, John-Michael continued, "Mother's still here for the same reason."

He didn't dare ask her to return to him. He wanted to, but the time wasn't right. He knew Olivia's analytical, researcher's brain. She would want time to think things through. So the question of her returning to him for good was left hanging in the air, unasked, but greatly hinted at.

"You believed me capable of destroying our children." The accusatory statement fell flat. She dreaded his answer. Like a child watching a Freddie Krueger movie, she was afraid to see and hear, but more afraid not to.

"I never believed that, Olivia." John-Michael shifted closer to her on the bed. "Yes, I know I repeated Mother's words, but I did it out of anger. I was frustrated and blinded with fear. I was losing you, and didn't know how to reach you, so I tried to bait you." John-Michael ran a hand over his head. "I was wrong. I know you would never hurt *anyone*."

A lengthy silence permeated the air. He could almost see Olivia's calculator brain figuring out all the puzzle pieces and putting them together.

"Does your father have anything to do with your feelings toward the farm and your mother?"

Dead air. John-Michael stared directly into Olivia's eyes. A faraway look rested in his eyes, then flitted away. She thought she saw a flash of pain skitter across his handsome face. She recalled the scene in the barn, and she knew she was on to something. "My father ran off and left the care of everything to me."

Empathy flooded her body. The pain in John-Michael's voice was unmistakable. Taking his hand in hers, she tried to assuage his hurt. "I'm sorry, John-Michael. Believe me, I understand." Although her parents had been present and accounted for, they really hadn't been there. They had never come to one of her spelling bees. They hadn't been at the PTA meetings to see her receive first place ribbons in the science fairs. They hadn't been at her graduation from high school. They had left her to figure out her own emotional lessons.

The mattress lightened and Olivia looked up from her memory movie to see John-Michael standing. "Anyway, I just wanted to apologize for being so cruel and harsh with you. Please forgive me." His feet were heavy as he dragged them slowly away from her bedside.

"John-Michael."

He turned to face the only woman he'd ever loved.

"I think you're a very admirable man." Olivia blessed him with a small smile.

John-Michael walked back to the bed and laid a hand on the side of her face. He leaned forward and kissed her on the forehead. "I love you, Olivia."

Olivia closed her eyes so he wouldn't see the tears shimmering there. Even after she heard the door close, she kept her eyes shut. The tears fell anyway.

Seven

"I'll be back in a few hours," Olivia threw over her shoulder. She could have saved those few words, since Dan and Micky didn't even look up to acknowledge her departure. On the edge of the test field, the guys continued mixing the compound that Chem-Co claimed would help regenerate the soil, allowing farmers to have higher yields. After mixing, they would spray the test area and then take the rest of the day off to enjoy a relaxing afternoon of fishing and eyelid watching.

Olivia's plans for the rest of the day weren't as simple as her co-workers'. A trip to Tuskegee University's library for some additional research information and to say *Hi* to former professors was her order for the day. Olivia was looking forward to the trip to town. She hadn't been there since Founders' Day, and now that the town knew she was back, she didn't feel nearly as self-conscious. *Heck, who knows? Maybe, on the way back I'll even treat myself to a slice of carrot cake and a cup of coffee from JoJo's.* With a spring in her step and a smile on her face, she entered the house through the back porch.

Lena was standing over the double white ceramic sink, washing fryers.

"Hi, Lena."

The friend and housekeeper turned her head toward Olivia, granting the younger woman a favorable smile. "Morning, Sugar. How are you?" It crossed Lena's mind that it was highly unusual for the graduate student to be in her kitchen during the day. A hybrid expression of confusion and happiness showed on Lena's ageless face. "What you doing here?" Lena squinted at the square wooden clock on a far wall. "It's not time for lunch yet, is it?"

"No, no, don't panic." Olivia chuckled at Lena trying to make out the time. "The guys won't be ready to eat for another couple of hours." Olivia thought about her comment. "Well, let me rephrase that. The guys are always ready to eat, but lunch*time* is still two hours away."

Lena relaxed, returning to her task. "Oh, good. I didn't think I had let the morning get by me."

Olivia grabbed a glass from a frosted-glass fronted cabinet and filled it with water from the dispenser on the refrigerator. "Where are your glasses? I thought you were supposed to wear them at all times."

"Ohhhh, they're around here somewhere." Lena chuckled. "I would wear them, but they keep getting away from me." Wiping her hands on the cotton shift that she wore on top of her day dress, Lena reached into a lower cabinet and pulled a boiling pot from underneath. She held it under the faucet and began filling it with water. "Thought I'd do chicken and dumplings. Dan mentioned he loves it."

Olivia swallowed a big gulp of the cleansing liquid. "Dan loves food, period. I'm sure that whatever you cook will be fine with him . . . and Micky too, come to think of it." Olivia finished her drink and placed the empty glass in the dishwasher. "Don't set a place for me. I don't think I'll be back in time." She leaned her back against the counter and crossed her arms, watching Lena as she returned to the fryers and cut them up in thirty seconds flat. Amazed, Olivia continued, "We decided to take the afternoon off, so I'm headed to the university. Do you need anything in town?"

"Nope. I'm fully stocked. Thanks for asking."

The four panel, distressed wood door which opened onto the main hallway pushed inward, and John-Michael walked in, rolling up his sleeves. With his head bowed, intent on his mission, he was oblivious to the extra company in the room.

"Lena, I'm headed to town. You want—" He stopped when he saw Olivia poised by the sink. "Good morning. What are you doing here?" His heart responded to her appearance by galloping like a wild stallion. It took an inordinate amount of willpower to stay still and not rush to touch her. It had been many days since they'd talked in her bedroom, and since then he'd kept his distance. He'd hit her with some pretty heavy-duty things that Saturday night, and he knew she needed time to digest it all. So, he'd resigned himself to just enjoying meals with her and the crew until she made the next move.

Olivia smiled. "That's the same thing Lena asked."

Lena piped up, fiddling with the flame gauge on the stove. "And, what are *you* doing here? Lord, I swear I've never had so much company."

John-Michael flashed a boyish grin at his surrogate mother. "I'm on my way to town. I stopped in to see if you wanted anything." John-Michael walked to a cabinet, snared a glass, and filled it with tap water. "Oh, by the way, before I forget, Walter won't be here for lunch Thursday. I'm meeting with him to review some quarterly reports. I hope we can take care of everything today."

"Fine." Lena set the pot with the chicken and seasonings on the stove. "Olivia needs to go to town, too. Might as well ride together and save the gas." Lena washed and dried her hands quickly, pleased with the way the two of them were being thrown together. "And, if you can wait a second, I'll even pack you a lunch. Days like this were meant for eating under the sky."

John-Michael turned to look at Olivia. *Wait for her to make the next move? Forget it.* He'd not continued the success of this farm by sitting around waiting for opportunities. No, he had proactively created opportunities, and here was a delicious chance just dropped in his lap. He wasn't about to ignore it or leave it to Olivia. "Where you going in town?"

"The university. But, if you don't have time to drop me off I can drive the van. I had planned on it, anyway." The words rushed out of Olivia's mouth and her body temperature began rising.

She wiped her palms on her jeans, wondering why she was nervous. She had these reactions during test times and on first dates, not standing in a kitchen talking. *What's wrong with me? Why am I so nervous about being with John-Michael?* No sooner had she posed the question than the answer came to her. It was a first date! During their last discussion John-Michael had shared information with her that had positioned him in a new and different light. Subsequently, her viewpoint had been re-shaped, and she could feel a change budding within her. Armed with new views, she could allow the three year buildup of poisons, misunderstandings, hurts, and anger to seep out of her. She knew it would take time for the poison to completely wash away, just like it takes time for a house to settle in its foundation.

In unison, John-Michael and Lena spoke. "Nonsense."

Eager to be alone with his wife, John-Michael assured her, "I'll drop you off. It'll take me about three hours with Walter. Does that give you enough time to do what you need to do?"

"Plenty. Thanks." Olivia had to admit her nervousness had turned to excitement. A second first date with John-Michael . . . who would have ever thought it?

As they talked, Lena bustled around the custom-designed, gleaming, steel blue and white kitchen, pulling down a wicker basket, throwing in napkins and utensils. She took ham and roast beef from the refrigerator and onion rolls from the bread box. Fresh fruit and cheese, condiments, a thermos of water, and wine followed. For a woman well into her sixties, she moved with the grace and speed of a young ice skater. In a flash, the basket was packed. She almost threw it into John-Michael's arms.

She dashed into the washroom adjacent to the kitchen, and a few seconds later emerged with a queen-sized, burgundy-colored blanket with tassels on the corners. She tossed it in Olivia's direction, then shooed them out of her kitchen.

Breathless, she suggested, "The northeast pond has the most beautiful view. Stop there and eat on your way back." Waving to their backs as they made their way to the truck, she thought, *They still gonna need my help.*

Waving to their backs as they made their way across the porch and down the steps to the yard she thought, *They still gonna need my help.*

She returned to the kitchen and stood in the middle of it with a balled fist on her hip. *Both of 'em hurting and don't know how to stop it.*

Lena patted her foot in time with her churning thoughts. "Let's see . . . What else can I do?" The seconds passed as she bantered thoughts about in her head. Finally, she lighted on an idea she liked. She wasn't sure with her lack of formal education if she could pull it off, but it was worth a try. The boys will be working for a few more hours and John-Michael and Olivia will be gone for a good while so now's as good a time as any to tiptoe in the barn and see what I can do.

She reduced the flame on the stove and hurriedly untied her apron. Lena entered the barn just as John-Michael turned onto the blacktop farm to market road.

John-Michael briefly glanced at Olivia as he straightened the truck. "Micky still doing okay?"

"Oh, yeah. He's fine." Olivia laughed. "You should have seen him dancing a jig when Dan told him the rodeo folks were shipping a pig to his dad's farm. He was so excited." Olivia angled her body toward John-Michael. "His dad was happy, too. I guess it gets lonely for him, what with his wife gone and Micky, his only child, living so far away. And, from what Micky says, they've had to sell most of their farmland to pay for his dad's treatments, so there's not a lot to occupy his dad's time. Micky knew what he was talking about when he said the pig would be a perfect pet for his dad."

"Then, despite it all, everything worked out just fine."

"Yeah." Olivia thought about their conversation late that Saturday night. She wondered if John-Michael would have come to her room to talk if Micky's accident hadn't happened. She had a strong suspicion that it was their prior time at County that had stimulated his need to talk, and her need to listen. Oh, well, it didn't matter. Micky's accident had happened, and she and John-Michael *had* talked. And, he had told her he still loved her! "It did."

"So, how's the study coming along? You going to give us farmers more fertile soil for more bountiful crops, or what?" John-Michael took his eyes off the road long enough to glance at Olivia.

"I'm going to try." A frown crossed Olivia's face. "The actual experiment's had a few quirks that I hadn't anticipated. Some of the numbers don't match. But it's really too early to tell. When I get back to Huntsville, the lab will run the stats, and we'll see what we're faced with then."

John-Michael made a noncommittal response. His mind had latched on to her mention of returning to Huntsville. A bitter draft of wind dampened his joy of finally being alone with her, then he strengthened his resolve. *I still have time to convince her I'm sincere about patching up our marriage. I just need to make the most of this time.*

A comfortable silence settled between them. Rhythm and Blues hits floated from the radio, offering a calming background to the silence. A romantic tune by the Stylistics—"You Make Me Feel Brand New"—drifted toward them. John-Michael reached out to turn up the volume and started singing along with the group, even though he couldn't sing worth a flip. Olivia smiled just the same. She closed her eyes, leaned her head back, and daydreamed about a different ending to the argument that had driven her away. They were drowned in their own pleasant thoughts, dreams, and the words to the song. The ride to town ended way too quickly.

The breeze floating through the halfway open windows of the truck was soothing. Olivia silently agreed with Lena: *It is too beautiful of a day to be inside.* From the minute she stepped into the university's library, then visited with former professors and stepped back outside, she had missed the warm sun, the rustling of the leaves in the wind, the chirping of the birds not quite ready to fly south, and the busy antics of the squirrels gathering food. By the time John-Michael had returned to pick her up, she had claimed a stone bench near their predetermined pick up point and was basking in nature. Now, riding in the Ford with her husband, she stared out of the window with fresh eyes, noticing the minor changes that had been made in the past three years.

"Tired?" John-Michael spoke softly, gently disturbing her study.

Olivia turned her head in his direction. "Sorry?"

"You sighed. Are you tired?"

Olivia resumed her relaxed pose. "No, just appreciating the day. It's beautiful out, isn't it?"

"Not more beautiful than you."

Olivia's heart thumped and raced with pleasure. "Thank you." Dynamite couldn't have kept the smile off her face.

"Thank you," John-Michael parroted, rewarding her with a smile that matched her own. "We should be at the pond shortly. Just sit back and relax."

Olivia didn't need John-Michael to tell her that. She was already as relaxed as a boiled noodle.

With her eyes closed, Olivia felt him turn off the main highway and onto Bear Creek Road. Only another six miles and they would be at the northeast pond, the place where John-Michael had taken her on their third date—many years ago. They had spent the afternoon fishing and later, after they had scared all the fish away with their nonsense, they had played card games and talked and talked. It had been a memorable occasion.

Now, history—or their courting ritual?—was repeating itself.

Olivia swayed slightly in her seat as John-Michael turned the two ton truck onto an unmarked road that signaled the beginning of his property. Still, with eyes closed, she could visualize the posted notice warning trespassers they were about to enter private property. With her mind's eye she could see the bank of old oak trees lined up near the water's edge like matches in a matchbook. Her swaying grew as gravel gave way to a dirt trail marked by tire tracks. Now they should be parallel with the trees. In a second, he would curve to the left, following the dirt track. Unless he'd done some improvements out here, which she doubted—it was impossible to improve upon this natural habitat—they would have to stop shortly, get out, and walk to the bank of the pond. She was right. Within seconds of her prediction, John-Michael brought the vehicle to a stop.

"We're here."

Olivia sat up and gazed around, testing the accuracy of her memory. She had passed! The place was as serene and untouched and green as she remembered. A profound feeling of what she'd lost swept through her. She wanted to moan, thinking about this and the other natural gifts—the forest, fields and creeks—she had given up when she left Johnson Farms. Not to mention the loss of love.

John-Michael opened her door, reminding her that for the time being she was back in Johnson country. She was determined to enjoy it while she could.

Plucking the picnic basket and blanket from the cab, John-Michael gallantly held out an arm for her. He mimicked an English accent. "Milady."

Olivia smiled at him and looped her arm in his. She joined him in his playful mood, "Why, thank you, kind Sir."

Matching his steps to fit her shorter stride, he escorted her through the calf-high grass, forging straight to the exact location under the trees where just enough sunshine and shadow met to create the perfect picnic spot. Here the grass was a hunter green and ankle high. Fallen tree limbs were scattered throughout, and most alluring of all was the background music—the lapping of the water and the fluttering of birds' wings.

While John-Michael spread the blanket, Olivia re-introduced herself to the beauty of it all.

Rapture covered her from head to toe. "Oh, John-Michael. It's even better than I remember."

"You mean they don't have scenes like this in Huntsville?" John-Michael kidded.

Olivia laughed. "Not by a long shot. There's no comparison."

"Good. Then that should make my selling job easier." John-Michael deposited the wicker basket in the middle of the blanket, then stretched out on one end of the covering.

Dropping down on the other end, Olivia kicked off her shoes and asked, "What do you mean?"

"I don't think it's a secret, Olivia. I want you back here permanently." John-Michael stared at her as if she were a national treasure. "That's all I'm saying. I want you back here with me."

Olivia paused in the midst of spreading out Lena's tasty fixings. Her hand stilled in midair and then landed on her chest. "What?" she mumbled as if the breath had been knocked out of her.

John-Michael hadn't planned to pose this important statement at this time. He would have preferred a more structured approach, but seeing her face glowing with happiness, hearing her glorious laugh, sensing her contentment, he had acted impulsively. "I know we've got some negative history to overcome, but Honey, I want you to give me a second chance—give us, our marriage, another try."

Trepidation seeped into her heart. The sun, previously brilliant, seemed to dim as his words fully sank in. Oh, but this was getting out of hand. Back in Huntsville, she had not anticipated any private moments with John-Michael. She had not planned to renew her feelings for him, and she certainly hadn't planned to consider any proposals for permanent residency. But, here she sat in the middle of a fall meadow thinking how nice it would be to call Johnson Farms home, and call John-

Michael husband and really mean it. On the other hand, she couldn't disregard years of pain and hurt. After all, they'd only had one conversation regarding their past problems. They'd only taken one step toward erasing the past disappointments. She had no guarantee that he meant the words he spoke, that he was a changed man. Was he really willing to displace his mother and hire a foreman? Did he really believe she didn't intentionally kill their children? Was he really still in love with her? She knew John-Michael was not a lying man, but would she be putting her education goals at risk again if she gave in to his request? Would he truly live up to his husbandly duties? If not, could she survive another heartbreak? Still, she knew he had power over her. With a smile, a wink, or a simple glance, he could make her feel like a teenage girl with a severe crush. And she had felt a release—a thawing of sorts—from his insightful disclosure. Oh, what did it all mean?

The conflicting thoughts flew back and forth like a pendulum, causing Olivia great discomfort. "John-Michael, I'm not ready for this. I came here for my study."

"Do you hate me, Olivia? Am I that despicable to you?" The ghost of his father floated before his eyes. John-Michael sat up and swatted a handful of the sweet grass, symbolically swatting away the image of his father.

"No, John-Michael! Absolutely not. I just—" If she could just have proof of his feelings. After all, she was a researcher. She dealt in facts . . . in observing and recording and making decisions based on results. She just didn't have enough data to answer him.

Urgently, John-Michael pleaded, "Just what? Tell me what's going through your mind, Olivia. I promise this time I'm listening."

"I didn't plan for this. I don't know what to say," Olivia answered truthfully.

"Say you'll at least think about it. Tell me that you care enough about us to consider it."

Looking at John-Michael's pinched face and seeking eyes,

Olivia could see how critical this issue was to him. He was right on one account. She did owe their past relationship a complete and honest evaluation. A thought occurred to her. Why not put him to the test? Why not observe his actions over a period of time, and see what the results proved?

In her research projects, Olivia usually had a control and test group. While the control group was the benchmark, the test group was the one acted upon, and they didn't know it. She hastily made a decision to put John-Michael under the microscope without his knowledge. To tell him would be tampering, and that was one of the worst things a researcher could be accused of. Still, Olivia hedged, searching for the right words. She didn't want to send him the wrong signals, or give him—or herself—false hopes. "I don't know, John-Michael. Let me think about it, please. You caught me off guard. As I said, I was only prepared to focus on my experiment. I hadn't anticipated any personal interactions."

Tell her you're the reason she's here. Tell her you want her back so desperately that you were willing to partially fund her study. The thought flew through John-Michael's mind, and just as quickly he discarded it. Olivia was already iffy. He didn't know how she'd react if he told her, and he couldn't risk her running off again. He shrugged it off, promising himself, *Later. I'll tell her later.*

"Baby, I know this knocked you off your feet. But, all I'm asking for is your free time." Powerful shoulders shrugged up, then down. "Concentrate on your study. I won't stand in the way. But give me the evenings, Olivia. Please."

Olivia stared into his face. Seeing nothing but honesty, she blessed him with a tentative smile. "You're asking a lot of me."

"Maybe this'll convince you that I'm serious." In seconds, the basket of goodies was brushed aside and inching closer to her, he gathered her, hugging her tightly to his chest. For several minutes, he was content just holding her in his arms. It calmed his exposed nerves and fed his fantasies. Then, his bodily needs aròse, calling for an even more personal contact. Planting a quick kiss on the top of her curls, he shifted slightly, lowering her to the blanket, never letting more than two inches separate them and never giving up eye contact with her.

"John-Michael. I don't—think—" Olivia tried to stop the heat that flowed from him to her. She was too late. Desire kicked in, and she surrendered to it.

He lowered his head to kiss her chin, then lowered it more so he could caress the soft skin of her throat. With one hand behind her back, he let his other hand travel the expanse of her arm, damning the longsleeved T-shirt she wore. He gathered her hand in his and brought it to his face. His lips and tongue worked magic on the crevices and grooves in her palm, and finally landed at the base of her hand, where a rapid beat could be seen. He licked, teased, the visible blood vessel.

Her moan was his undoing. Clasping their hands together and lifting them high above her head, he searched her eyes. "Stop me now or—"

Even if she'd had a thousand red and white stop signs, Olivia would not have been able to stop herself, let alone him. She was too far gone. She wanted his affection as much as he wanted to give it.

Reading the green go-ahead sign in her eyes, he kissed her. It was as soft as rain, and as life-giving. One, two, light kisses with imperceptible pauses in between. He lifted his head lightly, to nuzzle her nose making her smile. He outlined her lips with his tongue, then used that tempting instrument to probe the inside of her mouth. It was more moist and sweet than a chocolate cake, and just as satisfying. It wasn't long before Olivia's arms snaked around his neck, pulling him closer. Their tongues began a duel, moving first within her mouth, then his. The kiss deepened as she gave into the exquisite beauty of it. Unconsciously, her body pressed into his. John-Michael groaned, and in one fluid movement he rolled on top of her and parted her legs with his knee. Cradled between her jean-clad legs, he delved into the interior of her mouth, ravaging it, taking what he wanted.

And she gave to him willingly. Her hands took pleasure in smoothing the muscles and planes of his back and shoulders. As she heated she grew bolder, and reached lower still to knead his tight buttocks.

John-Michael was holding his own until she began rotating her hips.

As soon as he was on top of her, he was gone. Sitting back on his haunches, between her legs, looking down on her, he was tempted to reclaim his spot, but he forced his mind to clear. He was not interested in fulfilling their desires on a whim, a one time shot. When he made love to her, it would be with the understanding that it would be for a lifetime. Slowly, he moved away from her.

Olivia was slower reaching earth than John-Michael. On her back, she looked up at him and saw the passion roaring in his eyes. She knew her own reflected the same depth of wanting.

"Baby, I'm trying to be a gentleman."

She knew he was right, but it didn't make it easier for her to forget the urges and wants thundering through her body. Three years was a long celibacy period, and she had been accustomed to ardent lovemaking. Lovemaking had never been a problem for them. John-Michael had the damning ability to stoke her fires at will. Staring up at him, with her chest heaving for breath, she could only say one thing. "You've convinced me, John-Michael. I'll give you my free time."

The little boy grin on John-Michael's face was almost worth the frustration she was struggling with. Falling on his hands and knees, he swung low, kissing her loudly on the lips. "Good. Now let's eat, before I forget my pledge."

He moved to retrieve the basket.

Olivia smiled and rolled over onto her side, watching John-Michael as he unpacked the goodies. Wickedly, she asked, "So who asked you to be a gentleman? I don't remember doing so." She smiled sweetly, innocently.

John-Michael looked over at her, lying in the middle of the blanket and smiling like a wicked nun. "Don't start, Olivia." Tossing the water thermos in her direction, he said, "Here—this'll cool you down."

Their eyes met, and they both laughed.

Lunch was a comfortable meal during which they discussed everything from apples to Zululand. Appetites sated, they took a leisurely stroll near the pond's edge, where John-Michael tried to teach her to skip rocks. It didn't take long for them to realize Olivia would never have a talent for skipping rocks, so they returned to the blanket to lie on their backs to watch the clouds change shapes. Just as Olivia started feeling drowsy, John-Michael pulled a surprise from the basket. Retrieving a deck of red and white Ace playing cards, he challenged, "Gin rummy? Best of three."

It seemed he hadn't forgotten their earlier date many years ago, either. Olivia laughed and dealt the first hand.

The trip home was all fun and laughter. John-Michael ribbed Olivia about losing their impromptu gin rummy tournament. Olivia accused him of cheating. It didn't bother him in the least. He continued to toss out favors the loser would have to give to the winner.

"A back rub after a hard day in the fields?"

"Maybe."

"How about you spend the afternoon with Walter doing the books next time?"

"No chance."

"How about a kiss at sunset?"

"Maybe."

"A kiss at sunrise?"

Olivia shrugged her shoulders, pretending disinterest. Her blood was still percolating from his previous kisses. Any more kisses and her body would overheat and explode.

John-Michael snapped his fingers. "I got it. How about you put on that red teddy I bought you for Valentine's day, and those red high heels?"

Playing his game, she said, "Okay."

John-Michael almost drove off the road. Olivia screamed in laughter.

"Teaser." He pouted. He pulled into the side yard and parked the truck. "Thanks, Baby, I had a good time." He leaned over and kissed her on the cheek.

"So did I."

Laughing and teasing each other about his wanton suggestions, they walked through the back door and into the kitchen—straight into Roberta.

Eight

"John-Michael—*finally*. This place—" Roberta stood in the middle of the kitchen near the island. Her golden eyes were trained on John-Michael until she noticed her daughter-in-law. A mixture of shock, confusion, and annoyance resided on her honey brown face. She stared at Olivia, seeing and yet not seeing her.

"Olivia?" Roberta exclaimed. "What are you doing here?"

John-Michael stepped forward. He placed the basket on the nearest counter and circled the island to hug and kiss his mother. "Mother, you're back early. I thought you had another week."

"Well, I do . . . did . . . but your relatives were starting to get on my nerves." For once, she didn't give her son her complete attention. She looked around his massive shoulders to stare at Olivia. "Cousin Hattie was becoming a real whiner."

Olivia stared back, refamiliarizing herself with the woman who had made her final years at the farm hell. Time stood still for the Johnsons. She, like John-Michael, had not aged one iota. In her mid-fifties, Roberta could easily pass for forty-ish. Her light brown skin, tinged with yellow, was stretched taut against her bones—high cheekbones, broad nose, and prominent chin. A short layered haircut which brushed her collar and a five-foot eight stature which belied her size eighteen figure completed her person. She was a beauty, yet the only feature she had passed on to her son was the light eyes. Olivia was thankful for that, for John-Michael was even-tempered, friendly, and caring, whereas his mother was uptight—especially when it came to her son or the farm—a snob, and selfish. Olivia remembered telling John-Michael during one of their disagreements that his mother lived by one motto—My way or the highway—and she meant it.

"Well, I'm glad you made it back safely." John-Michael ended his hug, but kept an arm draped loosely about his mother's shoulders. Turning to Olivia, he said. "As you can see, Olivia's back."

"Yeah, I see. How did this come about?" Roberta spoke slowly, trying to clear the fog of confusion. She spoke to John-Michael but her eyes were fixed on Olivia.

Olivia moved toward mother and son. She needed to let Roberta know up front she was not going to deal with any foolishness. "I'm here on business, Roberta. I'm here on behalf of the state ag department, the university, and Chem-Co, to test the effects of an unpatented compound on Johnson soil."

"I see your focus hasn't changed." Roberta moved slightly so she could have a full, uninterrupted view of Olivia. Her accusatory tone was unmistakable. "Still putting all your time and attention to learning."

"If, in some roundabout way, you're asking about my educational pursuits, I can tell you this also happens to be my Ph.D. study."

"Then I should congratulate you?" A sneer twisted Roberta's face; the sarcasm in her voice dripping like venom with each word. "Should I call you Doctor Foster?" The use of Olivia's maiden name punctuated the air.

Unfazed by Roberta's antagonism, Olivia adopted a flat though urbane tone. "It would be premature to do so. I still have orals, a presentation to my major committee, written exams, and the study to complete. It'll probably be another year before you can call me *Doctor Johnson.*" It was petty, but Olivia couldn't resist.

"So you'll be here for a *year,*" Roberta screeched.

"Off and on," Olivia replied, stone-faced. Inwardly, she chuckled at Roberta's expression. It was obvious she had gotten one over on the other woman. As she observed her mother-in-law's expression, a thought suddenly occurred to Olivia. *John-Michael must have made all the arrangements when he was notified by the ag department of the use of his farm. I wonder why he didn't tell his mother. They always discuss matters pertaining to the farm. Maybe this is a sign that John-Michael is really taking control of his life and the farm, that he really has changed.*

"Mother, why don't you go upstairs and get ready for dinner? Lena should be setting the table soon." John-Michael had heard enough. His expectation that Olivia's extended leave would force civility between his two favorite women was quickly dashed to the ground. They had picked up right where they left off.

Roberta turned back to her son. Annoyed with her disastrous homecoming, she sighed. "What I was going to tell you before I got sidetracked—" she afforded Olivia a scant glance, making it clear she was the interruption—"this place is in shambles. One of our combines is sitting, abandoned, on the road. There are weeds in the flower beds. And what has Lena been doing? The floors look like they haven't been scrubbed in years, and there're three inches of dust on the furniture. Earlier, two men passed through here as if they owned the place, and the barn has a bunch of equipment in it that doesn't belong to us." Roberta gave Olivia a pointed look. She realized the culprit for some of her issues. "Now, I know who the two men are, and what the equipment is for." Returning her attention to John-Michael, she continued. "But where's Lena, and what has she been doing? And more importantly, what have you been doing while the farm's wasting away? Where were you this afternoon?"

John-Michael put his hands on his mother's arms and gently steered her toward the door. "Mother, you're being overly dramatic. Nothing's wasting away." John-Michael walked as he talked. "I'll go check on the equipment in the road. Lena will call Grady tomorrow, so he can come spruce up the garden and flower beds. Now, go. Once you've eaten and rested, you'll feel better."

Roberta looked skeptical, but allowed her son to direct her, anyway. "We need to talk later tonight, so I can get caught up on things."

John-Michael shook his head affirmatively. With one large hand on the door, he pushed it outward. "After dinner. I promise."

Stopping on the threshold, Roberta looked backward over her shoulder at her daughter-in-law. "Do they take meals with us?" she asked.

Somewhat surprised, John-Michael frowned. "Of course, Mother. That's what we always do when we have guests."

Roberta started to say something, closed her mouth, and without another word walked out.

The door swung shut behind her. John-Michael leaned his tall, lean body against the door frame and crossed his arms across his chest. His eyes beckoned to Olivia to come to him. She acquiesced.

"Sorry about that," he murmured as he slid his arms possessively around her waist.

Olivia smiled softly, running her hands up John-Michael's arms to rest on his shoulders. "That's okay. It's not your fault your mother and I have a personality conflict."

"Mother's never liked any of my girlfriends." John-Michael leaned forward to touch their foreheads together. "I was surprised when she took to you initially. But then, you're so lovable. Who couldn't care for you?" John-Michael didn't allow her to respond. He captured her lips in a kiss so full of tenderness that Olivia could have cried.

"Get out of my kitchen with that mess," Lena instructed as she entered the kitchen via the washroom. The harshness of her words was offset by her sunshine smile and bright eyes, which radiated happiness.

John-Michael ended the kiss, but kept his arms loosely wrapped around Olivia. "Earlier this morning you practically pushed us together, and now you're turning your back to us."

"Don't give me that puppy dog look," Lena laughingly teased him in return. "Olivia, get your husband out of here. Dinner's almost ready."

Olivia's heart jump-started at the mention of the word *husband*. It had been years since she'd heard that title and her name used in combination. Hearing it had been a bit of a shock. She had to admit it sounded good, and felt even better. She looked up into John-Michael's smiling eyes and knew he felt the speeding pace of her heart. "Yes, Ma'am."

As the couple straightened up and pushed away from the doorjamb, John-Michael threw over his shoulder, "Oh, Lena, did you know Mother's back?"

"What?"

John-Michael had his answer.

The door swinging back and forth, back and forth, signaled the couple's exit.

Olivia was the last person at the dinner table. She had stood in front of the closet for many minutes trying to decide what to wear from her meager wardrobe. Her wardrobe was not as extensive as *Cosmopolitan* magazine would recommend. Because most of her adult life had been spent in the school system, her clothes consisted predominantly of jeans, shorts, and T-shirts, with a few sweaters thrown in for winter. With just the four of them for dinner, Olivia had had no problem throwing on anything that matched. Now, with the matron of the house in residence, she felt she needed something a little more "adult". Something that would give her that extra boost of confidence, since Roberta had made it clear that the lines were still drawn.

She had had the foresight to bring a couple of dresses, some high heels, and a pantsuit, thinking she would need them for church. And, it was one of the dresses—a little red, brushed silk number—that she finally decided on. It had a pleated, circular collar which brushed her shoulders, buttons down the front, tucks at the waist, and a flared skirt which ended at the knees. Secretly, Olivia admitted she would get a thrill seeing John-Michael's expression when she made her entrance in the dress. Her petite, curvy figure offered a perfect silhouette.

Olivia flew down the stairs, a good twenty minutes later than everyone else.

"Here she is," Dan remarked as Olivia finally walked through the door.

"Gosh, Olivia, it's about time. I'm starved," Micky whined as he pinched off a piece of a dinner roll and popped it in his mouth.

"Sorry. Some of my buttons were uncooperative," Olivia apologized as she approached the antique dining table where the others sat. Roberta occupied her usual spot next to John-Michael on his left. An empty seat for her was on his right, with Micky seated next to her and Dan next to Roberta. The French doors, covered with sheer, embossed, lilac-colored panels, were tossed open, allowing a late autumn breeze in to lift their spirits.

At the head of the table, John-Michael sat with an elbow resting on the armchair and a hand framing his chin. With his eyelids half-closed, his eyes scanned her from top to bottom and silently communicated that the wait had been worth it. Within those sun-tea brown depths resided a multitude of emotions—including admiration, pride . . . and desire.

The look he telegraphed to her was so full of tenderness, so fiercely loving, that Olivia shivered. It reached down and touched her heart, stirring a cedar chest of memories. In past times, his loving look would have been accompanied by a touch—a hug, a caress of her lips by his finger, his hand tenderly disturbing the curls on her head.

The memories became more vivid. She recalled times when they had snuggled together on the couch in his office in front of the fireplace, when they had walked in the garden holding hands, talking in their own silent language, times when they had tiptoed downstairs to raid the refrigerator, only to end up making love on the counter, the table, or any flat surface. At the back of her mind, she had dressed for dinner to please her husband, and now she was paying the cost.

Shaking the memories, she broke eye contact with John-Michael and took her seat. The inane actions of shaking out her napkin and draping it across her lap hid the impact of his invisible touch.

As if on cue, Lena hustled through the connecting door between the kitchen and the dining room with a silver-footed casserole dish in her hands. She placed her famous goulash near the center of the table. A leafy lettuce salad and a steaming platter of corn on the cob occupied places by the centerpiece. "Dig in," she commanded.

John-Michael said the quickest prayer ever, and no sooner had the *Amens* left their lips than Dan and Micky flew into action. Watching the endearing looks of anticipation on their faces, she wondered how they would ever leave Lena's home-cooking and return to their bachelor, fast food lifestyle. She didn't have time to wonder long, for Roberta interrupted her musings.

"Since you were late for dinner, John-Michael formally introduced me to your co-workers. They tell me y'all have been together for about a year now, planning this little study."

"Yes, we have." Olivia knew Roberta well enough to know she didn't engage in nonproductive talk. She had always been a polite, attentive hostess but she was also the type to walk away from a conversation gleaning more information than giving. Olivia would have to play along until she could reverse the dealing hand.

"When you walked in they were telling us about their backgrounds, and how you all came to meet." Turning to Dan, Roberta asked him to continue.

Having long since savored that first bite, Dan took to hi
next favorite activity—talking—loudly.

"I've been with the state ag department for going on twent
years. They hired me right after I got my masters, but the rea
learning didn't come until I went to work for them. Boy, ol
boy." Dan chuckled. "Back then, what we learned in the class
room was way off target compared to what really goes on i
the workplace."

"What do you mean?" John-Michael asked.

"Well, take Olivia's work for example. What she's studyin
is real life. If this compound does what Chem-Co claims
will, farming will be revolutionized, so to speak. That's a direc
relationship between school studies and the real world. It hasn
always been like that."

"That's true," Micky piped in. "I finished my masters thre
years ago, and even in that short time the school curriculur
has gotten even better. The administration and teachers are t
be commended for making education more useful."

"So, Micky, tell us about yourself. How is it you came t
meet Olivia?" Roberta smoothly guided the conversation bac
to her original intent. She wanted to find out what Olivia ha
been up to in the past three years and, more importantly, wha
she wanted from John-Michael and Johnson Farms.

"Well, I'm a country boy from Altus, Oklahoma. My folk
used to own farmland thereabouts, but we had to sell it whe
Ma got sick and died."

Collectively, there were sympathetic expressions from
around the table.

"I was just starting work on my Ph.D. at O U, but Dadd
took my ma's passing so hard I dropped my studies and move
back home to be with him. I love my dad, but after a year o
subbing I was itching to get back into school. Of course, ou
money supply, what with Mama dying and Daddy's doctor bill
from the cancer, was extremely low, but as luck would hav
it one of my professors told the Alabama State Department o
Agriculture about me. They called and offered me a job, an

my first assignment was working with Olivia and Dan on this project. So, that's why I'm sitting here."

He paused before continuing, a frown creased his brow. "I really would like to start working on my Ph.D. again but things just aren't working out. About six months ago, my dad's health started getting even worse. Even if I had the money for school, it would be hard to concentrate."

During Micky's discourse John-Michael had laid his fork down. Drawn into the young man's plight, he inquired, "Have you considered taking a job with the ag department back home, where you'll be closer to your dad?"

Roberta jumped on the idea. "That's a great idea. Especially since you see the importance of balancing your education with the needs of your family. Not everyone's capable of being so multi-focused."

No one seemed to notice the quick glance she threw in Olivia's direction, except Olivia. *Score one for Roberta,* Olivia thought. She narrowed her eyes and pinned her mother-in-law with a cold stare. *She got that punch in, but she won't get in another.* The conversation continued without a hitch.

"I signed up for this project and, no offense, Olivia, but I'm stuck until it's completed. If I'd have known Dad's health was going to head south, I wouldn't have taken the job. I've made it known that as soon as this project is over, I'll be seeking a job transfer to Oklahoma. Right now, the main thing is ensuring he has the best possible care, and a paycheck to pay for it."

Dan lifted the serving fork to dish up another helping of goulash. "Olivia and Micky have the same goals. They both have this desire to teach at the college level, and or do free-lance research work for companies or agencies. Personally, I could live the rest of my life, never go into another classroom, and be deliriously happy. I've discovered in my twenty some odd years with the state that field work is the thing that makes me jump out of bed in the morning."

Micky's brown eyes lit up, excitement made them twinkle

like stars. "Oh, for me, it's that combination of teaching and research." Turning to Olivia he said goodnaturedly, "I really envy you, Olivia, you're so close. I mean, you only have another year and you'll realize your dream."

Olivia's derisive smile told the truth. "It hasn't always been smooth sailing. I ran into obstacles, too. The important thing is to stay focused, no matter what."

If Roberta and John-Michael inferred from her pep talk to Micky that they had been some of the obstacles, they were right. Even though she now had a little bit better understanding of John-Michael's reasons for asking her to sit out a semester, she couldn't totally forget the sacrifice that would have been required on her part. She was surprised, though, that the old anger and pain she usually felt when she thought about her former life at Johnson Farms was just a flicker. *Two months with John-Michael, and the memories are starting to fade.* Olivia didn't know if that was good or bad.

With a gracious smile dotting her honey-colored face, Roberta turned to Olivia. "So, Olivia, that's your plan when you get your Ph.D? To teach and conduct experiments?"

"Yes. You may remember my greatest role model was a teacher. Dr. Hill was a fantastic teacher, both in and out of the classroom. Anyway, I think teaching is an admirable profession, and the state ag department always needs freelance researchers to help with their projects."

"Any particular school in mind? Or one you'd like to teach at?" Roberta sat on the edge of her seat waiting to see if Olivia would say Tuskegee. It was world renowned for its agriculture program, and it was less than two hours from their home.

"I really haven't given it any thought. I'm just trying to make it through this next year. The fine details will have to wait." Olivia met Roberta's direct stare. She could have sworn she saw a flash of disappointment cross Roberta's face. *Was this the whole point of Roberta digging into everyone's background? Is she trying to figure out my future plans? I wonder if she thinks I'm going to try to come back to John-Michael.*

I'll bet she doesn't even know he's asked me to come back. Well, she'll just have to find out when the rest of the world finds out.

"And, in the last couple of years, you've been doing what?" Roberta opened her hands and waved them in a flimsy gesture. "Finishing your masters, working on your Ph. D. in Huntsville?"

"Yes." Olivia had had enough of Roberta's probing and prodding. She took advantage of a slight pause and inquired, "And you? What have you been doing with yourself since I last saw you?"

"Oh, you don't want to hear about my boring life." That flimsy hand gesture filled the air again. "Yours is so much more exciting, what with all those goodlooking boys on campus and . . ."

This time John-Michael, Dan, and Micky did stare at Roberta. Everyone at the table knew John-Michael and Olivia were still legally husband and wife, and for Roberta to insinuate disreputable conduct by Olivia was shocking.

"Mother!" John-Michael's stern voice broke the stillness. There was a veiled warning threat in that single word.

"I hope you boys saved room for apple pie and ice cream." Lena's timely entrance with dessert washed away the embarrassing moment. She set the pie and ice cream down at Roberta's elbow. Then poof, like a magician, she was gone.

Roberta picked up the pie knife and began cutting lumberjack portions. She was not a woman given to embarrassment or defeat. "Oh, let's see. You asked me what I'd been doing. Well, the same ole things—the Women's Society, the Tuskegee Historical Foundation, and of course I'm still one of the mothers of the church." Smugly, she added, "And of course you must remember all that's involved with running this house and taking care of John-Michael. I swear my son is all work. It's a full-time job getting him to take care of himself."

"Mmmm." Olivia couldn't bring herself to form words, and it took all her home training not to sneer. Of course she had no idea what it took to run the house! Roberta had never transferred the reins of responsibility. And as for John-Michael, the only rights she'd had were conjugal.

Roberta continued, pride coloring her words. "I am so proud of him. After Daddy's death he just stepped right in, and has maintained the success of our legacy. Did he by chance tell y'all he was asked in D. C. to speak at a congressional hearing on the state of farming in America? He was the youngest, most handsome farmer there. You should have seen those young female aides ogling him."

"Mother, I'm sure as Ag employees they hear and read enough about state and federal legislature and happenings in our industry," John-Michael remarked, looking slightly embarrassed. He continued, hoping to divert his mother before she got started good. "Dan, you look like you need another piece of pie."

Right at that moment, seeing John-Michael fidget in his chair, Olivia could imagine him as a youngster preparing to make his speech at the PTA or perhaps delivering a line of dialogue for the Christmas program. Olivia could just visualize Roberta, the consummate stage mother, pushing him forward, mouthing the words with him. The image of her man as a shy, insecure youngster brought a smile to her face and her heart exploded with tenderness and . . . love? The thought froze her from the inside out. Love. Dare she use that word in conjunction with John-Michael? What in the world was she thinking of? Things had not changed. Roberta was still attacking her on all fronts, and John-Michael had allowed her to. *Now, Olivia, in all fairness to John-Michael, he did shut her up when she was ready to unjustly accuse you of adultery.* Even given that fair assessment, Olivia had encountered too much talk today about love and reuniting. Those words were way off her game plan. Feeling the overwhelming desire to delve into something far more safe than her emotions, she stood.

"Excuse me. I really need to do some work in the barn. Good night, everyone."

Olivia hit full stride in less time than it took to flip a pan-

cake, and was upstairs in her room changing into a pair of
jeans and a sweater in the time it took for Lena to fry an egg.

The old college try to avoid thoughts of love and John-
Michael failed. The more she tried to ignore what her heart
was trying to tell her, the deeper it rooted itself in her gray
matter. *You can lie to the world, Olivia, but you can't lie to
yourself. You're still in love with John-Michael and nothing—
not even a lengthy absence or the pain of a broken heart—will
ever change that.*

Olivia plopped down on the side of the bed. As if summoned
by some spiritual force, a memory she had almost forgotten
rose to her conscious mind. It was a scene from long ago
involving Dr. Hill and a lesson in forgiveness and reconciliation. . . .

Cold winds, snow, and ice had forced the schools in Meridian to close down one day earlier than scheduled for the
Thanksgiving holiday. While the other kids had excitedly made
their way home to seek permission to build snowmen, go ice-
skating, or make angels in the snow, Olivia, a middle schooler
at the time, had stopped at Dr. Hill's house for her usual after
school visit. Dr. Hill already had the hot chocolate with small
marshmallows floating on the top ready. As always, they talked
about Olivia's schoolwork, her homelife, and a new agenda
item Dr. Hill had recently introduced—boys.

The telephone had rung, interrupting their discussion, and
during that brief phone call, Olivia remembered she had heard
Dr. Hill laugh as she had never laughed before. It was a co-
quettish laugh, a seductive laugh, but also a bittersweet laugh.
When the call ended, Dr. Hill had returned to the living room
and had informed Olivia to never martyr herself in favor of
love. Dr. Hill had laughed at Olivia's confused look and had
gone on to explain that she had just spoken to the man who
should have been her husband. William Patterson, another professional in the education system, and a married man, called
every year around Thanksgiving to check on Dr. Hill. They
had been engaged once, a long time ago, and were all set to

marry on a Thanksgiving weekend when Dr. Hill had seen him out on a date with another woman. She had been furious, and called off the wedding. She had sadly told Olivia that she had never tried to understand why William had done such a thing. Being young and naive, she had simply used her hurt feelings to erect a barrier between her and the man she loved. A year later, William had married the woman she had seen him with, and Dr. Hill had gone on to acquire her doctorate, shunning love and all the headaches that went with it.

William and his wife had moved on to another city, and it was years later when Dr. Hill finally saw him again. At a National Education Association convention, they got the opportunity to sit down, and talk about what had gone wrong. Dr. Hill had learned that William had only gone out with the woman as a final fling before making a lifelong commitment. He had explained that he had loved Dr. Hill and that the date with the other woman had proved that. His interest in the other woman didn't root until Dr. Hill turned her back to him, refused to take his calls, refused to see him, refused to listen to him. Much too late, Dr. Hill learned that her unwillingness to listen, forgive, and reconcile had cost her a lifetime of happiness. Although that spark of awareness was still there, she and William had ended the evening as just friends. At the end of the convention, William had returned to his home to be the loving and devoted husband and father he was, and Dr. Hill had returned to Meridian wiser and lonelier. She had warned Olivia to learn from her mistake.

Listen, forgive, and reconcile. Forgive and reconcile. The words of Dr. Hill's lesson thundered through Olivia's head until they forced her off the bed. On the heels of admitting she was still in love with her husband, she wasn't ready to take it a step further. She understood what Dr. Hill had taught her, but it was far different putting the theory into practice. Olivia did what she'd done in the past. She ran from the mental and emotional work that needed to be done—to her schoolwork.

Outside, the temperature had turned on them. The earlier

beautiful, unseasonable springtime weather had given way to a frigid chill and gusty winds. Olivia was oblivious to the weather, intent on reaching the barn to immerse herself in her work. With her schoolwork, she knew she could escape, if only for a short time, from her troubling thoughts.

His dinnertime meal wore off around midnight, making Micky's stomach growl uproariously. "Time for a midnight snack."

Micky closed the book he'd been reading and got up from the desk. Taking the stairs two at a time, he zeroed in on the kitchen. With his hand on the door, he was ready to sail through, straight to the refrigerator, when raised voices stopped him.

He stood indecisively outside the door, debating the soundness of entering. Straining, he could just barely decipher words and recognize voices. John-Michael mentioned Olivia's name in his deep male voice, and seconds later Roberta made an unintelligible response. The pleading in her voice was unmistakable. His stomach growled again, reminding him why he'd left his room. He was tempted to walk in, grab a hunk of banana nut bread and a glass of milk, and quickly make an exit. But, even through the thickness of the wood door it was evident that Roberta was not happy about something, and her distress clinched it for him. Disappointed, he gave in to etiquette and went back upstairs.

In the kitchen, with the overhead lights blazing like daylight, Roberta was standing within a ruler length of her son. With a frown on her face and hands planted on her hips, she queried. "Why would you do that?"

"Because I'm miserable, Mother. I want her here with me." John-Michael, tired and ready for bed, used his arms for support. They were braced against the island, stiff and straight. His lean body was positioned in a skier's forward position, with one knee cocked.

"She's not interested in being a wife, and she doesn't want your children. Why are you putting yourself through this again?"

"Mother, I'm going to tell you this one last time, and after this I don't want to hear it anymore. Those children didn't die by Olivia's hands. She's a woman who gives life, not destroys it. Heck, look at the work she's doing here. She's trying to feed the world, and at the same time save the soil."

"Oh, bravo! Bravo!" Roberta cocked her graying head. "That doesn't mean a thing. A lot of people are one way at work and totally different in their personal life. So what?"

John-Michael abandoned his stance. Pulling a stool from under the counter, he sat down heavily. He ran a hand across his face and responded wearily, "I know Olivia loves me. We went to the pond this afternoon for a picnic lunch and she responded to me as if this separation had never happened. It was like the first couple of years we were together." His tiredness lifted for a minute as he remembered.

"You took her to the pond! No wonder you two looked so . . . refreshed . . . when I saw you come in." Roberta spat the word "refreshed" out as if it were dirty.

"Oh, Mother, it isn't what you're thinking. It was . . . innocent. It was like reliving old times. Very pleasurable." A faint smile lit his face.

"I'll bet." Roberta expelled a huff. "Anyway, you've got to let this unhealthy infatuation you have for her go. You don't need her." Roberta spoke as if it was a done deal.

"That's where you're wrong, Mother. I need her like I need food and oxygen. I arranged for her to return because I need her."

Roberta took a step closer to her only offspring. Softly, warningly, she asked, "What do you mean, you arranged for her to return?"

Rubbing his forehead, John-Michael explained. "I worked with the state department to ensure that her experiment was conducted here."

"You mean to tell me you're responsible for her being here?"

"I donated thirty thousand to this research project with the stipulation that the experiment be conducted here. Chem-Co funded the balance. The folks at the university and the ag department were so excited that they didn't have to come up with any money that they agreed to my demand."

Roberta couldn't say anything for a while. Shock and fear paralyzed her vocal cords. Finally, she managed a response. "And it just happened to fall into the time period I was gone on vacation."

"Now, that was indeed a coincidence. The first confirmation letter vaguely referenced sometime in the fall. By the time I got the final letter, which only gave me a week's notice, you were well into your vacation."

Throwing her hands up in the air, Roberta belted out questions in step with her nervous pacing. "Hasn't she hurt you enough? Can't you see the handwriting on the wall? Son, I don't understand you."

"Mother, we both know the demise of our marriage can't fall totally in Olivia's court. We both made mistakes. I recognize now that I wasn't a very good husband, and there are some things I'm going to do differently the second time around."

Roberta's fear erupted. She felt as if she were living the nightmare dream that occasionally played behind her sleeping eyes.

She had started having the dream when John-Michael reached puberty, and as his age progressed so had the occurrence of the nightmare. When he married, it had become a nightly movie.

The dream started out with her walking leisurely on the bank of a pond. John-Michael was happily swimming in the water, taking lazy, unhurried strokes. It was obvious he was having a good time playing in the water. And it was obvious that she hadn't a care in the world, was totally free of stress, until his final lap. It always happened on his final lap. A "thing" with a womanly shape and as many arms as an octopus rose from the bottom of the pond and grabbed his legs. Slowly, she began pulling him under. He cried out for his mother to help him, but she couldn't. She didn't know how to swim . . . and she was afraid of that unrecognizable monster woman. While her son fought valiantly for his life against the unknown demon she stood by, hysterically crying and shaking with fear. The dream always ended with her seeing the tips of John-Michael's fingers as he slowly went under. Roberta always woke up in a sweat, with tears on her cheeks.

Although the monster woman's face was never revealed in the dream, Roberta now suspected it was Olivia. She was the only woman except her who had ever wielded so much power over John-Michael. The dream always scared her. Juxtaposed on the present situation, it made her jittery and angry.

Reacting from gut level fear, Roberta screamed at John-Michael. "I can't believe it! You're acting just like your father! John-Michael, you have a legacy to uphold. You can't throw it away on some educated floozy!"

John-Michael sat up straight, concerned about his mother's sudden outburst. He reached out a hand to her, anxious to still the trembling of her body. "Mother, calm down. Please. There's no need to get so upset." For the time being, he could ignore that she had once again compared him to his father.

Roberta tumbled into the safety of his hard, tangible arms. Crying noisily into his chest, she asked, "What about Alexandria?" Roberta lifted her head to look deep into her son's eyes. Tears lined her own. "I hear she's back in town, looking as lovely as ever. And what if she's not from the best family in town? She would uphold her wifely duties. She would make a good wife."

"Mother, what are you talking about?" John-Michael was confused. His mother, usually so strong, was shaking like Jell-O. He couldn't figure it out.

Roberta grabbed the front of his shirt. Her voice caught,

mixed hiccuped words and tears making it difficult to decipher
her messages. "Alexandria . . . a wonderful wife. You used to
like her. She wouldn't drown you."

John-Michael loosened his hold on his mother and leaned
back so he could study her and try to pinpoint the source of
her erratic behavior. He hadn't seen her this upset in years.
"Mother, Alexandria and I dated back in high school, and besides it's a moot point. I'm married to Olivia, whom I love
with all my heart."

"But, you could grow to love her."

"No, Mom, I couldn't, because there's only one woman I
want. It's just a matter of me convincing *her* of that." John-
Michael spoke patiently, even though he had explained this to
his mother an unrecorded number of times.

In the face of reality, in the security of her son's arms, the
nightmare dream started to fade, along with the fear and her
agitation. Her thought processes cleared, and her arguments
became stronger, more convincing. "John-Michael, think about
what you're doing, what you're saying. Don't make the same
mistake twice. Olivia only wants her education."

John-Michael sighed. "Mother, it's been a long day. We can
discuss this again later if *you* still think it's pertinent, but for
now, I think you need some rest."

"Don't send me to bed now, please. I won't be able to sleep."
The threat of the nightmare still loomed.

"Didn't Doctor Miles give you a prescription for sleeping
pills before you left for vacation? Take one of your pills."
John-Michael spoke matter-of-factly, not fully understanding
his mother's dilemma.

Roberta closed her eyes for a minute, fighting for full control. He was right, of course. She could take some pills and
not worry about that dream disturbing her rest, and the anxiety
of a few seconds ago had lessened. But John-Michael had to
know the danger Olivia posed to him. She made one last attempt to save her son. "I will take a pill, Honey, but John-
Michael, promise me you'll think about what I said." He

frowned and she clarified, "About Alexandria. Exchange Olivia for Alexandria."

Exasperated and growing more than warm under the collar, John-Michael explained. "Mother, when I first brought Olivia home to meet you, you welcomed her with open arms. You couldn't speak highly enough of her. And even after we married, you continued to praise her. Sometime throughout the years, you adopted a completely different viewpoint about Olivia. What happened to make you change your mind? Why don't you like the woman I love?"

With heat in her voice and desperation coloring her eyes, Roberta responded fervently. "I told you. She doesn't fit in. She fooled us, making us think she wanted what we want. But all she's interested in is her education, her degrees, her books. She kept bucking my authority, and she doesn't want children. That became apparent to me when she aborted that first child. And, son, we need a boy child to continue on with the Johnson name." Roberta lost some of her fire and resorted to exaggeration. "John-Michael, she only married you for your money. Look at it from her angle. You paid for her school expenses, you bought her that little red car. You positioned her at the head of society in Tuskegee, and you even loaned her family money."

"It was only five thousand, and I would have done it for any African-American who wanted to create jobs and economic independence for other blacks. It just so happens it was Olivia's sister, and look at how well Vivian's recycling business is doing. When I spoke with her a while back, she was in the process of hiring more staff. I was so filled with pride you'd have thought it was my enterprise."

In an ugly tone of voice, Roberta spoke her thoughts. "Well, then, maybe that's the sister you should have married. One who understands loyalty to family, not self-centeredness."

John-Michael dropped his arms, losing contact with his mother. Anger warped his voice. "Mother, I'm not going to stand here and let you demean my wife. I love Olivia, and nothing's going to change that. Nothing! Now, goodnight."

"John-Michael—" Roberta reached out a hand, but it was too late. Her son was gone; the swinging door proof that he was headed for the master bedroom.

Alone, she twisted her hands and paced the floor. With her head hanging low, thoughts circled within like planes waiting to land at an airport in foggy weather. *He's changed. He never talked to me like that before. What has she done to him?*

Roberta stopped in her tracks. Bracing herself against the island, she crossed her arms across her chest and lowered her head so that her forehead rested in the palm of one hand. "What is this nonsense, John-Michael?" she moaned. "Why do you persist in wanting someone who's bad for you?"

A thought occurred to her. Roberta nodded her head affirmatively. "Ahhhh, *that's* it. This afternoon when they were together, Olivia must have laid the loving on him pretty thick. His head's messed up because of that."

Warming to the idea, Roberta's thoughts secured the notion. *After all, as far as I know John-Michael hasn't dated or been with another woman since Olivia left. And he is his father's son. His father was weak when it came to sex. It stands to reason that John-Michael is the same way. So, Olivia's learned that little trick, I see.*

Roberta stood up straight as if preparing for battle. Striding to the door, she flicked off the lights and headed down the hall to her bedroom suite. "Well, Miss Olivia's going to learn that sex can't outweigh a mother's love."

Relieved that she had figured out why her son had discarded her advice—advice that he usually accepted without argument—she made up her mind to talk to him again after Olivia's loving had worn off.

Although exhausted from her travels, the mentally taxing dinner, and the emotionally charged argument with John-Michael, Roberta couldn't fall asleep immediately. After washing up and changing into her bedclothes, she reclined on the bed, pulling her Holy Bible onto her lap.

As she straightened the covers over her lap, she thought about the scene in the kitchen. It dawned on Roberta that the only real arguments she and John-Michael had ever had involved Olivia . . . and now the little vixen was back, causing more trouble. *Oh, yeah, at first she had me fooled. She came to us looking so sweet and innocent. But, she proved that it was just an act. She was only looking out for herself. She doesn't give a flip about my son. Well, I'm not going to let that woman destroy my plans for John-Michael. I need a wife for John-Michael who will let me handle his affairs the way I deem best. He'll need someone who will birth a host of children. Someone who will let me raise the kids and run the household. She can't have other priorities. Making John-Michael look good has to be her focus.*

Leaning her head back against the headboard, Roberta continued her requirements list. *I know what's best for my son, and although God has yet to make a woman who can care for him better than me, Alexandria can at least birth his children and be a makeshift wife. She's a beautiful girl, and if I help her get out of that little crowded house she lives in, she will do anything I ask of her.*

Smiling at how nicely the pieces were coming together, Roberta turned to the ribbon which marked her reading place and finalized her tentative plans. *The trick is convincing John-Michael to divorce Olivia. Once that's done, I can get John-Michael and Alexandria married in no time. Then they can start immediately on the first Johnson child.*

Nine

"Morning, Olivia." Dan strolled into the barn as if he'd been out taking a leisurely jaunt. Micky followed close behind, as animated and lively as a dancing pony. Lena's country breakfast rested comfortably in their stomachs.

"Hi, guys." Olivia looked over the top of her glasses. She tried to stifle a yawn, but it would not be gated. She'd ended up working past midnight last night—much later than she'd intended—and had risen at five this morning to be in the barn by six. In the early days of their arrival at Johnson Farms, she had worked long hours so she could finish the experiment and hightail it back to Huntsville, where she could resume her safe life. Now, she forfeited sleep in order to quell nagging doubts and troubling thoughts. In addition to dealing with John-Michael and her feelings for him, the research project had started to bother her.

Last night, she had decided to unearth her reason for questioning the project. She had started over again from step one, reviewing the research plan. She'd even gone so far as to reread her hypothesis and research questions. She'd examined the validity and reliability types, and reviewed all their data. The numbers they had recorded daily looked okay, for the most part. There were a few days where the data didn't look quite right, but once she compared them to the handwritten notes in their research notebooks and found them to match, she convinced herself that she was being paranoid, that she was letting the pressure of ensuring this initial phase be wholly right—or else admit contamination and tampering—get to her. Telling herself the university's computer lab would put her qualms to rest once they ran the numbers and validated the statistical accuracy and significance of her data, she had trudged up to bed.

Still, sleep had been long in coming. Her troublesome thoughts and skepticism followed her to bed. When a person had been involved in as many research projects as she had, intuition and "fretting" were almost as good barometers as the actual research results. Determined to address her woman's intuition and fretting again—she had risen early this morning.

Olivia yawned again. "How's it going this morning?"

"Great!" Micky exclaimed. It was obvious he was in a good mood as he boot-scooted up to the table where Olivia sat.

Dan patted his belly as if the fullness of it was the gauge for his happiness. "Lena almost killed us again. I swear I'm going to kidnap that woman when we leave."

"Hey. Hey. Speaking of leaving, we're on the countdown," Micky half sang. "Only three and a half weeks, and we're back in Huntsville."

"Right-o, Kid. As great as this place is, I miss my little old apartment," Dan continued, massaging his belly.

Micky *humphed.* "You gotta be kidding. I could live here forever. All this farmland and water, a great historical city nearby, a house that looks like it belongs on TV, and a fabulous cook. Olivia, how in the world could you have left this place?"

The question caught Olivia way off guard. She just stared at him while her mind went through a dozen abbreviated renditions of the truth. Seconds ticked off as she developed her response. "Ummm, Micky. It's a little complicated, and very personal. I'd really rather not get into it."

Still standing, Micky leaned forward placing his elbows on the table. He lowered his voice conspiratorially. "Does it have anything to do with the argument I overheard last night between John-Michael and his mother? Your name came up."

Olivia's head snapped back, and her mouth dropped open.

"Micky!" Dan rumbled. "You were eavesdropping?"

"No, I wasn't." Micky straightened up, looking offended. His tenor voice had climbed higher. "I went down for a midnight snack and almost walked right in on them. I was really hungry, and waited for only a few seconds to see if they would leave." Micky stopped to catch his breath. "I went away quietly when I realized they were going to be talking for quite some time."

Olivia's mind, processing faster than a Pentium, had trouble digesting Micky's comments. *Five years I lived here and they never argued. Amazing . . . I wonder what it was about. I wonder if John-Michael is starting to see his mother's true colors.* A nudge in her side pulled her from her internal thoughts. She gave Micky her undivided attention.

He asked somewhat timidly, "Olivia, can I ask you something personal?"

Olivia raised her eyebrows. "You can ask."

"But you may not answer."

Olivia nodded.

Micky thought about it for a second. He decided to take his chances. "Okay. Back in Huntsville, why didn't you tell us you were married?" Micky tapped the sparkling rock on the third finger of her left hand. "I thought you were wearing this ring because your husband had died or something."

Cryptically, Olivia commented, "My marriage died, not my husband." Again she was surprised that the old anger and pain had diminished to a dull, empty throb.

"You've been in Huntsville for years, and with all the projects you've been on for the school and the ag department you've worked with a lot of us, yet you never mentioned a husband to anyone."

Even though she thought the world of Dan and Micky, she wasn't ready or willing to share her wedding diaries with them. Both she and John-Michael were very private people, and even with the best intentions people were prone to spread other folks' business. No, no, best to keep mute on this subject. To cover for the slip of the tongue earlier, Olivia tried humor. "So you all have been talking about me behind my back, hmmm?"

Jokingly, Dan started softly whistling and looking off into space. Rocking back and forth, heel to toe, he wasn't admitting to anything.

Micky smiled apologetically. "Of course. In case you haven't noticed, Olivia, you're a woman. Our office is mostly guys, and you know how men are when it comes to a pretty girl. Especially a mysterious pretty girl."

Olivia smiled, shaking her head. *Yup, I can well imagine the comments.*

"A couple of guys at the office are interested in you, but no one has the courage to ask about your availability. You always shut down when it comes to personal business. That makes it hard to get to know you."

Dan joined in, considering it safe territory since Olivia was smiling. "Yeah, Olivia, imagine our surprise on the first day here when John-Michael announced you were his wife. We've been together now for a year. We deserved better than that."

Olivia nodded her head in agreement. "You're right. You're both right." Olivia shrugged one shoulder. "I wasn't looking at the whole picture. I was only concerned with staging this study. You know, making sure it would be a success." Olivia sighed and shifted on her stool. She didn't want to discuss her and John-Michael's past or evolving present, but she did owe them something. "John-Michael and I didn't agree on some pretty important things. We separated. That's it." Olivia held up a finger. "But . . . our separation has no bearing on the work we have to do here. We're still going to do a bang-up job on this research project, despite the fact John-Michael and I share the same last name."

Dan, thinking aloud, said slowly, "I just hope this doesn't backfire on you, Olivia."

Frowning, Olivia questioned him. "What do you mean?"

"Do the folks at the ag department and the university know he's your husband?"

"Well, I really don't know. Everyone knows his farm is on the field site list. A lot of people would like to use Johnson Farms for research. It's such fertile land, and there's so much of it. You can really get a good size control and test field without interfering with his income. I assume that's why we didn't have a choice of where to conduct this experiment. But again, I don't see how my being married to John-Michael has any bearing on the research work."

"It doesn't, in my opinion. But, you know how small-minded some people can be." Dan waved a hand in resignation. "Awwww, forget it. Just call me Mister Looking for Trouble."

"Well, Mister Looking for Trouble," Micky teased. "if you're through with your questions, I have a few others."

Dan bowed to the younger man. Olivia smiled. She didn't know what she was going to do with these friends of hers.

"So, are you still in love with him? Does Marvin back at the office stand a chance?"

Olivia threw her head back and laughed. "Oh, God, Micky! You're too much." She sobered enough to tell him, "Please let Marvin know that I'm honored and flattered, but it's not in the cards."

"So you still love John-Michael?" Micky persisted.

Olivia waltzed around the question. "Micky, have you ever thought about pursuing a career in matchmaking?"

"No, and you're not answering my question. Are you?"

Olivia nodded her head. "Right."

Dan snickered.

Undaunted, Micky continued. "Okay, how about this? Was his mother the problem? She wasn't friendly to you last night. And later, in the kitchen, I could tell she wasn't happy about something."

Her smile slipped a little, but she held on. "I'm still not answering."

"Okay, so, why haven't you divorced him?"

Olivia held up her right hand. "I plead the Fifth."

Acting out his interrogating detective role, Micky strolled around the table, chin in hand. "Did you marry him for his riches? If you divorce him, do you get anything? And, if so, can I borrow some money?"

Dan threw in his two cents. "You'd be stupid for divorcing him, since it's obvious you two are still in love, but if you do, ask for the northeast acreage. It has the richest soil and it has a natural irrigation system."

The ribbing from her friends was on full speed. Even though Olivia laughed with them and teased them back, her mind was stuck on Dan's comment. Were they that obvious—her feelings for John-Michael? She had tried so hard to discount it, even to herself, and yet Dan had been able to pick up on it. She wondered if Roberta was also aware. That would explain her behavior yesterday.

"Boy, I wish I could find me a honey with some money. I'd retire and fish for the rest of my life," Dan remarked as he headed toward the kitchenette to start a fresh pot of coffee.

"Oh, man! If I ever win the lottery or come across a large sum of money I'll tell you exactly what I'd do." Micky rattled off his priorities. "First, I'd pay off all my dad's medical bills, then I'd buy back the land we had to sell. Then, me and my dad, we'd go to Nashville. He always wanted to see the mecca of country music."

"I hate to punch a hole in y'all's dreams, Dan, but since you haven't found a rich damsel yet, and Micky hasn't won the lottery, maybe we'd better get down to the jobs we have today. How'd the spraying go yesterday?"

"Killjoy," Micky retorted playfully.

Olivia stuck her tongue out at him.

Dan returned with the coffeepot in one hand and three cups in the other. A hint of humor lined his voice. "While you and the master of the farm were frolicking in the meadows picking wild buttercups and holding them under each other's chins." Dan, a two hundred pound plus man, stood on his tiptoes and splayed his arms out full length in first one direction then the other, mimicking a ballerina. "But we were hard at work, sweating, swatting flies, bemoaning our fate." Micky and Olivia howled with laughter.

"Oh, Dan!" Olivia gasped, holding her stomach. "Quit. You're killing me."

Dan did, but only because he was out of breath. He set the coffeepot and cups down and, bending from the waist, spoke in puffs. "Some . . . body . . . pour . . . me a . . . cuppa . . . coffee."

Micky raised his head from the table. Happy tears streamed down his face. "Here. Let me help you."

Dan stood up straight to accept the full cup and met Micky's eyes, and all three fell out again. Not much work got done that morning.

John-Michael glanced up at the sky, trying to predict rain the way his grandfather had. He'd never been as accurate as granddad, but he was pretty good. This evening the purplish blue sky, growing darker by the minute, was telling him no rain was in sight. For October it was unseasonably warm, but the rainfall was good, and for that he was thankful. He was also grateful for the second chance with Olivia.

As he opened the door to the barn, anticipation tap danced along his spine. It was Friday night, when most people spent the evening at the movies or eating out, or bowling—like Micky and Dan were. He was in the barn, headed upstairs to meet Olivia. Her idea of relaxing after a hard work week was geneology.

This wasn't exactly what I had in mind when I asked her for her free time, he thought. It wasn't that he didn't care about his family roots; on the contrary, history had been the only non-agricultural subject he'd enjoyed in school. He simply would have appreciated being alone with her in a more intimate setting such as a drive-in movie, or cuddled up on the couch in front of the fireplace. But she was calling the shots, and if studying his family tree was how he could garner time with her, then that's what he would do.

As he made his way up the stairs, he tried not to think about what a good researcher Olivia was. He knew with her determination to ensure that her research projects were one hundred percent right, she would want to discuss his father. Apprehension knocked in his chest, reminding him about the consequence of accepting her "date." Yes, it would be good to spend time with her, but it was going to be trying. He'd prepared a tale that skimmed the truth. However, he prayed she wouldn't get too detailed, or his story would fall apart. If that happened, she would know what he knew—that he was his father, through and through. With that knowledge, she would never consider returning to him permanently. Olivia was an intelligent, well-grounded individual with valid expectations of her man to provide and protect. She would not stomach a man who was irresponsible about family and business. His dreams depended on her not discovering the truth.

"Hi, there. How was your day?" Olivia called out as he planted one booted foot on the uppermost step.

"Good. We finished turning the land—" John-Michael's breath caught in his throat; his heart did a somersault. She had on jeans and a ribbed cotton sweater which hugged her breasts. The sweater was tucked into the waistband of her jeans, showing off her narrow waist and nicely rounded hips. It was her usual casual attire, made all the more comely because she was who she was.

"Are you sure you don't mind working on this geneology chart?" Olivia turned an inquisitive, open face to him. "I know it's a Friday night and you probably want to do something more exciting."

"Nope," John-Michael lied as visions of her sprawled naked on the bed whipped through his head. "This is fine. I appreciate your offer to help."

Olivia, already seated, pulled out a chair for him. She patted the seat; her eyes were bright and dancing when she offered him a final out. "Are you sure you don't want to run into town for a movie or something?"

John-Michael shook his head. "Not interested." An image of her in that red lace teddy and high heels flashed through his mind's eye. He prayed God wasn't keeping score of his sins tonight. "But tell me why you're so keen on helping me with my family tree. I haven't seen you this excited since you've been back."

Olivia's smile intensified. "I really enjoy the research aspect. It's very gratifying to discover that missing piece, and even more fulfilling to know there are real lives attached to your work." Olivia shrugged her shoulders. "Who knows? Maybe when I get through with my Ph.D. I might start researching the Foster's roots." She paused for a moment, looking into John-Michael's eyes. "Besides, it's something we always talked about doing and never did."

John-Michael was touched by the wisp of nostalgia in her voice. Maybe he had a better chance of convincing her to stay than he realized. Maybe she was finally replacing horrible memories with joyous recollections. John-Michael prayed that was the case.

"Well, let me tell you where I got stuck." John-Michael positioned the chair she had pulled out so that the back of it bumped the edge of the table. He swung one long leg around, straddling the chair. Pulling the charts toward him, he pointed to a good starting point. "This is Madison's father's—"

"John-Michael, let me interrupt you." Olivia put a detaining hand on his arm. "Can you back up for a minute and tell me again why this entry is blank?"

John-Michael almost groaned aloud. Her finger was pointing to the spot where his father's name should have been listed. *Boy, she ain't wasting no time,* he thought. Clearing his throat, he recited his story. "Mother and Father weren't married that long, number one. Number two, listing his name would raise

questions about the differences in our last names, given the
fact that I'm also a John-Michael."

"Oh, yes, I see." Olivia leaned an arm on the table and
crooked her elbow to prop her head in a hand.

John-Michael almost sighed with relief. *Thank goodness!
That wasn't too bad.* "Madison's father was born—"

"Just a second. I'm still thinking about your father's situation." Olivia tapped her finger. "There's got to be a way
to . . ." Her words trailed off as the wheels in her mind turned
faster.

John-Michael resisted the temptation to lay his head down
on the table in defeat. He had forgotten how tenacious Olivia
could be. Just looking at her, he could almost see her mentally
fitting the puzzle pieces together. He was going to have to
come up with something else to divert her attention from his
father. *Maybe this wasn't such a good idea, after all. I should
have been honest with her and told her I wanted to take her
out on a real date.*

"I'm sure there's a way you can list your father, explain the
differences in the last names, and maintain the validity of the
document. Possibly—"

"The only way I can see it is by leaving his name off, which
is what I've elected to do." John-Michael hadn't meant for the
words to sound so harsh. He had schooled himself to try to
go with the flow, but the lesson had already worn off. The
subject matter made him extremely uncomfortable; it was a
constant threat to his existence, made more pronounced these
days by the presence of the woman who held his future in her
hands. He rubbed his head, trying to rub away the images of
a failed husband and father.

Olivia sat back, shocked at John-Michael's inflexibility. It
was totally out of character for him to be so closeminded. His
willingness to try new farming methods was one of the reasons
his farm was so successful. She couldn't understand why he
was being so unreasonable about his father's name on a piece
of paper. "Just because you want it so doesn't make it right,

John-Michael. You have to think about the generations coming behind you who will look to this family tree for their history." Olivia got goose bumps just thinking about the positive impact this study could have on future Johnsons. Knowing their history, and the great men and women who sustained life and love through slavery, the Great Depression, racism, and segregation, and the many other atrocities heaped on the African-American race would serve as a beacon of hope, a reason to push forward despite the curve balls that would be thrown at them. John-Michael was building a wonderful tool for ensuring his family's future, yet his stubbornness was threatening it.

Olivia felt her anger rising until she looked at John-Michael. His head was down, his shoulders slumped, and he was breathing deeply. He looked defeated. This was not the strong, confident man who ran one of the most successful farms in the state. What was it about his father that made him lose all reasoning and common sense? What was it about his father that made John-Michael less compromising and more cutting with his words and temper? *Okay, so he was abandoned by his father. That is devastating to a child, but he's a grown man now. There's got to be more. Something he elected not to tell me.* Olivia looked down at the family tree. Her eyes zoomed in on Roberta's name. *There are some skeletons here,* she thought, *and somehow those skeletons are controlling John-Michael, manipulating him as if he were a brainless mannequin.* She thought about the incident not too long ago when she had tried to write his father's name on the chart and he'd exploded. She thought about the years they had lived together, and how his father's name had never been uttered. She knew, looking at John-Michael, that she wasn't going to get the answers from him and she darn sure wouldn't go to Roberta. But, there was Lena. Lena had been with the Johnsons for more years than not. She would know what hold John-Michael's father held for him.

Olivia spoke softly, in a mother's soothing tone. "John-Michael—" She cupped his chin and turned his head to look at her. Their eyes met. Hers communicated trust and caring, his fear, before he blinked it away. "I'm here for you."

John-Michael spoke quietly. "If that's true, then don't leave me again. Stay with me." He ran a finger down the side of her face, tracing the outline of her cheekbone, the curves of her lips, the line of her jaw. In slow motion, he brought their faces closer together and lightly touched his lips to hers.

Olivia tingled from the inside out. She closed her eyes to savor the delicious feel of his lips against her own. His kiss was as light and tender as his words had been truthful and appealing. Right now, in the midst of surrendering to him, she was ready to tell him she would stay. That she would never leave him again. She opened her mouth to speak her wish.

Roberta stopped her.

"John-Michael! Oh, John-Michael! Are you up there?" Roberta called out from below.

"Damn." John-Michael pulled back, apologizing with his eyes. He got up from his seat and walked to the balcony railing. "Up here, Mother."

Olivia remained seated, praying Roberta wouldn't stay long. She admitted she wanted this time alone with John-Michael. She really was concerned about John-Michael's issue with his father, but most importantly she wanted him. She needed to fill her eyes with him, smell him, and listen to his slow, easy way of talking, touch him, love him.

And what if he continues to place his mother's needs above yours? a devilish imp inside her head prodded her. That thought doused the flame of desire that had ignited and spread within her. *It's possible. He's done it before. What then? You'd be right back in the same spot,* the voice continued. Olivia was rudely dropped back into reality. *I almost surrendered to his wish. What was I thinking of? I don't have any proof that he's changed. And, if there's one thing I learned from the last time, it's that love and passion aren't enough.* For once, Olivia was glad about Roberta's interference. It had saved her from a terrible mistake. She would not make another commitment to John-Michael until he passed her test.

"I'm not walking up those stairs. They seem unstable. Would you please come down?" Roberta half-demanded and half-pleaded.

"If you don't want to walk up, then just stay where you are. I can hear you from there." John-Michael leaned his elbows on the railing.

"Oh, I don't know why you're being so difficult." Roberta moved closer to the balustrade. "I need a ride to town. Bernie said if I get there within the hour, she can get me in and out. Otherwise, I'll be at the beauty shop all day tomorrow, and I don't want to waste my time like that."

"Mother, why didn't you say something earlier? Olivia and I are working on our family tree."

Olivia took the opportunity to make her presence known. She joined John-Michael at the rail and waved. "Hi, Roberta."

Roberta snarled in response. "It just came up. Just run me to town and bring me back. I won't be in the chair for more than an hour. Come on, now."

"Sorry, Mom, you'll have to drive yourself. Olivia and I made plans days ago for this evening."

"But, John-Michael, you know I don't see well at night," Roberta whined.

"Then keep your regular appointment tomorrow." John-Michael was growing antsy. With Olivia standing so close to him, he could smell her soft, flowery perfume. Her body heat wrapped around him, calling his flesh to meet hers. His lips ached to reclaim hers.

Roberta paused, trying to keep a lid on her anxiety. John-Michael had never given her this much trouble about running an errand. She knew what Olivia had been doing to her son, but now she wondered what Olivia had been whispering in his ear. Rattled, she desperately pleaded, "John-Michael, would you *please* come down here? I need to speak to you privately."

Olivia moved away from the balcony and reclaimed her seat.

Picking up a pencil, she twirled it around and around, wondering for the millionth time what mother and son had argued about days ago, and how she figured in the picture.

"Mom, if you'd have caught me earlier we could have worked something out. But, we've already gotten started."

"John-Michael, *please.*" Roberta crossed her arms across her heavy bosom. "You know I can't drive myself."

"If you're afraid to drive at night then wait until tomorrow. I can take you then, since I've got to be downtown for the auction by nine, anyway."

"If I wait until tomorrow, I'll be in the shop all day, and I don't have time for that," Roberta pouted.

John-Michael just looked at her, signaling with his eyes and body language that the conversation was over.

They stared at each other for minutes. The creaking of the wood settling for the night was the only sound that filled the air. Roberta had a few more things she could have said, but she held her tongue until she could be alone with him. She refused to give Olivia any more ammunition than she already had.

In a huff, Roberta twirled around and exited, leaving the barn door standing wide open.

John-Michael made his way back to the table and straddled his chair. "So, where were we?"

Olivia knew they hadn't settled the issue surrounding his father but she had enough smarts to not bring it up again. She pointed to the chart. "Are you sure you want to do this? We can always work on this another time."

John-Michael shrugged his shoulders. "I'm okay."

Olivia shifted in her chair so that she faced him. "John-Michael, may I pass on an observation?"

John-Michael smiled. "Sure. Please."

"There seems to be a change between you and your mother. I noticed it at dinner the other night, and just now things seemed a little stressful. Is everything okay?"

John-Michael pinpointed her with a direct gaze. "I've tried

to tell you that I'm not the same man you left. This may be difficult for you to grasp. I mean, it's hard for me to explain, but when you left my eyes opened. I realized I had taken too much of a hands off approach concerning our marriage. I guess I thought marriage would be like an automatic car. Just put it in gear and it runs itself. Well, much too late, I realized it takes constant time and effort."

John-Michael blew out a deep breath. "I've tried to share this learning lesson with Mother, but she ain't hearing it. She loves me, and thinks I was faultless in the break up."

"And, according to her, I'm the screw-up, hmmmm?"

"Right. But, it's not her opinion that counts. It's mine." He captured her hand and kissed her wrist, her palm, her wedding ring. "Olivia, let me prove to you I've learned my lesson. Make me a happy man and say you'll stay."

"I wish I knew that it really would be different this time, John-Michael." Olivia gently pulled her hand from his. Anguish was written all over her face. "I don't want to be hurt again. It almost killed me. It almost destroyed my dreams. Can you guarantee that I won't be hurt again, John-Michael? Can you promise me that this time love will be enough?"

"Do you love me, Olivia?"

With her heart ripping in two, she whispered, "Yes."

"I love you, too . . . more than you'll ever know. I could say sorry a million times and it would still not make up for the pain I caused you. I can only tell you that from this point I will do anything and everything in my power to keep from hurting you again. I'll make that commitment to you, Baby."

Dr. Hill's forgive and reconcile lesson rose from her subconscious, imploring her to learn from her "adopted" mother's mistake. It challenged her to let go of the past forever and live for the present. Olivia wanted to, but the remembrance of that life-threatening pain remained. "I . . . just . . . need more time, John-Michael. Please be patient with me."

John-Michael placed a hand alongside her cheek. "Before your experiment ends, I want an answer from you."

She gave him a weak smile in agreement.

He kissed her lightly on the lips. "Now, I need to come clean with you."

Olivia raised her brows.

"I really don't want to work on this family tree, at least not today. I was thinking we could, say . . ." John-Michael cut his eyes to where the bed stood in one corner of the room. He nodded his head in that direction and wriggled his brows, making his intentions known.

Olivia laughed and shook her head. Standing, she conceded one point. "We don't have to work on the tree. But I'm not going over there with you."

"Why not? Are you afraid, little girl?"

"Yes." Olivia answered honestly.

Looking in her eyes, John-Michael could see that she was. She did indeed need more time. He wouldn't pressure her. "Well, how does raiding the refrigerator and watching a few movies sound to you? We could cuddle on the couch, and I promise not to touch any of your sensitive parts."

Olivia smiled. *I really love this man,* she thought.

Taking his hand in hers, she headed for the stairs. "Deal."

Ten

Lena sat at the table shelling peas for tomorrow's dinner at the church. The smell of a smoked ham hock boiling on the stove wafted through the air. Olivia sat on the opposite side of the whitewashed pine table, snapping green beans. Other than the popping and crackling sounds from the stovetop and the few occasional snatches of conversation between the friends, the house was quiet.

John-Michael, Dan, and Micky had left the house around three in the morning to go hunting. They weren't due back for a few more hours. Roberta had gone to her standing Saturday morning hair appointment. She, too, was not due back until early afternoon, since she planned to stop by the church after her appointment, to prepare for the afternoon Stewardship service.

As Olivia sat in companionable silence, her fingers automatically snapping the ends off the beans, her mind was busy fashioning sense out of the last conversation she'd had with her husband regarding his father. It had been eight days since they had met in the barn to work on his family tree, and still she had questions.

"Lena—"

"Hmmmm?"

"May I ask you something personal about the Johnsons?"

Lena's head bobbed up. Her beautiful bronze face gave no hint to her thoughts. "What you want to know?"

"It's about John-Michael's father."

"Oh." Lena shook her head very slowly. "I see." She moved the plastic bowl full of peas from between her legs and placed it on the table. Wandering over to the counter where the coffee machine sat, she refilled her cup. She raised the pot, asking without words if Olivia wanted thirds. Olivia refused. Returning to the table, she sat down hard, nodding her head for Olivia to shoot.

"John-Michael's been working on his family tree and last weekend we were reviewing some of his work. Well, I noticed his father's name was missing, and when I tried to convince him that his father's name needed to be on the tree, he absolutely refused. He wouldn't listen to reason; it was like he shut down. And this isn't the first time he's refused to discuss his father. Well, I got to thinking and realized that John-Michael senior is rarely mentioned around here. I don't recall his name being spoken even when I lived here. Why is that? Why is he taboo around here?"

Lena sat back in her chair. For the time being the peas, the beans, and the dinner at the church were forgotten. "What did John-Michael say when you asked him?"

Exasperated, Olivia reported, "Nothing. He clams up."

Lena thought about Olivia's question. *The girl's playing with a hornet's nest, and don't even know it. If Roberta hears she's been asking questions about the senior, hell will rise up and claim us all.* "I think you'd best leave that subject alone."

"Why? You can't just wipe a person out of your history."

"Sounds to me like John-Michael's doing just that."

Ordinarily, Olivia appreciated Lena's matter-of-fact attitude, but not today. Today she wanted answers; she was tired of blank cartridges. "Well, it's not right! I can understand not wanting to release personal family information to just anyone, but that's not the case. I married John-Michael, and I can't help but feel that this—" Olivia searched for the right word— "*secret* has somehow affected our marriage."

"Could be." Lena shrugged her shoulders. Slowly, her head began to bob up and down. "Yep, could be."

"What, Lena? What could be?" Anxiousness moved Olivia to the edge of her seat.

"I was just thinking about what you said. It's very likely the past had a bearing on your marriage." Lena stared at the young girl. Seeing Olivia perched on her seat, witnessing the co-mingling of trepidation, frustration, and anger on the young girl's face pierced a hole in Lena's usual mind-your-own-business mindset. Putting aside one of her guiding principles, she said, "Olivia, you know I really don't like to get involved in other folks' business, but I'll tell you."

With her decision made, the words came easier. "You walked into a fine mess. A mess which started years ago. Roberta was just finishing at Tuskegee. 'Course, the only reason she went to college was to find a husband in one of those agriculture classes. All along, all she ever wanted was a smart, handsome boy who could eventually step into her father's shoes. Well, she didn't find that boy in school, but months after she graduated from college, a tall, slim, good-looking man drove up to the house."

Lena's eyes took on that faraway look and she chuckled softly. "My, my, my. He was a sho' nuff looker. Shoot, Honey, my husband was still alive at the time, but this man made me stop and take a good long look."

The older woman's speech grew more relaxed as she traveled, in her mind, back in time, but not so far back that she didn't occasionally return to the present. "They really are good men—those John-Michaels—but it only takes one misguided woman to ruin a good man. Anyway . . ."

Olivia forgot all about the beans she was supposed to be snapping. She was seized by Lena's story.

"The senior John-Michael had this air about him. Confident but not boastful, reserved and respectful, but no pushover. And, smart. Girl, he was sharp. Oh, my, you should have seen him. But then, what am I saying? All you gotta do is look at John-Michael, and there's the father."

Lena leaned back in her chair and folded her hands over

her generous belly. "So, he came to the house to interview with Madison and got the job heading up the northwest fields. Miss Roberta took notice immediately. In her heyday, she was a downright pretty girl. She went after him with everythin' she had. The poor man didn't stand a chance. He wasn't even on the payroll a year before they got married. She came up pregnant almost instantly."

Lena clucked her tongue and shook her head. Compassion and sympathy made her voice lose some of its earlier enthusiasm. "Bless his heart, the senior took Roberta's abuse and demanding ways for as long as any real man could. But Roberta ignored the fact that he was a man, not a puppet, and every man's got his limit. Before he lost himself, he left. It must have been hard for him, because he loved John-Michael. He'd get up early, early in the mornings, and feed and play with him. I really think he stayed as long as he did because of his son."

Olivia couldn't keep quiet any longer. A frown carved a groove in her forehead and around her lips. "Does John-Michael know any of this? What you just told me, does he know?"

"I doubt it. You see, Roberta was bitter, very bitter, after the senior left. Her pride wouldn't let her go after him, and her ignorance prevented her from looking inside herself to see why he'd left in the first place. Roberta did the only thing she knew to do—filed for divorce. When she did, she had the lawyer change their names back to Johnson, and she wouldn't let the senior have any custody rights. He tried to fight it, but he didn't have Madison's money. Then Roberta forbade anyone to speak about her marriage or the senior."

Lena clucked her tongue again and stood up to check on her ham hock. With her back to Olivia, she continued. "I don't think John-Michael knows anything about his father except what Roberta has told him, and that can't be positive, knowing Roberta. She hates to lose."

With her chin resting in the palm of one hand, Olivia murmured reflectively. "Lena, that's so sad. I can't—well, yes, I can—believe Roberta can be so mean."

"Roberta is spoiled. Her mother died at childbirth, and her father, scared of losing her because she was such a sickly child, gave into her. And she has a controlling personality."

Caustically, Olivia replied, "Don't I know it."

Lena *humphed* on her way back to the table. Pulling the bowl of peas to her, she resumed her chore.

"Roberta'd have a fit if she knew that about once a year I get a letter from the senior, asking about his son. He even sent me a letter to give to John-Michael, but told me not to give it to him until Roberta had loosened her hold on him. I still have the letter, and it's getting close to that time."

Wanting to be certain that she and Lena were on the same wavelength, Olivia invited clarification. "You're going to have to explain that to me."

"John-Michael started changing after you left. He pulled back from asking Roberta's opinion. He started saying no to her, and in the last year or so he's been spending his little free time doing what he wants to do and less on what she wants him to do. He's finally realizing he's gotta live his own life."

Olivia's mind flew back to the afternoon she and John-Michael shared at the pond, and the Friday evening they'd talked in the barn. She spoke softly to herself. "He told me he'd changed. I was skeptical."

Lena stared at Olivia, praying she was getting the message. "I think Roberta realizes her hold is slipping. Now, you're back. You'd better watch yourself."

Alarmed at the ominous threat in Lena's voice, Olivia sat up straight. Her deep brown eyes popped open wide. "Roberta's more bark than bite." Olivia thought about it a second longer, then asked, "Isn't she?"

"Is a cornered animal more likely to bark, or bite?" Lena didn't expect an answer. "You're the one person who can upset her world. Her life consists of her son, this farm, the few people she calls friend, and Saint Stephen's A.M.E. church.

You have the power to strip her of two of those. They also happen to be the most important. Of course, she'll do whatever possible to keep life the way it is . . . or rather, the way it was before you showed up."

Lena finished her peas. Moving the bowl and empty hulls to the side, she grabbed a handful of the green beans in front of Olivia and started snapping. "I was rooting for you, Olivia." Lena thought about Roberta's selfish plot to break up her son's marriage. She had overheard many of the lies Roberta had told John-Michael about Olivia, and she had witnessed so many of Roberta's successful attempts to shut Olivia out of the social, professional, and personal sides of the family business. Two lives had been damaged needlessly because she had been unwilling to get involved in other folks' business. "I should have warned you what you were up against. I'm sorry she ran you off, but I'm glad you're back."

Olivia reached out a hand to cover Lena's timeworn one. "Lena, despite it all, you are a dear friend to me. I always knew you were in my corner, and many times that was enough to help me to continue."

"That's good to hear. Now, I need you to do something for you and John-Michael. Be right back." Well into her sixties, Lena jumped up and out of her chair with the agility of a pre-teen. She trotted through the hallway that connected the kitchen to the laundry room, to the back stairwell which led either up or down. Lena lived down. She hadn't always lived at the Johnson farmhouse, but when she moved in after her husband's death she took the living space downstairs, preferring the quiet and solitude. Her quarters consisted of a combination sitting room and bedroom, a standard size bathroom, and a mini-kitchen area like those found in efficiency apartments. Furnishings were sparse. In one corner of the sitting room was an antique rolltop desk which served many functions for Lena. She headed for the desk, and within seconds found what she needed. Within minutes she was back in the kitchen, carrying an empty envelope. She placed it beside the bowl of green beans.

"What's this?" Olivia asked while scanning the paper. The address of Johnson Farms was written in the middle of the envelope and the return address was John-Michael Taylor's. With eyes full of questions, Olivia stared at Lena.

Like a wise old owl, Lena looked through Olivia's unstated inquiries and calmly spoke the obvious. "I thought you might want to write him."

Olivia jerked back and let the paper fall to the table. Her mouth fell open and her eyes grew as round as a ball. "Why?" Laying a hand on her chest. "What would I say to him? John-Michael is the one who needs this."

"You can help John-Michael need that." Lena leaned her hands on the table, propping up her heavy body. She spoke softly; her eyes drilled into Olivia's. "You said earlier he doesn't want to acknowledge his father. Everyone needs a mother and a father."

Olivia's eyes dropped down to the envelope. She touched it lightly as if it were the original Emancipation Proclamation. She spoke slowly, the idea still very uncomfortable to her. "I don't know, Lena. John-Michael has a major problem with his father. I told you, he won't even talk about the man. And you're suggesting I write to him?"

"Don't you think John-Michael deserves to hear both sides of the story? Isn't that what they teach y'all in school? That there's two sides to every story?" Lena stood with one hand on her hip.

"Well, of course, but I don't think *I'm* the one who should initiate their coming together," Olivia protested, shaking her head.

Abruptly, almost rudely, Lena jumped in. "Why didn't you divorce John-Michael?"

Olivia frowned. "What's that got to do with this?" She pointed at the envelope.

"Three years is plenty of time to get someone out of your

life you don't care about." Lena straightened to her full height
and shrugged her thick shoulders. She measured her words,
making sure Olivia understood. "You cared for him enough
to keep your love going strong for three years. Surely, you
love him enough to help him with this problem." After a slight
pause, she continued. "No matter how hard you want it not
to be so, you do love John-Michael. It shows."

Olivia collapsed mentally and physically. Her shoulders fell,
her head dropped, and the weight which had held her heart
prisoner lifted. The crack John-Michael had wedged open
weeks ago—and the admission to herself of loving him yet
fighting it—widened to Gulf Coast proportions. The game was
over, the liar in her exposed. "I tried not to, but I do love him,
Lena. Very much." A drop of wetness splashed on her hand.
Dabbing at her eyes, she rounded the table and walked straight
into Lena's waiting arms. She didn't realize until she luxuriated
in them just how desperately she had needed a hug. "Why
can't two people just love each other and that be enough?"
she mumbled into Lena's bosom.

"Oooooo. Now. Where's the adventure in that, huh?"

Olivia pulled back and looked deep into Lena's soulful eyes.
She managed a crooked smile. "Yeah. You're right. But I can
do with less adventure, that's for sure."

Lena chortled and released her hold on Olivia. "Go on upstairs and write your letter. I'll finish up down here."

Even though Stewardship service was slated to start at four
that afternoon with a dinner for guests, church family, and
visiting dignitaries scheduled for two, church service ended at
the usual one o'clock.

John-Michael and Olivia vacated their pew seats as soon as
the last amen was said and headed for the vestibule to wait
for Roberta.

"I hope she doesn't take long," John-Michael whispered in
Olivia's ear so none of the passersby could hear. Loosening

his tie, he smiled and issued pleasantries to the church folks. Olivia, standing by his side, itched to shed her pantyhose. *There should be a warning label on pantyhose packages that two hours is the most time a woman should wear these things,* she thought as she smiled pleasantly and nodded good-byes, *otherwise you run the risk of grouchiness.*

Fifteen minutes later, the sanctuary and the parking lot were nearly empty, and still no Roberta.

"Where is Mother?" John-Michael growled. He was tired and wanted nothing more than to go home and sleep. Although he had had a good time hunting and hanging out with Dan and Micky and some of the locals at Jo-Jo's afterward, it had been a long day. They hadn't made it back home until some time after midnight. On his way to the master bedroom, he'd been tempted to knock on Olivia's door. Since that afternoon at the pond, sleep had been near impossible, knowing his wife lay next door with a flimsy sleeper on. But, the good news was that he felt they were inching closer to a permanent reconciliation, and for that reason, along with the anticipation of a lifetime of loving, he'd continued on to his room. Still, his sleep had been troubled with desire.

"She should be out soon." Olivia laid a hand on his arm, trying to soothe him. She could feel the tension, brought on by tiredness, building in him. "You know the mothers of the church come out last."

"Yeah, well, I'm ready to go. I need some sleep and I've got work to do."

"I'll go check on her." Olivia took two steps and halted. Roberta, with the pastor by her side, walked through the double door entry and into the lobby. Their eyes met and she could see the disdain in Roberta's.

Pasting a smile on her face for the reverend's benefit, she closed the gap of a few feet and held out her hand to the pastor. "I really enjoyed the service. That was a wonderful sermon, Pastor Clark."

"Thank you. Thank you, Sister, er, uh . . ." The reverend

shook her hand then ran a finger around his neck, hoping to loosen his stiff white collar. He had already shed his black, ankle length robe. It lay carelessly in his arm, along with his *kinte* cloth scarf, but still he sweated.

Pastor Clark resembled a black bear. He was six foot, three inches tall, as dark as a Michelin tire, and burly. His wife joked constantly about his enormous appetite and it showed in his massive bulk. The man made Dan look like a Richard Simmons graduate. To look at the reverend, one would expect him to be a formidable opponent, and he was. He was highly intelligent, had two masters degrees and was extremely articulate. To complement his smarts, he was street-wise and had a love for his race that matched a mother's love for her children. Pastor Clark had been appointed to St. Stephen's two years ago, and although the younger people adored him the older, monied members of the congregation complained about his contemporary sermons.

Roberta was one of the chief complainers. She now had his ear, and Olivia could only imagine what imaginary fault she had found in today's service.

Smiling sweetly for Roberta's benefit, Olivia supplied, "It's still Johnson."

"Why aren't you all down in the fellowship hall?" Roberta ground out between clenched teeth. Roberta raised her voice to attract her son's attention. "Olivia, you could be setting the tables and John-Michael, you can help the men bring in more chairs."

Sensing some underlying currents, Pastor Clark smiled and excused himself. "Mother Roberta, we can finish this discussion after Wednesday Bible Study." He shook John-Michael's hand and was gone.

"Mother, we'll help get everything set up, but Olivia and I aren't staying. She has schoolwork, and I'm tired."

Roberta's eyes cut quickly to Olivia. "Was this your idea?" The evil thought that passed through her mind did shame to all the amening she had done in service.

"I—"

John-Michael cut Olivia off. "No, Mother. It was a mutual decision. We both have other things to do."

Roberta petitioned. "John-Michael, you know how important this service is to the church. And, I have worked very hard to prepare a nice dinner. Now you're telling me you're not even going to stay and fellowship?"

John-Michael cupped his mother's shoulder with one hand. He bent slightly at the waist to peer into her face. "Mother, I'm not staying. I've already completed my pledge card and I wrote my check. As soon as we finish setting up, we're gone."

"You don't even have time to eat?"

Olivia spoke up. "Lena whipped up a casserole before she left for her church this morning. She didn't think the boys would make it out of bed today, since they had such a late night."

Roberta turned on her. Her face contorted in anger. "You and your crew are disrupting my household. That was extra work for Lena." Roberta pointed a finger at Olivia. "You're not paying her." She turned her finger toward herself. "*I* am."

"Mother, calm down. People are looking." Indeed, a few stragglers were staring at the trio. John-Michael lowered his own voice. "This isn't a federal issue. Olivia didn't keep the boys out all night. Anyway, Lena loves to cook. She didn't mind in the least." John-Michael shifted on his feet. His eyes were getting heavier by the moment. "Lena will be here this afternoon for the dinner and the church service. She'll drive you home this evening."

Roberta bristled. "Lena doesn't drive well."

Although weary, John-Michael managed to hang on to some of his good humor. "Lena drives better than me." He kissed her on the cheek. "Now, where are those chairs?" John-Michael walked off to huddle with one of the male elders of the church. They headed downstairs to the storage room.

"I guess you're pretty proud of yourself," Roberta said in a fierce whisper, "taking John-Michael from a service he enjoys."

Olivia wanted to avoid a fullblown argument with Roberta. She was not about to engage in an emotional battle with her mother-in-law. She thought about Lena's words yesterday afternoon, and knew the housekeeper was right. She now knew it wasn't a personal thing between her and Roberta. Roberta was afraid of losing her only child. She would act the same if any other woman married John-Michael. Unfortunately, what Roberta failed to realize was that more than anyone else she was hurting her son. The thought saddened Olivia. "Roberta, I'm not taking John-Michael from you. I could never do that. For God's sake, you're his mother!"

Olivia's words washed right over Roberta. The look she X-rayed Olivia with contained pure venom. "Your little plan to steal him from me won't succeed, you know." Before Olivia could open her mouth to try to reason with Roberta, the older woman stomped off, leaving Olivia to stare, openmouthed, at her back.

Shaking her head, Olivia followed.

In thirty minutes, they were finished and headed home. Olivia drove while John-Michael slouched in the passenger seat with his eyes closed. Olivia noticed that his breathing was suspiciously deep. She smiled, appreciating the time to survey him at her leisure. As she Ping-Ponged her eyes between the road and her husband, she thought about the spider's web he was caught in—wife or mother, which would he choose? *Does he even know he has to choose?* Olivia wondered. *I know he doesn't know about his father, but I wonder if he knows about Roberta's background. It's quite possible he doesn't. He may just think, like I did, that it's a personality clash between us.* Blowing out a deep breath, she looked over at her sleeping husband. *Gosh, I love him so much.* Her heart swelled as she caressed him with her eyes. *What can I do to help? Is there any way everyone can be happy?* she wondered. *Maybe his dad will have a clue. He probably knows Roberta better than anyone. I'll just have to wait patiently for his response. Thank goodness I had the foresight to give him both my addresses.* Olivia slowed the car to turn into the driveway. *What if he doesn't write back?* a tiny voice inside her head prompted. Then, somehow, she answered it, *I've got to help John-Michael understand the true depth of his mother. If that turns out to be the case, he's the only one who can help her.* She stopped Roberta's Benz in the sideyard and switched off the motor. With both hands on the wheel she stared straight ahead into the garden, thinking about how innocently their marriage had started and how twisted it had become. Feeling weighted down by the magnitude of her thoughts, she reached over to John-Michael and cradled his cheek with a hand. "I love you, John-Michael Johnson, and today I'm going to show you just how much." Leaning over, she kissed his forehead.

John-Michael woke with a start. He looked around, orienting himself to his surroundings. "Oh! That was quick," he muttered thickly.

John-Michael unfolded his limbs from the car and stretched full length. "Boy, I'm hungry. I wonder if your comrades are still asleep."

Olivia spoke over the roof of the car. "I'm sure their stomachs have driven them downstairs by now."

They entered the house from the back door and as soon as they walked into the kitchen they spotted Dan and Micky—one at the refrigerator; the other at the counter.

"Hello, hello, hello, all." Dan spoke in his loud, boisterous tone. He was at the counter dishing out a huge chunk of the casserole Lena had prepared.

A round of greetings circulated throughout the room.

"I see we're just in time," John-Michael remarked, stripping off his tie and throwing it haphazardly over a chair.

Olivia bumped Micky out of the open door of the refrigerator to pull out a fresh garden salad and a pitcher of tea. "How about we keep it informal and eat at the table in here?"

"If that means I can eat that much quicker, fine with me," Micky replied. He moved over to the counter to serve himself a fairly reasonable portion of the casserole.

Moving at rocket speed, Olivia hastily put bowls, silverware and glasses for four on the table in the alcove of the kitchen. Dinner was a hastily consumed affair during which Micky gave an hour by hour report of the fun he'd had the previous day. With appetites sated, the men offered to pitch in and help clean the kitchen. Olivia shooed them away. She didn't tell them she needed the chore to work off nervous energy.

Dan and Micky headed to the family den for a leisurely afternoon of napping and watching football. John-Michael headed upstairs for a quick nap before starting work on a presentation he would be delivering next week to stock exchange trading analysts who dealt in cotton futures.

With a very small portion of leftovers stored in the fridge, the dishes stacked in the dishwasher, and the counters wiped down, all was spic-and-span again. With tap dancers still dancing a jig in her stomach, Olivia headed upstairs to initiate her plan.

After two hours of primping, Olivia wrapped her terrycloth house robe around her. "I wish I had something more fancy," she muttered. "Oh, well, this'll have to do." Stepping into the hallway, she scanned it quickly then headed in the direction of the master bedroom, a few feet away, where her husband slept. Opening the door, she tiptoed across the massive, fan-shaped room to the king-sized, oak sleigh bed. John-Michael lay smack-dab in the middle of it, face up, with one arm thrown over his eyes and the other outstretched. His legs were parted wide.

For several minutes, Olivia stared down at him, surveying his perfectly made face and body. He had stripped down to nothing, but had covered his middle with a throw. His arms, although relaxed, bulged with the muscular strength gleaned from years of hard physical labor. His legs, long and dark brown, were perfectly formed: bulging thighs and calves, narrow ankles. His torso was her favorite. She had loved to curl up against his hairless barrel chest. She had loved running her hands along his well-defined pecs, down to his flat stomach.

Here, on the part of his body unexposed to the weather or his demanding work, his skin was smooth and baby soft.

Olivia's heart swelled just looking at him, and her nervousness evaporated. This was her man! Her husband!

Eager to enact her seduction, she reached out a hand and shook his shoulder. *I wonder if I can wake him?* Olivia thought. She remembered John-Michael had an internal biological clock like none other. He could stay up half the night but when it was time for work the next morning, his eyes automatically flipped open without the aid of an alarm clock. This had been a tough, long, workweek for him, though, and with the additional male-bonding hunting excursion this weekend, he might not respond. She shook him again, harder this time.

He didn't respond.

She shook him again and called his name. This time he murmured something and turned his head. That murmur made Olivia happy. She stripped out of her housecoat and tossed it on the bench at the foot of his bed.

Crawling on her knees to his side, she ran a finger along his forehead, down his cheek, landing at his lips. She followed that same path along his smooth, unblemished features with her lips.

"John-Michael," she breathed. "Wake up."

He murmured again and rolled his head to the other side. Not at all perturbed, Olivia continued to plant light kisses along his face, throat, and torso. The moment she kissed his chin, her breasts scraping lightly against his chest, his eyes creaked open.

"Olivia?" he croaked, his voice made deeper by sleep.

"Yes, it's me." She smiled down at him. "I've come to pay my debt." Shifting from her crouching position, she sat back on her haunches, parallel to his knees. "I hope I'm not disturbing you." The girlish grin on her dark face belied her statement.

John-Michael struggled from the hold sleep had on him. He

rubbed his eyes, blinked several times, and rubbed them again. Finally, they opened fully . . . and John-Michael like to have had a heart attack. He couldn't talk, couldn't do anything but stare at her nearly naked form. Raising up on his elbows, he surveyed her from head to toe and back again. "Am I dreaming?"

Olivia chuckled, backing completely off the bed so he could get a better view of his gift. Earlier, she had tiptoed into his bedroom and retrieved the red lace and satin teddy he had purchased for her as a Valentine's Day gift. Now, for the first time, he saw his shopping efforts come to life. Standing straight, she slowly twirled around so he could truly appreciate his purchase.

The naughty was one piece of red satin and lace, cut high at the legs. It had three heart-shaped holes down the front: one placed over her belly button, the other right below her breasts, offering a sneak preview, and the final one in the V between her legs. A big red bow served as the convergence point for the thong in the back and the straps which lifted the lace and satin bra and pulled together what there was of the sides and the upper back.

To the naughty, she'd added three-inch red pumps, and a red garter circled one thigh. "I know you're tired, so if you—"

"Shhhh." John-Michael's voice had turned gruff, and she saw hard evidence that indeed he was well pleased with his purchases.

Olivia did as instructed and continued twirling around and around, slowly, until she heard the bed shifting. Looking behind her, she saw that he was off the bed, closing the gap between them. Almost reverently, he began touching her. A light caress on the shoulder, a sliding hand down her back to land on her buttocks. Fingers smoothing a thigh and climbing upward to play in the hole at her belly button. An arousing squeeze of a breast, the flick of a nipple. As he explored with his hands and fingers, Olivia could hear his breathing become more labored, and she herself had trouble staying clearheaded.

When he dipped his head to add his lips to the exploration,

she gave up trying to remain levelheaded. The feelings he evoked were too sensational. She felt her body shudder alive. Spasms of electric shock waves jarred her into mindless oblivion. Her breathing matched his in its rapidity, and she grew moist. John-Michael, replicating her urges, turned her to face him and married their lips in an uncontrollable, desire-wrenching kiss. Their bodies pressed close together, and she could feel his arousal pressing against her stomach. Raising her arms, she circled his neck as the kiss grew more intense, more devouring. It erased the last shreds of sanity.

Suddenly, she was free. Her eyes popped open, and she instantly knew the reason why. John-Michael was stripping out of his briefs. Seconds later she was back in his arms.

"I'm sorry, Baby. I can't wait." With those few words, John-Michael pushed her backward against the nearest wall and preceded to devour her. His lips and hands savored her skin. No less needful, Olivia basted his body with her own hands and lips. Love mixed with need, driving her to match him kiss for kiss, caress for caress, stroke for stroke. Finally, when their primitive urges could no longer be sated as two, he pulled the satin of her crotch aside and entered her in one long, smooth stroke. The intensity of that movement made them cry out and shudder. When the light show inside his head dimmed, John-Michael pumped slow and steady at first, but quickly escalated to hard and fast. Olivia responded to the urgency of their bodies by wrapping her legs around his waist. With deeper access to her treasure chest, it wasn't long before a gut-level moan erupted from John-Michael. He shuddered more violently, and a final stroke pushed them both over the edge. A symphony of black and white stars exploded behind her closed eyes. In her heightened sensory state, she could still feel the minor tremors that played throughout their joined bodies.

Slowly, their bodies grew still; their breathing returned to normal. As they stood chest to chest, thigh to thigh, their lips mingled in a long, satisfying kiss. They ended the kiss to caress each other with their gazes. No words in any language could capture the message they sent to each other.

Taking her hand, he led her to the bed. Stripping her of the garter, which was greatly askew, and her one remaining pump, he pulled her down on the bed with him. They lay on their sides, facing each other.

Staring into her eyes, John-Michael caressed her face. "Tell me what this means?"

"It means I've been a fool." Olivia smiled at him. "A dear, old friend once told me not to turn my back on love. So, I'm facing you front and center. I love you, John-Michael."

John-Michael was afraid to ask the question. His heart was beating fast, his stomach had dropped to his toes. Fear almost made him hold back, but love and need pushed the question out of his mouth. "Are you going to stay here . . . with me?"

"There's no place else I'd rather be . . . than here . . . with you." Olivia sealed her commitment with a kiss.

John-Michael expelled the breath he'd been holding, and at the same time expelled the ghost of his father. He wasn't like his father. He was not a loser. Everything would be all right. He kissed Olivia's nose, forehead. "I love you, Olivia. There's never been another woman for me but you."

With the luxury of love on her side, she could afford to tease him. "You mean to tell me that in the three years we've been apart, you've never been with anyone else?"

"Of course not." John-Michael was serious. "I'm not going to lie to you, Olivia. I did take a couple of women out. But your ghostly presence always interfered. As soon as the date was over, I'd go running up to Huntsville to try and talk to you."

"And I always turned my back to you." Sadness colored her words. "I'm sorry I was so stubborn. I'm sorry I hurt you."

"Honey, that's in the past. Today we start building a glorious future." John-Michael sealed his promise with a tender kiss.

"I need to call my major professor in the morning and make arrangements with him to designate a surrogate major professor. Perhaps someone from Tuskegee will be willing to serve in that capacity."

A shadow crossed John-Michael's face. It was unbelievable, yet believable, that her most pressing thought would be of her schoolwork. "Baby, do you remember a while back, we were in the barn and I mentioned to you that perhaps this Ph.D. was more than just a love for research?"

"Yes, I remember." Olivia propped her head up with a hand, curious about his question and where it would take them. "And?"

"I think you're using that Ph.D.—for that matter, your entire school career—as a crutch."

Olivia sat up. "No, I'm not. I've told you before that I enjoy school."

John-Michael got the awful feeling that he should have delayed this conversation until a later time. It was too late now. "Olivia, here we are in the midst of renewing our love, and the first thing you mention is your studies. Why is that?"

Olivia grabbed for an explanation. "I . . . well, I was just planning ahead."

John-Michael slowly nodded his head and pinned her with his gaze. "If for some reason you don't get your Ph.D., what will you do?"

"I've never thought about it."

"Think about it now," John-Michael directed. "And tell me what you will do."

Silence filled the room as Olivia thought and thought. She couldn't come up with an answer. "I guess I'd keep trying."

"My point, exactly. You can't imagine life without a Ph.D. Why not?"

"John-Michael, let's not talk about this right now. We have three years of loving to make up for." Olivia leaned over and outlined his lips with her tongue.

John-Michael allowed her to sidetrack him for a few minutes, but before he got too heated he pulled away. "I think you've allowed that degree to become as important as breathing. And, I think that's because *you think* it will fill that empty cavity your parents didn't fill."

Olivia tried to laugh off his deduction, but it came out as a harsh, grating noise. "John-Michael, that's ridiculous. My parents were good to us. We never lacked for anything."

" 'Anything' being defined as material possessions, or 'anything' meaning emotional?" John-Michael continued, cutting off her possible objections. "I'm sure they took care of your physical needs quite well, but parenting is more than providing food and shelter and clothing and medical care. What about hugs and praise, and discipline, and positive affirmation? Somehow I think you latched on to this Ph.D. as a means to compensate for your emotional neglect. Think about it, Olivia. How many hugs did you get growing up? Do you remember the first time your parents told you they loved you? How often did your mother or father tell you they were proud of you, that you're unique?"

Casting her eyes downward, Olivia traced the striped pattern in the fitted sheet. She heard, but didn't hear, John-Michael's words. Her mind was trying to piece together the validity of his comments. *Is it possible? Was I neglected emotionally as a child? Is that why it became so important for me to visit Dr. Hill every day? Because from her I always got kind words, and praise about my report card, and participation at my school events, and lessons in living?*

John-Michael lifted her chin. "Your parents had the monumental task of raising ten children. I'm sure they did the best they could. But now, it's time for you to think seriously about your goal to obtain this degree and how that goal played into your past, and how it will play into your future." John-Michael wrapped his arms around her and lay them both down. He kissed the top of her head. "You don't need a Ph.D. to make you feel important. Just your mere presence speaks to your significance. But, if that's too vague, hear me." He tilted her head back and stared directly in her eyes. "I love you. I want to be your lover in every sense of the word . . . emotionally, physically, mentally, however and whatever you need. All you gotta do is face the truth and open up to me."

This was a paradigm-shifting concept John-Michael was throwing at her. She needed time to think about it. Time to really analyze it and come up with an answer. As an immediate response, Olivia snuggled closer to him, holding on to him for dear life.

For the rest of the afternoon, they remained in bed, alternating sleep with lovemaking with whispered talks.

A dark blanket of sky covered the earth when Olivia stirred again. Without moving a muscle, she could feel and hear John-Michael's deep breathing behind her. His arm was draped casually over her middle, and one of his legs was thrown over hers. She had never known a more peaceful, a more weightless moment in her entire existence. Smiling, she moved closer to her husband, and was on the verge of a deep sleep when she heard a knock at the door.

Before she could respond, she heard the hinges of the door squeak open. The architecture and darkness of the room prevented her from seeing the newcomer. Squirming from under John-Michael's heavy limbs, Olivia was about to flip back the covers and throw on her robe when the lights blazed on, blinding her.

"John-Michael," Roberta called out. "John-Michael."

Olivia hurriedly adjusted the covers so that their private parts remained private.

Roberta came within several feet of their bed and stopped dead. Her mouth hung open, and the command she was about to give John-Michael hung uncompleted in the air. She stared at Olivia as if the younger woman had grown two heads. "What are you doing in here?" she spat at her daughter-in-law. In the space of five rapid heartbeats, Roberta felt a red hot comet of anger consume her. "Oh, never mind. I can see what you're up to." She wanted to slap the innocent look off Olivia's face. She wanted to throttle the little minx who threatened her peaceful existence.

"Mother? What are you doing in here?" John-Michael's groggy voice sounded in Olivia's ear.

Roberta's attention was momentarily pulled from Olivia to her son. "I came to wake you, but I can see she beat me to it." Roberta's gaze swung back to Olivia, her eyes filled with hatred. "Of course now I know the real reason you couldn't stay for service. Now I know why you disappointed me." She drilled her gaze into Olivia. "The devil got to you before I did."

Roberta turned around quickly and stomped out of the room, slamming the door closed behind her.

Olivia rolled over to face John-Michael. A concerned expression cut grooves in her face. "John-Michael," she breathed. "Your mother's really upset."

"Ummmmm." John-Michael didn't take his arm from over his face, didn't say anything.

"John-Michael?" Olivia shook his shoulder. "Didn't you see how upset she was?" She'd seen Roberta angry before, but this was beyond anger. This was close to madness.

John-Michael unshielded his eyes. He met her gaze for many seconds, then lowered his eyes to her exposed breasts. She didn't need telepathy, ESP, or any other psychic method to know what was on his mind. "I don't want to talk about it right now."

He pulled her into his arms and loved her concerns away.

Eleven

From infancy to high school, Mrs. Foster had preached to Olivia and her siblings that breakfast was the most important meal of the day. Indeed, every morning, her mother always had a big pot of grits or oatmeal or Cream of Wheat ready for her children to devour before school, or—if it was a week-end—before starting their chores. But, just as time lapses, customs lapse, and Olivia dropped the breakfast routine shortly after leaving home for college. However, this Monday morning was an exception. She was starved! The dinner she and John-Michael had eaten yesterday after church had long since worn off.

Descending the wide, wooden staircase, Olivia followed the aroma of a full breakfast to the dining room. Entering through the open double doors, she saw Dan, Micky, and Roberta seated at the table.

She wasn't surprised that John-Michael was absent. An hour ago, when she'd left his room, he'd been sound asleep; he hadn't even budged when she'd slipped from between the sheets. She had no doubt he would show up, though. Not only would his internal alarm clock wake him, but sometime in the darkness of night he'd promised her that they would talk to Roberta immediately after breakfast. She knew he would keep his promise.

Dan and Micky looked up from their plates as she walked to the table. Surprise registered on their faces.

"Olivia? Is it really you?" Micky teased, temporarily abandoning his need for food. He playfully rubbed his eyes. "I can't believe you're not in the barn."

Olivia wrinkled her nose at him. She could take any amount of horseplay and kidding today, because she felt good. Feelings of being loved and being in love radiated from within her. She was happy. She was at peace with the world!

"Good morning, Dan, Micky." She picked up a plate from the table. "How are you, Roberta?" Even her greeting to Roberta being met with utter silence didn't dampen her high spirits.

"Are you okay?" Dan joked. "Do we need to call a doctor?"

Olivia goodnaturedly rolled her eyes at him.

Dan laughed, a short burst that sounded more like a horse snorting. Energized by her response, he continued. "Look, Micky, she's actually headed for the spread. Let's see . . . oh, she's picking up two pieces of bacon, toast, hash browns. Uhhhh, I can't see the rest. She's blocking the plate with her body."

"Good," Olivia laughingly replied as she returned to the table and took her usual seat near the head of the table. "I think you guys watched too much football yesterday."

"Not enough, in my opinion," Micky countered seriously.

Dan agreed. This was a subject the guys didn't joke about. "I wish football was a year-round sport. I really miss watching those Cowboys during spring and summer."

Roberta cleared her throat. "Excuse me for interrupting." She actually smiled at the guys. However, when she turned to Olivia, her smile vanished.

Yesterday's remembrance of Roberta's frightfully angry face floated before her. Olivia hoped John-Michael would show up soon.

"Have you seen my son this morning? Usually he's had his breakfast by now. And I know he needs to get on with his busy day."

Olivia put her fork down and wiped her mouth, actions intended to buy her some time to think of a suitable response.

She knew Roberta's show of concern for John-Michael was a cover-up. She had no doubt Roberta's real intent was to make her squirm and to poke into their sleeping arrangements. Shrugging her narrow shoulders, she conceded, "I imagine he'll be down soon." She paused slightly. "Do you have big plans for the day?" Olivia hoped to navigate around the subject of her and John-Michael, at least until he showed up. And, when he did, she would gladly hand over the reins to him. No one could handle Roberta the way he could.

Roberta strained until she produced a plastic smile. "Why do you ask?"

"Good morning, everyone." John-Michael stepped through the door, saving Olivia the trouble of having to come up with a response. He was as singularly focused as Olivia had been, for as soon as he entered he headed straight for the buffet. "Boy, this looks good. I am starved!"

Various greetings followed his back.

"I'll bet," Micky remarked. "You didn't show up for dinner last night. You must have had a lot of work to do."

John-Michael sat down at the table with an overflowing plate. A little boy grin highlighted his handsome brown face; there was a mischievous sparkle in his eyes as he stared meaningfully at his wife. "You could say that."

Olivia felt the blood rush from her heart to the roots of her hair. Her food took on monumental significance as she dipped her head to hide the telling signs and stuffed her mouth.

Ignorant of the message passed from one lover to another, Micky felt obligated to tell John-Michael all about the Sunday sports action he'd missed. With that subject reintroduced, Olivia knew she could relax and enjoy the rest of her food. Heck, she might even get seconds.

The second after John-Michael finished eating, Dan stood up, automatically adjusting his pants under his belly. "Come on, Little Joe. We got work to do."

Micky stood. He turned to Olivia. "You coming?"

"Go ahead. I'll be there in a bit."

While Micky would have persisted in questioning Olivia, Dan nudged him and cocked his head toward the door. An understanding, conceived from a year of working together, passed between the odd couple. Micky closed his parted mouth and followed Dan out of the room.

Olivia thought, *Dan knows. He's so very perceptive. I'm sure he knows John-Michael and I were together yesterday. And by the time they make it to the barn, Micky'll know.*

John-Michael stretched. "Oh, boy, that was good."

Roberta wasted no time. Her voice was hard, her face harder. "John-Michael, do you want to tell me exactly what was going on yesterday?"

John-Michael lifted an eyebrow. "Exactly?" he teased.

Roberta just stared at him. John-Michael got the hint. He took Olivia's hand. John-Michael looked at his wife and smiled. "Mother, Olivia and I have decided to reunite. She's coming back home—for good."

He leaned over and kissed Olivia on the cheek. With his head turned away from his mother, he did not see the look of hostility stamped on her face. But, Olivia saw it. Olivia felt it. It bored like a drill into the core of her. Intuitively, she knew this second time around would be no easier than the first.

Olivia had hoped there was some way all three of them could live happily ever after, but Roberta's posture was making it highly unlikely. That left Olivia with two choices: she could stay and fight, or she could quit and run. To stay and fight would be to help Roberta understand that John-Michael loved both of them. To quit and run meant she would renege on her promise to John-Michael. Before the thought had finished forming, Olivia knew she could never do that again . . . back out on their love. She had no choice but to try to make Roberta understand she was not a threat.

An elated John-Michael faced his mother. "So, what do you think? Are you happy, shocked, what?"

Roberta averted her vile stare from Olivia and looked deep into John-Michael's eyes.

Olivia noticed that Roberta's expression changed instantly from one of antipathy to one of love. Olivia wanted to groan. *There's no denying it. She covets her son. This is* not *going to be easy.*

A warm, motherly hand fell on John-Michael's arm. "Son, are you sure this is what you want?" Roberta leaned toward him. The desperation in her eyes could not be ignored. "Sweetheart, you've been down this road before. Do you really want to open yourself up for more hurt and pain?" Her grip tightened on his arm.

"Mother, it's not going to be like the last time." John-Michael eased her hand off his arm and held it. "We know we made mistakes, and we've learned from those." John-Michael glanced at his wife. Olivia faintly nodded her head, signaling her agreement. "We're not in our twenties anymore. This time our marriage will be different . . . stronger, because we know the work it will take. We love each other, Mother. It'll work."

Roberta pulled back slightly. The light in her eyes dimmed. "Baby, I believe *you* believe what you're saying, but I don't want you to be in a position where you're making all the sacrifices . . . like last time." Roberta looked over at Olivia. "Olivia, are you willing to fully accept your role as his wife?"

"Mother—" John-Michael started.

Roberta held up a hand to him. In a stringent voice, she declared, "I'm asking Olivia."

Olivia's chin went up a degree. Defensively, she answered, "Of course, I'm going to be the best wife I can be."

"Then you're *sacrificing* your Ph.D. for the sake of the marriage? You're dropping your studies?"

"I didn't say that." Olivia flashed back to the conversation she and John-Michael had had yesterday. Was her desire for a Ph.D. replacing some other need? Could she give up her educational pursuits and concentrate only on John-Michael and her marriage?

The light in Roberta's eyes grew bright again.

"That still has to be worked out . . . along with some other issues." Olivia glanced at John-Michael. She was becoming more and more convinced that maybe she and John-Michael should have done more talking yesterday and less loving.

Roberta attacked. "Correct me if I'm wrong, but wasn't balancing school priorities with the demands of being a wife one of the difficulties y'all encountered?"

"Mother, we encountered a number of problems. Some of them were on my end. But, I told you, we're going to work through all that." John-Michael rubbed his forehead as if he had a headache.

Olivia put a hand on his neck and began massaging it. "And, Roberta, it's not as simple as you're trying to paint it. John-Michael knows how unrealistic it is to ask me to quit school just like that." Olivia snapped her fingers. "There's a process that's involved, and a desire to be considered. Just think of how unreasonable it would be if I asked him to quit being a farmer. Think about the difficult decision that would be for him. What we do is a fundamental part of us."

Sarcastically, Roberta retorted, "That's a neat little tidy answer, but it really doesn't address the underlying problem, now, does it?" Roberta continued her grilling attack. "What's your priority, Olivia? Are you willing to support my son and Johnson Farms? What will your decision be when you have to decide between a school project or accompanying John-Michael on an important business trip? Who wins, and who loses?"

"Why does it have to be win or lose?"

"Because that's life, Sugar." The words were spat out. They landed almost like a slap against Olivia's temple. "And I've got to know if you're really going to take care of my son, and of what we've built up here."

"Mother, Olivia understands the struggles previous Johnsons overcame to make this farm profitable. And I know the obstacles

Olivia has had to endure to get as far as she's gotten. I respect her goal just like she respects Johnson Farms."

Roberta continued as if her son hadn't spoken. "There has to be one hundred percent commitment to Johnson Farms. My father didn't compromise, and neither will you, John-Michael." The matriarch of the family sat back. Her face was twisted with wrath and consternation. "And what about children? How will this farm stay in family hands if she can't carry a child full term?"

In the blink of an eye, Olivia was on her feet and leaning over the table. A finger pointed in Roberta's face. "Roberta, I've sat here long enough listening to your crap. You just need to get the hell out and stay out of my marriage."

Slowly, Roberta rose to her feet. "How dare you?" Her voice trembled with indignation. "You selfish little—"

Sometime, in the midst of their exchange, John-Michael had also risen to his feet. "Mother! You've said enough."

Mother and son stared at each other.

Somewhere deep in his consciousness, John-Michael knew he had crossed a line that had changed his relationship with his mother forever. He spoke softly, but with an edge to his voice. "I wanted you to be happy for me. I wanted you to root for us, to tell us you would support our decision. I had dreams we could all be adults this time and live harmoniously—"

Roberta reached out a hand to her son. John-Michael shunned it.

"I can see it's not gonna happen." John-Michael had made up his mind. "Olivia's going to move back here permanently in about two weeks. During that time, either you can look for an alternate place to move to, or I can look for you. Just tell me which it'll be." His voice shook, his dream for the three of them vanished.

Roberta took one step, then two, toward her son. Her eyes were bright with unshed tears. "John-Michael. Please, Son. You're not thinking straight."

He held up a detaining hand. "I'm sorry, Mother. I really wanted it to be different, but I can't let you ruin our love."

Silence filled the large room.

Olivia stared at the silver salt and pepper shakers on the table. She looked at the napkin near her plate. She gazed at the thin gold band which circled the diameter of their breakfast plates. She looked at anything except the heartbreaking scene between son and mother.

Moments ticked by, and then a soft cry escaped Roberta as she ran from the room.

Olivia went to her husband. He accepted her unspoken love. Wrapping her in his arms, he hung on to her as if sinking in quicksand.

"John-Michael, I am sorry."

Neither spoke again until his trembling stopped.

"I never thought it would come to this. I had hoped it wouldn't." John-Michael loosened his grip, but maintained a solid hold on her. He leaned his forehead against hers.

Olivia kissed him softly on the lips. "I'm sorry. I know you really wanted your mother's blessings."

"It's obvious we don't have that." John-Michael looked helpless. "I really thought she would see things differently this time."

"Maybe it's not a total loss. Perhaps if you talk to her again, you know, convince her that I'm not stealing you from her. Maybe it'll help her."

John-Michael screwed up his face in confusion. "What do you mean, steal me from her? She knows I love her."

Patiently, Olivia recapped the conversation she had had with Lena concerning Roberta, editing it to give him the basic picture of a lonely, overprotective, domineering woman. She ended by restating her suggestion. "I think she needs reassurance that your love for her will never vanish. That you'll never turn your back on her. Perhaps you can teach her that love doesn't strangle or bind."

Slowly, he nodded his head. "Yeah. Okay. I see what you're

saying, and it makes sense." John-Michael dropped his arms and moved away from her. He re-claimed his seat at the table. "To think that all these years I never knew she felt threatened by anyone. I've always viewed my mother as a completely strong, self-contained woman."

Olivia smiled softly. "The viewpoint of a man who admires and respects his mother." Olivia followed him to the table and stood behind him, massaging his shoulders. "But, she's more than a mother, John-Michael. She's a woman who loves. She's a human being with human frailties."

"Ummmmmm." John-Michael pondered Olivia's observation. "I will talk to her. Alone." John-Michael sighed deeply. "I hope it helps."

Olivia bent and kissed the top of his head. "Me, too."

"If it does, are you saying you wouldn't mind Mother living here?" John-Michael twisted in his seat to look at his wife.

Olivia sat down in Roberta's chair. She knew this was an important issue for John-Michael. Just weeks ago, he had admitted he felt responsible for his mother. That he had made a vow to take care of her. She knew John-Michael didn't take his vows lightly. Taking his hands, she answered him truthfully. "If your Mother can honestly respect our marriage and if she can truly exhibit an unselfish love, she is welcome to live here."

She curved her arms around his neck and kissed him on his cheek, his neck, his throat. Standing, he gathered her in his arms and warned, "Keep that up and I'm going to carry you back upstairs. Neither one of us'll get anything done today."

She kept it up, leaving him no choice but to capture her lips in an arousing kiss. Minutes later, when they came up for air, he said, "I love you, Olivia. If it ever comes down to you or anything or anyone else, I'll pick *you*. Promise me you'll never forget that." His light brown eyes had grown dark with serious intent.

Olivia crossed her heart. "I promise."

"Thank you, Baby." Their lips met, acting as a pledge to

cement the promise. John-Michael used one long arm to plaster her to his chest. His other hand explored the outline of her shoulders, her back, her rear end.

That's the position Lena found them in.

"I wish y'all would get out of my way so I can clean up."

Slowly the couple came apart. Olivia smiled at the wise old mother figure. "Lena, is there anything that goes on in this house that you don't know about?"

"I ain't got nothing to do with these thin doors."

Olivia and John-Michael exchanged knowing winks. Smiling, she extracted herself from John-Michael's grip and hugged her treasured friend.

"So you two gonna renew those vows with a ceremony, or just sneakily move back in together?" It didn't require a Ph.D. to figure out Lena's preference. "You need to let me know as soon as possible, so I can get started with the shopping and cleaning . . ."

She ambled off, rattling off a list of activities she needed to do for the ceremony.

John-Michael smiled and held his hands up in a defensive position. Walking backward away from her, he stated, "I'm leaving that up to you and Lena. I don't want to get on either one of your bad sides."

"Chicken!" she called out to him.

John-Michael laughed and walked out of the room.

A tremor of pleasure raced through her as she watched him exit. She hugged her arms around her middle and thought how wonderful life was. The only dark cloud was Roberta, and with John-Michael making another attempt to speak with her later maybe that dark cloud would evaporate as well. *Boy, that would be a blessing and a miracle.* Olivia headed for the back door. *Let me go tell my co-workers that our time line has changed. This will be their last week at Johnson Farms.*

She almost skipped out of the house.

* * *

In her pristine room, Roberta paced like a caged tiger. Wringing her hands together, she let the tears fall softly down her cheek. "I can't lose him. I just can't. This has got to work."

Patience had never been a strong attribute with her. This situation—waiting for the phone to ring—clearly highlighted that fact. She was almost out of her skin with the lack of activity. *Oh, call. Call!* she demanded. *So much relies on you.*

Roberta backed away from the phone and took up her pacing near the window. From her first floor position on the northwest wing of the house, she could see a great expanse of the garden. She recalled the days when it used to give her pleasure, when it used to calm and soothe her. That was before Olivia Foster took up residence at Johnson Farms. Ever since she'd heard the name, ever since she'd become a part of their lives, life had not been as enjoyable. Well, she was tired of living in fear of a short, petite harlot. She was going to take care of that troublemaker today!

"If that little witch thinks she can come in here and use her body to make my son even *think* about putting his own mother out, then she has greatly underestimated me." Roberta thought about the careless words her son had tossed at her. "I'll have that little whore killed before I pack one single suitcase. This is where I was born, and this is where I'll die."

The phone rang, startling Roberta. She ran to answer it.

"Hello, this is Miss Johnson." She struggled to catch her breath.

It was obvious from the irritation in the voice on the other end of the line that it was way too early in the morning to talk. Unperturbed, Roberta informed the caller what she wanted to have done.

"How much you paying?" the woman demanded to know.

Roberta named her price.

"Bump it up another grand, and we've got a deal."

Roberta agreed to the price; the deal was done; the lines disconnected.

Walking to the rocker in one corner of her room, Roberta

sat down heavily. She felt a little better, but she knew she wouldn't feel totally alive again until Olivia was out of their lives for good. The soothing effect of the rocker moving slightly back and forth and knowing that her plan would be enacted shortly, knowing her fear of losing her son would soon be entombed in the past all allowed a settling feeling to overtake her. *Everything will be all right,* she thought. *Everything will be all right.*

Not even a grain of remorse did she feel, even knowing she would cause her son some pain. What she did, she did for them.

Twelve

Olivia sang along with the radio as she traveled on Interstate 85 toward Tuskegee. Monday morning traffic was light. She was glad, because her mind was not focused on defensive driving, traffic, or the roads, but on John-Michael.

Glancing at the clock in the truck, she guessed John-Michael's plane was probably nearing Chicago, the first stop in a week-long series of business meetings in several cities. She smiled as she recalled their parting at Atlanta's Hartsfield International Airport. While waiting for his flight to board, John-Michael had given her a small jeweler's box. Her hands had shaken when she slowly opened the lid. Inside, on a shocking blue, satin bed, lay a heartshaped, diamond necklace. He had whispered, as he put the necklace around her neck, that it would have to keep her company until they were reunited on Saturday. She had failed at keeping tears from sliding down her cheeks. John-Michael had done his best to kiss them away, but he hadn't been able to keep up. Shortly after that, he had walked away from her to take his seat on the northwest bound flight. She had walked, teary-eyed, to his truck, missing him already.

Several days ago, after one of their steamy lovemaking sessions, they had talked about her accompanying him on his trip, but had decided it would be more worthwhile for her to finalize her life in Huntsville. They had agreed that since John-Michael was due back in Tuskegee late Friday night, he would drive to Huntsville on Saturday morning to assist her with her packing.

Exiting off the highway and cruising into town, Olivia headed for the FedEx office downtown. As she searched for a parking space, she thought about how quickly her new life was shaping up. It had only been seven days since she and John-Michael had announced their decision to reconcile. After the talk with Dan and Micky last Monday morning, they had all agreed that cutting the experiment short by a few days wouldn't do any harm. They had a good size sample, more than enough for a statistically valid benchmark. A call later that afternoon to her major professor had garnered the same conclusion. As a matter of fact, it had been his idea to FedEx the data disc to the computer lab so they could start immediately on finalizing the models and running the numbers. It seemed the staff at the state agriculture department, the Ag dean at the university, and the scientists at Chem-Co were all eager to hear about the first round of results. A lot was riding on this study; to say it was under the microscope was an understatement.

The FedEx office was nearly empty. She concluded her business in record time, and in a hop, skip, and a jump was back on the streets headed for Johnson Farms.

To think my work on this Ph.D. brought me full circle to true happiness. Olivia thought it amazing that nearly three months ago she had come to Johnson Farms kicking and screaming. Now, she and John-Michael were back together, happy, in love, and making plans for the future. She wished the outcome of her relationship with Roberta had been different, but even the last talk John-Michael had had with her had failed. The cold war was on.

Unfortunately, you can't win them all. She was extremely sad for John-Michael, since he loved his mother so. She knew it must have been hard for him to make the decision to move her out, and then stick to it when Roberta refused to bend. Olivia was hopeful that over time Roberta would accept her, and come to understand that John-Michael would always love her.

Her mind turned to the conversation she and John-Michael had shared about her reliance on obtaining a Ph.D. After letting his challenging words soak in her mind for several days, she had to admit he had been right on target. All these years she had been pursuing a degree because she thought she wanted to be a Dr. Hill clone. She thought it would afford her the same admiration and respect the citizens of Meridian had had for Dr. Hill. Now, thanks to John-Michael's stinging, probing words, she knew that was only part of it. John-Michael had challenged her to seek out the true reason *why* she wanted a Ph.D. He had made her go beyond the surface level to see what lay under the half-truths. She had done so, and it had been a painful discovery. She had met a shy, lonely child who suffered from feelings of unworthiness. She had introduced herself to the child within her who was plagued with self-doubt and was afraid of and out of touch with her emotions. As she opened the door to her childhood, she recalled years where no form of affection was given, where no positive words were showered, where tokens of appreciation were not handed out as readily as chores.

Through a series of questionnaires in one of his college psychology books, John-Michael had helped and participated in her journey. As she had unlocked the keys to her hidden self, he had held her close at night and whispered in her ear that she was no longer that scared, emotionally retarded little girl. That she was a woman who was loved, who was worthy, and need not be afraid. He had even bought her a book of affirmations which she had added to her daily, morning ritual. When she thought about her budding liberation—she recognized she still had miles to go—she was thankful to John-Michael for spearheading the fact-finding mission. He was indeed a godsend, and why she had thrown him away the first time she could no longer fathom.

She turned into the mile long driveway leading to Johnson Farms. *Thank goodness all things conspired to bring me back here to conduct this study. I feel like kissing everyone on my committee, the Ag folks* and *the Chem-Co people.* With a light heart and buoyant spirit, Olivia stopped the truck near the back door. The unfamiliar car parked in the front circular drive didn't even catch her eye.

"Hello," she yelled as she walked into the kitchen. "Lena, where are you? I'm back."

Silence greeted her in return.

Shrugging her shoulders, she headed for the stairs. *I'll change clothes really quickly, then go help the boys break down the equipment.*

On the second stair from the bottom, she thought she heard a noise from one of the rooms on the west side of the house. Pausing for a second and cocking her head like a golden retriever, she listened. Silence. She took two more steps and was sure she'd heard a muffled noise. Delaying no longer, she backpedaled, turned the corner, and saw that the door to John-Michael's home office was partially open.

She rapped on the door and crossed the threshold. A little better than ten feet from her was a woman who could pass as the sister of Vanessa Williams—the short-reigned Miss America—if she were twenty pounds lighter. She had auburn hair with golden highlights which reached the middle of her back, gray eyes, and skin the color of caramel candy. She was one of the most beautiful and curvaceous women Olivia had ever seen. Even with all her outstanding attributes, the little boy who played patiently near John-Michael's desk was the showstopper, though. He couldn't have been more than four or five years old, and he was TV-commercial-adorable. He had big, hazel-colored eyes, thick, curly hair, and an aura of shyness that would have captivated even Scrooge. He was also the source of the noise. Even as Olivia's eyes bounced back and forth between the woman and the child, he made engine sounds with his mouth as he pushed toy cars over the thick carpet.

The woman had the wall safe open, and half of one arm was swallowed up in the safe. "Who are you?" the stranger

asked Olivia as she withdrew a packet of money bound together with the kind of paper band that banks use.

As she walked into the room, concern furrowed Olivia's
brow. *Who is this woman? And what the hell is she doing in
John-Michael's safe? Is she robbing him? How did she get the
safe open? Why would she commit a crime with a child in
tow? Are we . . . am I in danger?* The questions bounced
around in Olivia's head like wildly popping corn kernels.
"Who are *you,* and how did *you* get in here?"

"I don't think you're in any position to question me." The
woman turned face front to challenge Olivia. "Either you introduce yourself, or I call the cops and have you arrested for
trespassing."

Taken aback by the brazenness of the woman, Olivia sput-
tered, "You—you have to be kidding—I live here! You don't."
Olivia advanced a few more steps toward the woman. "Call
them, please. You're the one they'd cart away."

The woman's face brightened as if she were remembering
something, then darkened almost immediately. She looked
Olivia up and down, sizing her up as if she were planning to
sew her a dress. Dryly, she stated, "You must be Olivia."

"Yes . . . I am." Olivia spoke slowly, racking her brain, trying to place this woman. She crossed her arms under her
breasts. "And who are you? Should I know you?"

The woman opened a small pink purse and flung the banded
money into it. The laugh that accompanied her action was
jaded, hurtful. "Probably not." Lowering her voice, she lifted
her eyebrows. "I'm the family secret."

Olivia frowned. "The family secret."

The woman laughed again. "You weren't supposed to be
here. He told me you'd be gone for most of the morning."

"He . . . John-Michael? You talked to John-Michael?"

"I talk to him quite frequently. Did someone else take him
to the airport this morning?"

Olivia shook her head, trying to get back on track. "Excuse
me, but, uh, you haven't answered my question." Olivia walked

to the phone and picked up the handset. "I *know* I have a right to be here. You don't! Now, speak up. I'd hate to have this young man see you handcuffed."

"Calm down, Sister." The woman pulled off her full-length mink coat to reveal a two-piece jacquard silk jacket and dress, fuchsia in color. She tossed the coat carelessly across the arm of the couch. The purse, made of the same fabric as her dress, followed. Gingerly, she sat down and crossed her shapely legs. She reached for the cigarette holder on the coffee table and lit one of John-Michael's cigarettes. The boy, eyeing Olivia with huge button eyes, moved silently to the woman. He remained standing, half facing Olivia and half facing the woman, with a hand on her knee. Through a cloud of smoke, she remarked. "I guess secrets have a way of coming to light at the most inappropriate times."

Olivia's patience flew out the window. She started dialing.

"Okay. Okay." The woman held out her hands in supplication. "God! John-Michael said you could be stubborn. He wasn't kidding."

"I'm asking you one more time . . ." Olivia's heart began pounding; her palms were starting to sweat. She hated the level of familiarity this woman had about John-Michael—his whereabouts, his house, her characteristics. Olivia started feeling nauseated.

"My name is Alexandria." The woman snubbed out her cigarette and stood up. Holding out a hand to Olivia she continued, "Alexandria Simpson. And, this young man—" On cue, the little boy went to his companion and held out his arms to be picked up. She dropped the hand she had offered Olivia and picked up the boy instead. "This young man is John-Michael Johnson . . . the Second." The woman looked Olivia dead in the eye. "Your husband's son."

Olivia quit breathing. She quit thinking. Her gaze darted to the young man, looking for traces of John-Michael in his bearing, and to Alexandria. "No," she said, "it can't be." Slight resemblances existed—the shape of the eyes and head, the skin coloring, the light-colored eyes, the quiet, reserved manner. *But, it can't be. John-Michael couldn't . . . wouldn't have. He would have told me!*

"Oh, yes, but it is." Alexandria kissed the handsome little boy on the cheek and put him down. "Go play with your cars, Honey."

The little boy scurried to where he had left his Hot Wheels.

"My son wasn't conceived out of love but loneliness. John-Michael and I met, quite by accident, in town. We were both at the car dealership getting our cars serviced when we started talking." The woman shrugged her shoulders, "After a while, the talk led to . . . ummm . . . grown up things. I was on the rebound, and y'all were experiencing some marital difficulties. He said something about school taking all your time and his mother whining, and some other mess about refereeing. Anyway, we became—" she cleared her throat, searching for the least offensive words, "regular partners. One too many times we weren't careful, and voilá . . . nine months later, we had a son."

"No," Olivia shook her head. "You're lying. It can't be." Olivia's gaze traveled between the boy and mother. Looking incredulous, she whispered, "John-Michael would not have done that." With a hand to her throat, she kept shaking her head. "This isn't possible."

"Oh, but it is. Look at him. Isn't he as handsome as his daddy?" The woman said this as proudly as any mother.

"No," Olivia whispered. Her eyes were riveted to the young boy.

He seemed totally oblivious to the monumental happenings in the room. Quietly, he played with his cars.

Returning her eyes to gaze at Olivia, Alexandria said in a sincere tone, "Look, I'm really sorry you found out like this. I told John-Michael many, many times that he should confess, especially knowing you were coming back for this study. But what can I say?" The other woman shrugged her shoulders again. "He's a man."

The shock was starting to wear off. Olivia's brain began jamming, trying to piece the puzzle together. "How old is he?"

"Come on, you can say it. John-Michael Johnson, the Second." Alexandria held up two fingers.

Olivia stared at the young boy. "How old is John-Michael Johnson, the Second?"

"My baby is a whooping four years old, soon to be five. And, he's quite a handful. Just like his daddy." This time when she laughed, it sounded joyous. She sounded like a woman happy with her child and her man. "I'm always threatening John-Michael that I'm going to dump his bundle of joy off at his front doorstep and let him deal with his own flesh and blood." She devoured her son with her eyes. "But, I could never do that. He's too precious to me."

Seconds of silence passed during which both women stared at the child.

"Roberta . . ." Olivia was still trying to piece everything together. She couldn't make herself believe this was John-Michael's child, that John-Michael had an affair while they were still together. But, here was the woman. Here was the child.

"Ahhh, John-Michael's mother. I haven't had the pleasure of meeting your mother-in-law. But, I understand she can be quite the tyrant." Alexandria winked as if they legally shared Roberta.

Olivia shuddered at the action. She closed her eyes and gulped in huge amounts of air. *Oxygen. I need oxygen to think.* "Does she know?"

"Not that I know of." Alexandria put a finger to her temple and thought for a second. "But, maybe so. They are pretty close, you know." She laughed bitterly. "I'll have to ask him the next time we—" The woman let Olivia's busy mind finish the rest of her thought.

Olivia looked around for a trash can. She felt nauseated and lightheaded.

Alexandria watched as Olivia circled the desk. "Oh, my,

you don't look so good. We'll leave you alone to . . . recover."
Alexandria bundled her son up. "We just came to collect our
monthly child support. Usually John-Michael drops it off when
he comes to . . . check on us." Alexandria paused.

Olivia slumped over the desk as if a stake had been plunged
into her heart. She started shaking all over, and her body temperature began rollercoastering, up and down.

"With you in town and Roberta back from vacation, we
really haven't seen much of each other. John-Michael promised
me the house would be empty this morning. He told me
Roberta was spending the night in town, Lena would be shopping, and you would be in Atlanta. Boy, I'll have to tell him
he was really wrong."

Alexandria quickly scooped up the boy's cars and dumped
them in the pocket of her mink. She slung the coat over her
shoulders and took the little boy's hand in hers. "Again, I'm
sorry you found out like this, but I guess since you guys are
on the outs it doesn't matter, anyway. You probably don't care
what he does, do you?"

The lump in Olivia's throat wouldn't let her answer Alexandria.

Not that Alexandria expected an answer, anyway. She was
already headed out the room, and was almost through it when
she spoke again. "You have the best of both worlds, you know.
Your husband won't divorce you because he's afraid you'll take
everything. And he still finances your school expenses, so you
can get your blasted Ph.D. Sister, you really have it made."
Alexandria and John-Michael Johnson the Second left.

Olivia was slowly coming back to life. The bout of sickness
eased, and she could stand up straight again. *Four, almost five
years old! He had an affair while we were still together.* The
reasoning side of Olivia's brain caught up to her emotional
side. It cautioned her, *You don't know if that woman's telling
the truth. She could be lying! Recount down the facts,* the
emotional side of her brain demanded. *She had a key to the
house. She had the safe open, and only took a certain amount.*

She knew the comings and goings of the household members. She even knew about your study. She knows way too much to be lying. And what reason would she have for lying, anyway?

The tears started slowly, then fell in rapid succession. Olivia shook her head, trying to dislodge the facts, the emotions, everything that was rattling around in her head. The beautiful world she had envisioned for her and John-Michael crumbled. She had even thought that they might start working on a family soon. *Well, forget that. He already has a child, and apparently a woman whose company he enjoys.* Still, it was hard for Olivia to believe John-Michael was capable of such deception. *Why?* she wanted to know. *How could he have made love to me with such tenderness? Why did he tell me he loved me? How could he have disrupted his relationship with his mother unless he really loved me?* So many questions filled Olivia's head, but no answers came forth.

The only person who could answer her questions was hundreds of miles away, and there was nothing she could do until he called tonight. *Do I really want to talk to him about something this important over the phone? I need to see his face. I want him to look in my eyes and tell me the truth. I'll just have to fake it until I see him Saturday morning. Then, I'll know the truth.*

More than an hour passed before Olivia felt composed enough to go help Dan and Micky As she worked alongside the guys she valiantly kept the tears at bay, but the fear, bitterness, and bewilderment persisted, making her wonder if she would really return to Johnson Farms.

Thirteen

"Wake up, wake up, wake up! It's seven o'clock, and if you've nowhere to be today, stay in bed. It's cooooold outside," the radio announcer warned his listening audience. "Now, here's Joyce with the top of the hour news report for Friday, October twenty-seventh."

Olivia reached for the snooze button and missed the entire clock. "Auuuugggggg," she moaned. No way would she have guessed that in three months her body would have adapted to the sleeping environment at Johnson Farms. Now, she had to readjust to the setup in her apartment. She rolled over, pulling the sheet and blankets with her.

Swatting at the clock, she bingoed. Silence. Too silent. She threw off the covers and padded to the adjoining bathroom.

Since returning to Huntsville three days ago, she'd purposely kept herself day-to-night busy, writing her report, catching up with her staff assistant work, and bugging the computer lab about her test results. She thought that if she could keep her mind focused on work, she wouldn't think about John-Michael, Alexandria, or John-Michael Johnson, the Second. She had thought wrong! Images of couples holding hands while strolling across campus, snatches of conversations about children, John-Michael's telephone messages, all of these things blended to keep her insanely focused on the truth—or lie—she just didn't know which.

Even with the hectic schedule she had adopted, she'd been home one evening when John-Michael had called. When she heard his voice float through the answering machine speaker, she had been tempted to pick up the receiver and ask him about Alexandria and his son. Her hand was actually on the handset when an internal voice demanded that she see his face during the interrogation. She had withdrawn her hand and cried, listening to his deep voice tell her he loved her and couldn't wait to see her.

As Olivia performed her morning routine, she tried not to think about John-Michael's visit tomorrow, but it haunted her, just as it had in her sleep. A part of her wanted it over so she could quit agonizing and second-guessing; another part of her didn't want to face it, did not want to have this conversation with John-Michael for fear of what she would learn.

Walking back into her bedroom to throw on jeans, a sweater, and boots, she hurriedly brushed her curls and threw on a hat. Slinging her backpack over her shoulder, she locked the door behind her.

Last night, her major professor had called to set up an early morning appointment. As she trudged up the hill and across the campus in the crisp fall air, she had hoped to have enough time before her meeting with him to pop into the computer lab to see what progress they'd made with her data. The time on her watch told her she didn't have that luxury.

The door to Professor Standish's office was wide open. He rarely closed it, claiming that to do so would fog his mind. No one challenged his thinking, but rather, they allowed him his idiosyncrasies.

"Good morning, Olivia." Professor Standish looked over his half frame glasses to peer at her with his baby blue eyes. His gray-white hair, styled in a crewcut, stood all over his head, a testimony that he'd been wrestling with some major problem. In his forty years of teaching he'd adopted one dress code, and of course he sported it today: tweed jacket with suede patches at the elbow, twill pants, and a solid colored bow tie clipped to a white shirt.

"Good morning, Professor. Already got a problem, huh?"

Professor Standish was always amazed that she knew when he had a problem. "Yes, yes. Why, yes, I . . . um . . . do. Have a seat." The professor, devoid of a sense of humor but long on patience and understanding, got up and closed his office door.

Olivia raised her eyebrows in surprise, then grew nervous. She'd been with the university for almost three years, and in that time she'd only known him to close his door twice—both times to inform the students they were being kicked out of the Agricultural Studies Department. Olivia took a seat in one of the hardback chairs facing his cluttered desk and clasped her hands together between her legs. She thought it would keep them from shaking. It didn't.

"I don't quite know where to begin. My, my. This is terrible."

"Just come right out and say it, Professor." Surprisingly, her voice was calm. Inwardly, she was a mess. The sleepless nights, her poor diet, and the emotional overload had converged to make her a wreck. She had a pretty good idea now of what therapists meant when they referred to someone as a basket case.

Professor Standish cleared his throat and sat up straighter. "Your test results. They're totally useless."

A long pause followed his statement.

"What?" Olivia blinked. "I think you need to repeat that." Her heart was pounding like a jackhammer, causing a ringing in her ears.

"The numbers, the data, is so jumbled the lab can't make heads or tails of it. That's why it's been taking so long. The lab supervisor and his team ran and re-ran the numbers. They tried all sorts of variations, and the data always came out the same. Nothing. It told them nothing."

Telling herself to remain calm, that there was a plausible reason for this outcome, she asked, "Are you sure they ran the correct models, the appropriate formulas?"

"Olivia, they double and triple checked and quadruple

checked everything. Your data is coming out garbage. There's absolutely no correlation to the approval standards."

Olivia's mind shut down. She closed her eyes. Garbage. They considered her work garbage. That hurt. It hurt almost as much as her meeting with Alexandria. She tried to stop them, but several tears collected at the corners of her eyes and slid down her cheeks.

"Oh, dear. Oh, dear." Professor Standish pulled a hankie from his jacket pocket and handed it to her. He knew this work was not characteristic of Olivia's high standards. He was as concerned as she was. After she cleaned her face, he pursued his line of questioning. "Are you sure you didn't make a mistake in recording? Are you sure you FedExed the right disc?"

Like a little lost child, Olivia mumbled fearfully, "I'm not sure about anything anymore." She leaned an elbow on the corner of his desk and propped her head against her fist. Staring unseeingly, she continued. "I thought I was being careful, especially after I found some discrepancies early on in the study. Some of the numbers didn't look right, so I did a verification. They were wrong, but I fixed them . . . or at least I thought I had." Suddenly, Olivia didn't know anymore. *If I had paid less attention to John-Michael and his problems and more to my study, I wouldn't be in this mess. Without all those hours I wasted on social events with John-Michael, could I have prevented this fiasco? Why didn't I stick to my original plan—just complete the study, have limited contact with them, then get the heck out? How did I throw that plan aside? John-Michael! John-Michael!* her mind screamed. If she had known three months ago that all she would receive at the end of her time at Johnson Farms was a great big zero in love and school, she would have fled the state.

"The kicker to this is that the dean is very agitated. He wants you thrown out of the program, just so he can save his own butt with the state agriculture department and Chem-Co, you know." The professor sighed and shook his head. "Of course, John-Michael Johnson, the other investor in this project, won't be too happy about this, either."

Olivia's head shot up like a firecracker. She'd been half listening. "What! What was that about John-Michael Johnson?"

"John-Michael Johnson, the man on whose farm you conducted the experiment. He donated a nice sum of money for the project, as well. This was a highly political study. Unfortunately, a lot of reputations and money was riding on your work, and now the dean wants answers." The professor ran a finger around his collar. "More than that, he wants your head on a platter."

Olivia fell back into her seat, slumping like a rag doll. She was amazed that John-Michael was involved in the funding of this project and that no one had bothered to tell her. Not even him, her husband.

"Did he know I would be the lead on this project?" Olivia asked in a wooden voice. "That this was my study?"

"Well . . . of course, My Dear. Even months before you left Huntsville. We had to send names and bios, especially since the team would be living in his house."

It clicked! As soon as the words were out of the professor's mouth, everything fell into place. Now, she knew what Alexandria had meant when she'd mentioned John-Michael was financing her education. John-Michael was no dummy. He was probably the one who had sabotaged her work. *But, why?* her mind clamored. *Why would he want to destroy me like this?*

Olivia hid her face in both her hands. The tears she had managed to rein in earlier threatened to break free. But, she refused to shed another tear for the man, or the love she'd thought they had. Squaring her shoulders, she quickly swiped at her eyes and stood to leave.

"Uh . . . hmmm, Olivia. There's one other thing."

Olivia's mind screamed that she couldn't take one more thing. Couldn't the man see she was splintering into a million pieces? Couldn't he see she was hurting?

Professor Standish straightened his already straight tie. "The dean has given you till Monday to explain what happened. If they like your explanation you can stay in the program, and try again from scratch on a totally different project."

"And if they don't?" Olivia asked in a quivering voice.

"Then you'll be expelled from the program. Olivia, I'm sorry. I wish I could get more involved, but that would be highly improper. You're on your own."

"In more ways than you could ever know," Olivia cynically commented, with a catch in her voice.

"Also, Dan and Micky, your co-workers, have until five o'clock today to offer a complete report to their boss. They were questioned yesterday."

Olivia took a deep breath. She exhaled slowly. "So all this questioning and investigating and decision making was going on behind my back?" Olivia tried to get angry at them, at John-Michael, at everyone, but her emotional bank was empty.

"I'm sorry, Olivia. My hands were tied until late last night. The dean wouldn't let me talk to you until they'd completed a final check of the data last night. I'm sorry."

Olivia reached over the piles of paper and shook her professor's hands. "Thanks, anyway."

With head held high, she left his office.

My study's a complete failure. They want to kick me out of school. My husband financed my work to destroy it, and he cheated on me. By itself, she could have dealt with the school issue, but combined with John-Michael's damaging acts, it was too much.

As she stood outside the red brick building in the cool morning sunshine, the bottleneck of emotions exploded. Olivia kicked and screamed and cried.

John-Michael's eyes popped open, as if they were on an automatic timer. Despite the stressful week of business travel and the late return to the farm last night, he woke up alert and ready to go collect his woman. As he rolled out of bed, he prayed Olivia had had enough time to get everything settled so she could return with him. If not, a week or two of commuter marriage could be tolerated.

In no time he was dressed and headed for the kitchen. He was only mildly surprised that he hadn't heard from Olivia this week. Of course, he had been nearly impossible to reach. He hoped her unavailability meant she was busy snipping the ends of her life there in Huntsville.

"Good morning, Lena. How are you?"

Lena nearly jumped out of her seat when he walked through the kitchen door. "Oh, John-Michael. You're up early."

John-Michael smiled. "Yeah. I'm going to Huntsville." He headed straight for the coffeepot and poured a cup. "If Olivia has everything wrapped up, she's coming back with me." He felt like kicking his heels high in the air.

Lena matched his smile, but he noticed it didn't quite reach her eyes. "I'm glad for you, Honey. You two deserve to be happy."

"Thank you, Lena." John-Michael looked over the rim of his cup at the woman who had been a fixture in his life since childhood. In that length of time, he had grown to know Lena as well as he knew his own mother. She was rocking slightly to and fro. And, she didn't have a thing cooking on the stove or in the oven. That meant all was not right with Lena. "Have you by chance heard from Olivia this week?"

"No . . . well, yes. She called to say they made it safely. But, haven't heard from her again. She did say she was going to be busy with her schoolwork and might not get another chance to call."

"I figured as much." John-Michael leaned back against the countertop. "So, if you're not concerned about Olivia, and I made it home safely, and Mother's in her room, sound asleep—" John-Michael used his fingers to tick off the people she cared about. "Then what's got you worked up?"

Twisting her hands, rocking slightly, Lena just stared at him.

"Lena, are you okay?" John-Michael shoved away from the

counter and advanced on Lena. Her lack of words and the
dead look in her eyes scared him.

"I'm thinking how to tell you." Lena was staring through
him, shaking her head. "I don't know—"

A deep male voice, coming from the same door John-Michael
had just ushered through, interrupted her. "She's probably not
sure how you're going to take me being here."

John-Michael looked around Lena. His coffee cup crashed
to the floor. His heart started pounding, sending crazy amounts
of blood to his head. For a second, John-Michael was dizzy,
his vision blurred. He rubbed his eyes. The man was still there.
A clone of himself—about twenty years older—stood a few
feet from him.

"I haven't seen you since you were a baby." John-Michael
Taylor walked to his son, hand outstretched. "Hello, Son. I'm
your father."

A wooden puppet had more life in it than John-Michael, the
younger, had at the moment. His mind had gone numb. Words
were impossible. He had no control of his limbs. They were
frozen. Only his eyes moved. They examined the man from his
short Afro to the tips of his cowboy boots. John-Michael Taylor
was leanly built, an inch taller than his son, with the same skin
coloring. The only physical differences between the two men
were the sprinkling of gray in John-Michael Senior's hair and
the Hershey's Kiss coloring of his eyes.

John-Michael Taylor dropped his hand. Awkwardly, he suggested, "I guess this is quite a shock for you."

John-Michael looked at the hand the elder had withdrawn.
It, like his own, had long, thin fingers, and scratches, as if he,
too, had spent all his life meeting the physical demands of
farming. Of course, John-Michael knew that wasn't the case.
His father was afraid of hard work. He'd preferred to marry
rich, then depart with some of those riches, breaking the heart
of the young woman and abandoning his son. Those thoughts
propelled John-Michael to turn on Lena.

In a savage, ragged voice, he hissed, "What's he doing here?"

Nonplussed by John-Michael's threatening tone and posture, Lena went to him. She placed her hands on his arms and squeezed. "Honey, he came to meet you. He's not the man you think he is."

John-Michael heard, but didn't hear her. His mind was recovering from the shock of seeing the man whose ghost he had been trying to squash all his life. Breaking away from Lena's grip, he faced his father. Angrily, he asked, "What do you want?"

Neither paid attention to Lena as she quietly left the kitchen heading in the direction of Roberta's bedroom.

"Son, I—"

"Don't call me your son! Granddad was my father. A true father." John-Michael spat the words out. Like a slide show, his mind carouseled through his growing years: Him with Madison at the Boy Scout father son banquets. Madison coaching him on jump shots. Madison at his parent teacher conferences. Driving lessons, fishing, man-to-almost man talks about cars and girls, and crops and girls, and social responsibility and girls, and Johnson Farms. It had been Madison who had taken him to vote for the very first time. Madison had been there to get him out of jail when the cops had arrested him in a case of mistaken identity. Madison had paid his way through college. Madison *was* his father. His father was dead.

The elder John-Michael paused. His eyes seemed to mist. "I wanted to meet you. I've wanted to meet you for a long time now." He shrugged his shoulders, a mannerism passed on to his son. "It seemed like the right time."

John-Michael held his hands out and apart, palms upright, elbows by his side. "Well, now you've met me. So leave." John-Michael smarted from the pain, the anger, the audacity of the man. This man had hurt his mother, had hurt him. It was time for him to go. He should have never come.

Anticipating the cold welcome, but still not prepared for the sting of his son's words, John-Michael Senior flinched. His heart was heavy. "I'm not leaving until we've had a chance to talk."

"After thirty-five years you want to talk?" John-Michael laughed sarcastically. "It's way past time to talk." Sobering, he drilled his eyes into the man. "Why don't you tell me the real reason you're here? Let's get this over with."

"S . . . I mean, John-Michael, I was hoping—"

"For money. You were hoping you could extort more money from us. You finally ran through what Mother paid you, and now you're back for more. Well, there's no more," John-Michael yelled. He stalked to the back door and yanked it open. "Get out, or I'll boot you out."

John-Michael Senior maintained his ground. "John-Michael, I can understand how you're feeling." He took a step toward his son.

"Oh? Were you abandoned by your father, too?" Cynicism filled his voice.

The elder John-Michael sighed. His shoulders drooped. "I wish I could wipe away all the years of hurt and pain I've caused you, Son, but I'm not leaving until I tell you why I left, and why I haven't been in touch."

The cold air blowing through the back porch and into the kitchen didn't register with John-Michael. He was wrapped up in a personal fight. "I don't want to hear your excuses. There's nothing you can say that will change my feelings about you."

"You've been living under false pretenses long enough. It's time you heard the truth about me, from me."

"I know everything I need to know about you. You're a sorry excuse for a man. You're a liar, a con man, and a cheat. And you're not welcome in this house." John-Michael held up a lone finger, pointing it at his father. "Now, I'm telling you one last time to get out of here—or I'll physically throw you out."

John-Michael Senior wondered if Olivia had been mistaken, or if Roberta's fable was just that hateful and ugly. He wasn't making any progress with the boy, and he had no doubt John-Michael would throw him out on his butt if the tide didn't turn soon. He decided to pull out his trump card. "How do you think Olivia would feel about that?"

John-Michael Junior's head snapped back as if slapped. He blinked, and a deep furrow appeared on his forehead. "Olivia? How? What do you—"

"She wrote me and told me you'd reached a point in your life where you would be willing to listen to the truth." He reached into his jacket pocket and withdrew Olivia's letter. He tossed it on the table for his son to inspect. "Maybe she was wrong."

Like a bloodhound to a possum, John-Michael was on the letter as soon as it hit the table. He ripped the letter out of the envelope and scanned it.

The man wasn't lying! In Olivia's handwriting was her plea to his father to settle the past. John-Michael's hand started shaking so much that the letter fell out of it and drifted to the table. He stood stone-still, but his mind was whirling like a ride at the fair. *Olivia? Olivia brought this man here? Why did she do this? She knows how I feel about this man. How did she know how to reach him?*

A hand on his shoulder brought him out of his internal interrogation. Slowly, John-Michael looked at the hand so like his own. He backed away from it until it no longer touched him. "My wife didn't have my approval to send you that letter. And, it doesn't change a thing. You can leave by the back door." Some of the anger had evaporated from John-Michael's voice. Confusion had replaced it. *Why would Olivia betray me like this? I made it clear how I feel about this man. Yet, her letter clearly tells him I'm ready to talk.* He had to go to Huntsville. Now more than ever he needed to talk to Olivia.

The senior John-Michael shook his head. The snippet of hope he had brought with him died. His son hated him, and rightfully so. He knew now that he should have fought Roberta, should have fought harder for his son, his only child.

Now, it was too late. A deep sadness engulfed him. "For you to hate me so much, I can only imagine what your mother told you."

As if she had been listening on the other side of the door for her name to be called, Roberta flew into the kitchen. Guided by motherly sonar, she ran straight to her son and grabbed him around the waist, hugging him for dear life. "Whatever he told you, it's a lie." With her hair all about her head, her eyes wild and glassy, Roberta half turned to see her ex-husband. "You, get out!" she screamed. "Get out of our lives!"

All the anger he had for himself directed itself to Roberta. "Why, Roberta?" he yelled back. "So you can continue to squeeze the life out of him, like you tried to suffocate me?" John-Michael Senior had nothing to lose. All the words he'd wanted to tell Roberta and his son tumbled out now, with a force guided by anger, regret, and love. "Ask her, Son! Ask her why she kicked me out of her bed, out of your life and hers." Not giving either of them a chance to respond, he continued. "No, don't bother. Let me tell you. It's past time for you to hear my side, anyway. Your mother threw me out on my butt because I wasn't willing to be castrated. My parents didn't raise me to be no doormat for any woman . . . no matter how pretty she was, or how much I loved her. I wasn't then, nor am I now, willing to be less than a man."

"Rubbish! Pure rubbish. Don't listen to him, John-Michael. "Close your ears, Baby." Roberta stood up on tiptoe and put her hands over John-Michael's ears. "Don't listen to his lies."

"My lies or yours, Roberta? You've had thirty-five years with the boy. Can't I have five minutes?"

John-Michael had had enough. He didn't care what these people did. He was going to Huntsville. He looked at his mother, ready to tell her just that, but then he noticed her aggressive hold on him, her fearful eyes, the threat of tears, and remembered what Olivia had said—"She's more than a mother, John-Michael. She's a woman who loves. She's a hu-

man being with human frailties." A dark, sinking feeling replaced his need to leave. Could the same kind of threat Roberta
felt from Olivia be responsible for the separation of father and
son? *No, it's not possible. I can understand Mother being a
little jealous of Olivia, but not of this man. Mother wouldn't
feel that way about a father son relationship.* It was too damning a thought for John-Michael to dwell on. To avoid those
thoughts, he had to get rid of his father. The man was a threat
to their existence.

He pulled his mother's hands from his ears. Holding onto
her wrists and bending so he could look her dead in the eye,
he pleaded, "Mother, I don't know this man, but I know you.
All you gotta do for us to be rid of him is repeat what you
told me as a little boy. Say it loud, for both of us to hear. Then
he'll leave. He won't be man enough to stay."

Roberta put her hands over her eyes. The tears rolled down
her cheeks. Her shoulders shook.

Frightened, John-Michael grasped her wrists and pulled
them down. "Mother, please, just tell him the baldfaced truth,
and he'll leave. Please, Mother, say it."

"John-Michael, I did it for you." Roberta framed his face
with her hands. Her tears were flowing fast, making dark spots
on her terry cloth robe. "I did it for you. You needed to be
protected. You were just a little boy. You wouldn't have understood."

John-Michael let go of his mother's hands. "Mother, did
you—" John-Michael's eyes darted to his father, then back to
his mother. "Mother, tell me you didn't lie to me."

The elder John-Michael had remained by the table. His eyes
were downcast. He looked fatigued, and he had a death grip
on the letter.

Looking at him, John-Michael knew. Returning his gaze to
his mother, he studied her with new eyes. "Mother . . ." The
egg-size lump in his throat blocked the words. The pain ripped
him apart.

Roberta saw the shutters close on John-Michael's soul.

"John-Michael, please—you don't understand." She grabbed him around the waist and lay her head over his heart. "I was going to tell you but, the time was never right. I love you, Son."

In a thick voice, John-Michael muttered, "Mother, I built my life on a lie." John-Michael pushed her away from him. Holding her at arm's length, he repeated, "A lie, Mother. My whole life is a lie." He let her go and walked out the back door.

Roberta raced after her son. "Don't leave, John-Michael. Don't leave!" she screamed.

John-Michael Senior caught her halfway to the door. "Let him go, Roberta. He needs time."

Face streaked with tears, nose flared, Roberta turned on him "You bastard! Look what you've done." Arms flaying, she started to beat on his chest. "You've turned my son against me."

Capturing her wrists, he shook her until she sank, crying desperately to the kitchen floor. The senior John-Michael stared down at her bent head. With sorrowful eyes, he looked at the woman who had once made him the happiest man on earth. "Roberta, you've always held the ones you love too closely."

He walked out of her life for the second time.

John-Michael drove around aimlessly for more hours than he could remember. At times, he pulled over to wipe his eyes. Sometimes, he simply pulled over to get out of the truck, to throw or beat something. A litany became mixed with his other muddled, confused thoughts, to crowd his mind: *A lie. A lie. Your life is a lie.* He had built his life on sand, not cement. His father was not a liar or schemer. His mother was. His father had not abandoned his wife or son. His mother had driven him away. John-Michael now knew how that was possible. *Olivia tried to warn me. Olivia exposed the truth.* John-

Michael thought about his wife. He needed her. He needed to be held by someone who was real; someone he could trust; someone who was in his corner. Screeching to a halt, he looked around, trying to get a fix on his surroundings. After a few maneuverings, he headed north to Huntsville.

Fourteen

Her apartment looked deserted. No sliver of light escaped from under the door or windows, the drapes were drawn tight, and there was absolute silence. John-Michael knocked again, louder this time. He leaned against the door, and after a few moments he thought he heard shuffling.

"Olivia? Olivia! It's me, John-Michael." John-Michael used a lower than normal voice. For a Saturday evening in an apartment complex filled with college students, the place was eerily quiet. No loud music, no horseplay in the parking lot, no shuffling of bodies back and forth from apartments to the laundry room. Just silence. "Open the door, Baby, please. I need you."

A few seconds later, he heard chains jingling and then the door was slowly opening. It was late afternoon, but inside her apartment it looked like midnight in the country. Cautiously, John-Michael stepped across the threshold. Feeling his way through the room, he headed straight for a lamp. The wattage wasn't laboratory strong, but it was bright enough for him to see. And, the sight of her stopped him cold. "Olivia?"

Olivia had followed him into the light.

She looked a mess. Her clothes were classic laundry day: baggy sweats with holes in the knees and the elastic missing in one of the legs, oversized sweatshirt with irremovable stains and no socks. There were dark circles under her eyes, as if someone had punched her in both, and she was shaking like a brand new pup. It even looked as if she had lost weight.

"Olivia, baby! What's wrong?" He rushed to her. "You look—"

When he was within hugging distance, she lifted her hand and slapped him silly.

John-Michael's reaction was instantaneous. He grabbed the stinging cheek. She slapped his other cheek. With hands on his cheeks, his golden eyes open wide, he stared at her. "What the hell—"

Before he could finish his sentence, Olivia charged him with both fists. "You bastard!" she half-cried, half-screamed. She lit into him as if he were a mugger, and she high on adrenaline.

Stunned, John-Michael took a few blows before reality tapped him on the shoulder. Grabbing her wrists, he twisted around until her backside was against his front. He crossed her arms across her chest, stilling her. "What the hell are you doing? What did I do?"

Olivia, out of energy and out of breath, slumped in his arms. The tears, hot and scolding, came in a gush. "How could you? How could you do this to me? You said you loved me."

"Baby, I . . . what did I do?" The fog was not clearing fast enough for him. Actually, it was not clearing at all.

"Oh, yeah. Pretend you don't know a damned thing. That you're totally innocent. Why didn't you just leave me alone?" she screamed in anguish, and struggled anew. "Why did you have to destroy everything? My love, my goal, our plans." Olivia ran out of steam and slid against him, down to the floor. Her body shook violently with heavy sobs. She wrapped her arms around herself.

John-Michael knelt beside her. His hand hovered over her, then began stroking her hair, her shoulders, and back. Forgotten were his problems. He needed to erase the suffering his woman endured. "Baby, I'm sorry, I don't know what you're talking about. What have I supposedly destroyed? I promise you I haven't done anything."

The tears kept flowing while Olivia rocked herself.

Deciding she would tell him in her own time, John-Michael

patiently stroked her. The need to feel her drove him to circle his arms around her and draw her into his chest. They remained like that until finally Olivia's crying subsided.

Squeezed against his chest, her words came out muffled. "I'll give you your divorce. I don't want anything from you. Just please don't hurt me any more."

"Divorce? Did you say divorce?" John-Michael strained to hear her clearly.

Olivia took a deep breath, inadvertently inhaling his fresh male scent. The thought that she would never get to smell him again or take comfort in his arms after today made the tears start anew. She blubbered through the hurtful words, "I know about everything. The illegitimate child, the funding for my project, the sabotage, the affair. I'm sorry for whatever I did to make you hate me. I'm truly sorry."

John-Michael set her away from him. He studied her face, searching for signs that would help him decipher this mystery. "Olivia, I don't hate you. Baby, you mean more to me than anything or anyone on this earth."

With the shakiness diminishing, she spoke more clearly. "John-Michael, you don't have to lie or cheat or hide anymore. I'll give you your divorce." She accepted the handkerchief he handed her.

John-Michael ran a hand down his face and over his head. Suddenly, his mind and his body slumped. He was extremely tired. "God, what a day!" For the first time since seeing Olivia, he remembered the other reason he was in Huntsville. Pushing that situation aside until he could make heads and tails of Olivia's situation, he positioned himself more comfortably on the floor. "Okay, Olivia, from the time you dropped me off at the airport until I walked through that door just now, tell me everything—I mean everything—that's happened."

"Fine." Olivia sniffed. She twisted the hankie around her finger. "We'll play this little delay game if that's what you want."

Olivia started with her encounter with Alexandria. She told

him about their in-depth conversation, stopping occasionally to cry softly or take deep breaths to keep from crying. She relayed the context of her meeting with Professor Standish, informing him that he had paid for her education only to destroy it. She wrapped up with an explanation about her all nighter in the lab, trying unsuccessfully to piece back together the study and her life.

John-Michael's expressions during her discourse had ranged from angry to incredulous, to mad to disbelieving, to crushed.

At the conclusion of her tale, neither said anything for a while. Olivia, overwhelmed by the remembered hurt and pain, rested her head in her arms, which lay on the coffee table. She struggled for control.

John-Michael sat quietly to the side of Olivia with his back to the couch. His mind reeled with the facts he'd just heard, but uppermost in his thoughts was the fact that Olivia had seemed to accept her conclusions as reality, without giving him the benefit of the doubt. That more than anything else drove the life right out of him.

Not two weeks ago she had promised to love him and remember that he loved her. When that promise had been put to the test she had tossed it aside, preferring to believe that he was a monster. John-Michael didn't know which pain was worse: his mother's thirty-five-year-old lie, or Olivia's betrayal.

John-Michael wanted to walk out, but because he loved her so he held onto a thread of hope, praying there was a knot at the end to keep him from sliding into a bottomless hole of grief and despair.

"Olivia," he said softly, "let me get this straight. You think Alexandria and I had an affair while you and I were together, and that I have an illegitimate child with Alexandria. You also think I paid for your Ph.D. study so I could sabotage it. Is that correct? Did I cover everything?"

Olivia, sitting so close yet shut off in her world of pain, stared at the cheap still life painting hanging lopsided on the wall. Speaking to the object, she croaked, "Yes. That's enough, don't you think?"

John-Michael sat up straight. He forcefully turned her to face him. "Olivia, do you actually believe I could be so mean and hateful and calculating?" Shaking her shoulders, he forced her head up so he could see the truth or a lie. "If you really believe me capable of treating you so callously, just tell me, and I'll leave. You won't ever have to see me again, or worry about me hurting you, ever. Just tell me, Olivia."

With her eyes filling with tears, she thought about what he was asking. Looking into his eyes, she didn't know anymore. Her mind told her this was John-Michael, the man she loved who was her lover, her friend, her teacher. But, all the evidence pointed to him being the person responsible for ruining her life. Her mind was clouded over with reasons and emotions. She didn't know right from wrong or up from down. She only knew she hurt. "The facts say—"

"Forget the facts, Olivia." John-Michael ground the words out. "You just told me minutes ago that numbers—facts—can be rigged. What does your heart say?" John-Michael squeezed her thin shoulders as if trying to squeeze the right answer from her.

The battle ensued between Olivia the research scientist and Olivia the loving woman. If she sided with reason, was she sure she had all the evidence? John-Michael hadn't tried to defend himself in either situation. He had not offered one piece of proof to refute her claims. Was that because all the evidence was accounted for, and true? Was he playing a mind game with her?

On the other hand, if she sided with emotions what would she be opening herself up to? What further pain . . . or pleasure . . . would she encounter? And, if he had indeed done those things, shouldn't she forgive him, anyway? Did she want to repeat Dr. Hill's mistake? Did she want to risk obtaining the facts to end up losing out on love? Should she side with her heart, which told her to believe in her husband?

John-Michael dropped his hands from her shoulders. He stood up slowly. Her eyes had revealed nothing, and she was taking too long to answer. That was answer enough for him. Temporarily patching his broken heart, he headed for the door.

"Where are you going?" Olivia hopped up from the floor.

"Home." The word was out before John-Michael thought again about the fiasco that awaited him there. He cringed. *Can't go there,* he thought. He wasn't up to dealing with that mess, either. *A nice, clean hotel with no phone and a couple of days in seclusion sounds like heaven about now. I can at least fix my mind and patch my heart in peace.*

"John-Michael, I haven't answered you." Olivia swayed toward him. She stopped, afraid to go to him completely.

"Yes, you did." John-Michael didn't even turn around to face her when he answered. He opened the door and came face-to-face with Dan and Micky.

"Hello, boys. Go on in." John-Michael stepped aside to allow them entry. "I'm on the way out, but she's in there."

Sullenly, Dan returned the greeting. "I think you'd better stay. This concerns you, too." Dan didn't give John-Michael an escape. He gently pushed him back in and closed the door.

Dan spoke. "Hey, Olivia. Sorry about all this business with the study."

"Thank you." Olivia spoke to Dan, but her eyes were trained on her husband. He stood solemnly with his back against the door. His arms were folded across his chest, and his eyes were focused on the tip of his boot, which doodled in the carpet.

"Micky has something he needs to tell you." Dan pushed Micky forward. The younger man cleared his throat, staring at an invisible pattern in the carpet.

"Olivia, I . . . I messed with your numbers." He spoke in a church mouse whisper.

Olivia's mind was on John-Michael. She was trying to think of a way to get him to explain about Alexandria, and the study. She was sure she could eliminate some of her confusion if she could get him to stay and share his side of the story.

Putting her fingers to her temples, she lowered her head, trying to listen to Micky while plotting to get her husband to stay. Slowly, she picked up on some of his words. Finally, he got her full attention.

". . . needed money for my dad's treatments, and Chem-Co offered me ten thousand dollars if I would change the numbers to position their product in a favorable light. I took their offer, but since I botched it up, they refused to pay me. I lost all the way around."

Olivia stared at him as if he were an alien. "What's that? What did you say?"

Micky kicked at an invisible figure. Digging his hands deep in his pockets, he repeated his guilty admission. "I fudged your numbers. I wasn't trying to, but I completely ruined your study." Micky stared hard at the floor.

Her eyes swung immediately to John-Michael. Their eyes locked and a thousand sorrys were communicated from her eyes to his. His were void of any emotion except the pain she had put there. She took a step to him with her hand outstretched. But he was gone, out of the door, out of her life.

A strangled cry erupted from her throat. "John-Michael. John-Michael. Wait! Please!"

John-Michael didn't heed her call. He stopped only when he got to his pickup. She reached him as he put his key in the lock.

"John-Michael, I'm sorry. I'm so sorry." She grabbed his arm.

He shook off her hand and unlocked and opened his door. "So you got the facts you needed."

"John-Michael, please. I was afraid."

"And you think I wasn't?" he said harshly. Anguish ripped through his words. He climbed into his truck and started the motor. "We could have worked through this together, Olivia. But, you don't know how to love me unconditionally."

John-Michael pushed her out of the door opening and slammed the door shut. He cracked the window as he threw the truck in gear. "And if you check with Mother, I'll bet she could shed some light on the Alexandria situation. I'm finding out she's full of stories."

"John-Michael, please. I made a mistake!" Olivia begged.

"I will take credit, though, for funding your study. I simply wanted you back in my life. Stupid me!" John-Michael started backing out of the parking space.

"Please. Give me a second chance."

"In case your head got screwed up with all those other numbers, I'll tell you. This *was* your second chance." He kept backing up.

She kept her hands on the door. "John-Michael, don't leave." He rolled up the window and floored the accelerator. The sudden movement forced her away from the truck, and in seconds she heard the screech of his tires rounding the corner.

Fifteen

John-Michael was dog-tired. It'd been one hell of a long week, and there was still plenty of work to be done. There was one more round of fall harvesting to do, and they had yet to finish the winter planting. He scraped his boots on the welcome mat at the back door and decided the rest of the work could wait till tomorrow. For now, he was going to take a hot shower and give his paperwork some needed attention.

Heavenly aromas from the kitchen met him at the door, reminding him he had skipped lunch. *Thank goodness Pearl could start immediately.* She wasn't as good a cook as Lena, but with time she could probably get close. And, it was comforting to know someone else was in the house. He didn't feel quite as alone.

He walked in with a big ole smile on his face, prepared to give his recently hired household help a big compliment. Instead of Pearl's pleasingly plump rump bent over the open oven door, a smaller, rounder rear end faced him. The jumpstarting of his heart and the increased blood to his lower extremities told him who it was before she straightened up and turned to face him. The breath caught in his throat.

Olivia smiled timidly. "Hi, John-Michael. Dinner's almost ready." She pulled off the oven glove she had used to check the meat and laid it on the countertop. "Would you like something to drink before dinner?"

"What are you doing here?" he demanded, slapping his work gloves down on the kitchen table. His work jacket followed. In spite of the pain she had caused him, he couldn't stop his body from responding to the sight of her. John-Michael was splitting in half. He wanted to rush to her and kiss her till the cows came home, but he also wanted to hurt her as he was hurting.

She swallowed hard. She had known he wouldn't welcome her with open arms, but she wasn't prepared for out and out hostility. "I gave Pearl the day off. I thought we could have a nice dinner and . . . um . . . talk." Olivia didn't realize she was turning the meat fork around and around in her hands.

"You've got some nerve." He couldn't believe she had gotten more beautiful, but she was. In just ten days and three hours, her curls had grown longer, her lips and hips fuller. She was an oasis in the desert, a welcome neon sign for his lonely eyes and tortured feelings.

"Yes, I do." Olivia moved closer to the table. Closer to her man. She drew her boldness from the knowledge that she could not live another day without him. She was determined to fight for their love . . . and win. "I spoke with Lena several days ago. She told me she and Roberta had moved to the city."

John-Michael crossed his arms across his chest. He didn't say a word. He just watched her move closer and closer.

"She said Roberta was not doing very well. The adjustment's been hard for her."

In a voice as hard and cold as ice, John-Michael said, "Mother's tough. She'll survive."

Olivia blinked and wondered if this was a foolhardy thing she was doing—trying to prove her love to a man who didn't appear interested. She was daunted, but determined to give it her best try. "She also told me you'd been spending some time with your father."

"Lena ought to mind her own business." John-Michael was as still as an iceberg.

"Thank God she didn't, or we would all still be living out our lives as blind as bats and as ignorant as dunces. Anyway, Lena loves us. She can't stand to see the people she cares about miserable." Olivia had reached the table. She laid the fork down and ran her sweaty hands down the sides of her jeans.

John-Michael moved away from her to the cabinet and took out a glass. He filled it with water and drank half the content. Pigs would fly before he told her that simple act of wiping her hands had steamed his insides. He'd needed the water for more than just a thirst quencher. *Just leave, Man! Go upstairs. Shut the door. Get away from her. She'll get the message.* John-Michael knew he should listen to his internal messenger, but his feet were rooted to the spot. Now that she was within eye chart distance, he didn't want to quit looking at her. Wiping his mouth with the back of his hand, he ignored the voice in his head and asked matter-of-factly, "Since we're making small talk, what happened to Micky?"

"He was fired. He moved back home with his dad. I'm not sure what he's doing there. Dan would know. He talks to him almost every day."

"Are you still angry with him?" John-Michael's intent had not been to get pulled into the conversation to this extent, but he cared about this crazy woman standing just a few feet from him, and he had grown to like her co-workers.

"No. I understand his motives." Olivia shrugged her shoulders. "He loves his dad." Olivia thought about her own motives for not believing in John-Michael. When it came down to the bottom line, her excuse had been just as weak as Micky's. Who was she to not forgive a person for a mistake? She promised herself that if John-Michael forgave her and took her back she would sit down and write Micky a long letter.

"I'll call a buddy of mine who can probably get him on the corporate staff of Four-H there in Oklahoma." He wasn't seeking her approval, just telling her what he was going to do.

"Oh, John-Michael, thanks. I really appreciate that." Olivia's face lit up and she automatically took a couple of steps toward him.

"I'm not doing it for you. I like Micky."

Olivia's face fell. She was reminded that she was walking

on very thin ice. "Oh . . . well." Olivia averted her face, hoping he hadn't seen the pain he'd dumped on her. "The state ag department and the university have completely disassociated themselves from Chem-Co, and right now the patents office and the FDA are re-evaluating some of Chem-Co's other products which received approval."

"And, of course, that brings us to you." When she began to speak, he held up a hand and said, "No, no. Let me fill in the blanks. With Micky's confession, I'm sure you were completely exonerated of any wrongdoing. You are once again the Eastern Star at the university, and you'll be starting your next Ph.D. project in what . . . ummmm . . . six months? . . . a year?"

Olivia shook her head. "You got it completely wrong." She moved to stand directly in front of him. She left just enough room for a handshake. She wanted him to know she was completely sincere and honest. "Olivia Foster-Johnson officially withdrew from the university's doctoral program. She quit her staff assistant position and moved out of her apartment in Huntsville."

John-Michael lifted a brow. Actually, he was stunned. He never thought she would give up on acquiring a Ph.D. *Maybe those affirmations and lessons in self value did more good than I thought. Or maybe she's just burned out on school, and needs a break. I sure as hell know it ain't because she loves me. We both know that's old news.*

"Olivia has decided she wants to be the wife of a successful farmer. Through that major ordeal with the study and Roberta's scheming with Alexandria, she realized that the one true constant was the love she has for her husband. And, the love he has for her. And even though she didn't give him enough trust, deep down in her heart she never truly believed he had done the things she claimed he had. Olivia needs a good, loving, gentle man who cares for her and will be her lover in every sense of the word. A man who will continue to teach her about unconditional love and about the joy of forgiving and reconciling."

Olivia unbuttoned her jeans and pushed them past her hips. They fell to the floor with a soft thud; she stepped out of them. The sheer bottom of a black lace teddy showed off her legs and hinted at the excellence cushioned between them. "She, in turn, will worship the ground this farmer walks on. She will give him lots of babies, give him an unlimited supply of emotional support and love. Most importantly, she will help him finish his family tree, and let him win all of the gin rummy tournaments." She pulled the sweatshirt over her head. It joined the jeans on the kitchen floor. Its absence revealed Olivia's scantily clad body.

John-Michael sucked in his breath. His arousal was complete. The tips of her breasts showed through the bra of the teddy, and a string crisscrossing down the front tempted him to pull it to release the dual mounds of pleasure. John-Michael reached out a hand and fingered the string. He surveyed her body, being careful not to touch. He knew that if he touched, he would be lost. And, there was something important he had to say to her. He just couldn't remember what it was. "You think it's that easy, huh?"

"Nothing worthwhile is easy, John-Michael. I'm just asking for your forgiveness and love. That's all I want . . . it's all I've ever wanted . . . for you to love me."

Still fingering the string, greatly tempted, John-Michael looked her in the eyes. "I gave you love, and you tossed it out with the garbage. What's changed?"

"I have." Olivia couldn't resist touching him a second longer. She placed her hands on his face, caressing his cheek, his chin, his forehead, rubbing her thumb across his lips. "I don't know everything about loving a person, John-Michael. You must remember I had poor role models. But, if you're willing to be my teacher, I promise I'll be an A student."

"I told you once before I love you more than anyone or anything. You promised me you would remember that. When the chips fell, you bailed out." John-Michael was having trouble concentrating. His breathing was becoming more restricted.

"You're right. I could stand here and repeat a thousand times 'From now on, Olivia will believe everything her husband says' but you still wouldn't trust me. The only way I can prove to you that I'm in it for the long haul is for you to try me. Test me for a few years, and see if the new and improved Olivia passes the John-Michael Johnson course on love." Olivia took his hand and placed it over one of her breasts. "Or are you afraid to follow your own curriculum?"

A shudder coursed through his body.

Olivia smiled. She covered his other hand and excruciatingly slow, she helped him pull the string holding her little outfit together. "If you forgive me, I promise I'll never hurt you again." Olivia stood on tiptoe and touched their lips. "I love you. Let me come home," she breathed into his mouth.

John-Michael looked into the eyes of his wife and saw all he needed to see. "I'm going to forgive you this time. But, do it again, and I don't know what I'm going to do."

John-Michael bent his head and kissed the smile right off her lips. Soon, they were excitedly all over each other in a desperate attempt to ease their fears and frustrations. John-Michael plowed his tongue deep into Olivia's mouth. She responded with an urgency born of primitive need.

When his hands gripped her backside, pulling her closer to his stiff manhood, they both groaned at the presence of too many clothes. They came apart and together. They stripped John-Michael of his boots, his jeans, and his briefs. Reuniting, their bodies clamored for a complete union. Picking Olivia up, John-Michael dumped her on the counter. He entered her the moment her fanny hit the ceramic tile. Satisfying moans filled the air as they held on to each other for dear life. The rhythm was fast, and increased to a frantic speed until the momentum carried them over the top. Simultaneously, they hit the peak. Tremors racked John-Michael's body as the inconceivable pleasure spasmed throughout his limbs. It had never been that hot, that fast, or that good.

When the world quit spinning, he helped her off the counter. As she slid down the length of him, their lips met in a kiss born of promises and forgiveness.

"I think I tore your pretty outfit," John-Michael whispered into her mouth.

"That's okay. I stopped by the mall on the way here. More of these pretty little things are upstairs on the bed."

John-Michael's head snapped back and he looked deep into his wife's eyes. "Then what are we waiting for?" He grabbed her hand and they hurried up the stairs. For the rest of the night, Olivia modeled for him—in between other things.

Sometime, late, late, late in the night, or perhaps it was early morning, Olivia woke and pinched herself. *Thank goodness for first, second, and third chances.*

Olivia snuggled against her forgiving farmer and drifted into a deep, peaceful sleep.

And So . . .

The buffet was loaded with salads, meats, vegetables, and desserts. The drinks were cold, the music warm, and the guests slowly trickled in.

Lena and Roberta were the first to arrive. For this special occasion, they entered through the front door. They barely had time to place their gifts on the coffee table before the kids pounced. J M, five years old, grabbed his granny around the legs and squeezed as if he hadn't just seen her yesterday. Carter, the second child and three years old going on thirty, threw himself at Lena, and the twelve-month-old baby girl, Pamela, named after Dr. Hill, toddled over in the general direction of the fracas. With her white high-tops and precarious balance, she was much slower than her brothers.

"Hi Mom! Hi Lena!" John-Michael called out. He sat in the middle of the living room floor surrounded by puzzles, games, and toys.

After slobbery kisses, short-armed hugs and general baby talk babble had been exchanged, Lena excused herself to help Pearl in the kitchen. In less than a minute, she was back in the living room. In the six years Pearl had been working at Johnson Farms, she had marked the kitchen as her own territory, Lena didn't mind. It gave her more time and freedom to play with the kids.

The doorbell rang. John-Michael went to answer it.

Mr. and Mrs. Foster, Olivia's parents, several of her sisters and brothers, and a whole army of their kids trampled him.

He laughed, accepting their gifts and hugging as many as he could.

They all headed for the living room, and within minutes the noise level threatened to blow out the downstairs windows. The kids romped and played, the adults talked and laughed.

John-Michael Senior walked in from the direction of the kitchen. He had a handful of licorice sticks. The kids flocked to him as if he were the Pied Piper.

With the room a little more quiet since the kids had candy in their mouths, Mr. Foster asked the room in general, "Where's the guest of honor? Where's my daughter, the doctor?" He teased, but everyone could tell he was proud of his baby. His chest was stuck out, and his eyes were lit up like a Christmas tree light.

"I'll go check on her." John-Michael headed for their bedroom.

After minor construction, including the installation of an intercom system throughout the house, John-Michael and Olivia had moved into Roberta's old suite on the first floor, leaving the upstairs to the children. John-Michael opened the door. Not seeing her in the outer room, he walked into the bathroom.

"Honey. Everyone's out front. What are you doing in here?"

Olivia sat on the closed lid of the toilet with her arms crossed in front of her. She lifted her head.

"Baby, are you okay? You don't look so hot." John-Michael rushed to Olivia and knelt in front of her. He ran his hands up and down her arms. Her skin felt clammy and he could see a thin layer of perspiration above her lip. He put a hand to her forehead. She didn't feel hot, but that didn't mean anything. "Honey, you're sick."

"No, I'm just . . . I can't believe I finally did it. I really have my Ph.D." Amazement colored her words.

John-Michael smiled and rubbed her curls. "Do you want me to pinch you as a reality check?"

Olivia half-smiled. She slumped over and rested a cheek in

her hand. "After the fiasco with my first study I was so sure I didn't want anything else to do with school. But, after I moved back here and accepted that part time researcher's position at Tuskegee, my interest was rekindled."

"And naturally so. I don't think it's any mystery that you're a born researcher. It was as natural for you to fulfill your educational goals as it was for me to be a farmer." John-Michael kissed her lightly on the lips. "Have I told you I'm proud of you. For the past six years you successfully balanced school with motherhood with being a wife." He captured her hands and pulled her up off the seat of the toilet. Pulling her close into his arms, he nuzzled her neck, inhaling her clean, natural smell. "And, I know that just as you were successful in juggling multiple priorities, you will be just as successful in your new position as lead researcher at Tuskegee. Congratulations, Baby."

Olivia wrapped her arms tight around her husband and raising up on tiptoes, planted a kiss on his chin. "Thank you, John-Michael, for being so supportive. I love you so much."

They shared the most tender of kisses, then Olivia pulled back, grinning girlishly.

"Guess what else I have to tell you?"

John-Michael narrowed his eyes and screwed up his face. "What?"

"I wanted to be sure before I said anything." Olivia smiled brightly. "John-Michael, we're pregnant again."

John-Michael searched her eyes, looked down at her stomach, then up again. His lips moved, but no intelligent words came forth. Finally, he sprang up, as if he were on a Pogo stick. "All right! Holy cow!" He shouted. He gave the air high fives, and ran around in circles. Remembering his wife, he went to her and hugged her. Holding her tight, he swung her around. It was the wrong thing to do.

Olivia got sick. They barely got her to the toilet in time.

John-Michael stood behind her, massaging her back and shoulders. Excitement renewed itself, but he managed to contain it. "I'm sorry, Baby, I . . . I just got so excited." He laughed. "This is perfect. Absolutely perfect. We can toast you for getting your Ph.D., then we can toast us, for baby Johnson number four. What a day! What a fantastic day!"

Olivia flushed the toilet and turned to face her husband. "Give me a few minutes to wash my face and brush my teeth, and I'll be right there."

John-Michael hugged her and kissed her loudly on the lips. "I love you, Olivia Johnson."

The wave of nausea had passed. Olivia was beginning to feel like her old self. "I love you too, Mr. Johnson."

He kissed her again and left her to freshen up.

When he got to the door, Olivia cried out after him. "And don't you dare do like last time."

John-Michael looked as innocent as an angel. "What?"

"Tell everyone before I get there."

John-Michael smiled devilishly. "Then don't take too long."

He closed the door, and Olivia knew that as soon as he walked into the living room it would only be a matter of seconds before everyone knew.

She stared at her reflection in the mirror and smiled. She loved that man. How she had ever thought she could live her life without him, she didn't know.

Everything has worked out beautifully, she thought. *We have three, soon to be four, gorgeous, brilliant children. A successful business. A beautiful home. And so much love.*

Six years ago, if anyone had told Olivia she and Roberta could sit in the same room and be civil to one another, she would have laughed in his face. With the stunt Roberta had pulled and the lie she had told John-Michael, Olivia didn't see how she could ever forgive her. But, it had taken her teacher, John-Michael, to remind her yet again that love was forgiving. He had challenged her to forgive his mother as *he* had forgiven her . . . and as he had forgiven Olivia. Impressed by those simple terms, Olivia had changed her stripes. Although it hadn't been easy, she had made a sincere effort to include Roberta in family events and activities.

The most rewarding change had been John-Michael's acceptance of his father. Just as her acceptance of Roberta had not happened overnight, John-Michael had had trouble embracing his father. He'd had to work on it, but over time their relationship had blossomed.

John-Michael Senior had never given up farming. After he left Johnson Farms all those years ago, he had accepted a field supervisor position with a major farm in Mississippi. Naturally, upon learning this, John-Michael convinced him to quit his job and come to work with him at Johnson Farms. The elder John-Michael had been extremely quick to jump on his son's offer.

And she had maintained contact with Dan and Micky.

Tragically, Micky's father had passed away shortly after he moved back to Oklahoma. With his job at Four-H, he'd been able to get out of debt and buy back a lot of their farmland. He had ended up liking his job at Four-H so much that he had given up pursuing a Ph.D. About once a month, he and John-Michael exchanged farming stories. Sometimes, they even let Olivia in on the conversation.

Dan finally snatched his dream. He retired from the state job and got acquainted with every fishing hole in the great state of Alabama. He was harder to keep in touch with than Micky, since they didn't have telephone lines at his favorite fishing places.

The grandchildren were the big winners. They had a loving mother and father, and grandparents who spoiled them rotten. Their childhood was built on hugs, kisses, love, strict discipline, positive affirmation, and absolutely, positively, no lying.

Olivia turned off the water and wiped her mouth. Quickly, she applied a thin coat of lipstick then ran to the living room to accept . . . unconditional love.

Dear Reader,

At booksignings and various other appearances, I'm often asked where I get the ideas for my stories. My answer has always been from a variety of sources such as TV commercials, news articles, conversations with family, friends, songs, etc. Never once in reciting those sources did I mention dreaming as an origination point, but now I have to add that to the list because John-Michael and Olivia's story came to me in a dream.

I can't say I dreamt the book from beginning to end, but when I woke up, I remembered certain elements like: a strong bond between mother and son, a sexy farmer and a studious pixy of a woman. I also remembered that the "dream" was set in the south and that I would somehow reconcile a marriage. The rest of the "dream" I had to fill in as I wrote.

And, boy, did I have fun writing this book! The characters were so deeply rooted in my mind and the plot so clearly outlined that the book practically wrote itself.

My favorite character was Roberta. I had a great time writing Roberta's lines and delving into the reasons for her character flaws. So many times, in the telling of a story, I don't have time to examine secondary characters but with Roberta, I didn't have a choice. Once she came on the scene, she demanded her "white space" and threatened to overshadow John-Michael and Olivia. Talk about a character growing larger than life!

In any case, I hope John-Michael and Olivia's story was satisfying to you, the reader. I heard from many of you after the release of *After Hours,* my first novel, and I pray *Second Time Around* is the type of story that inspires you to write me as well. I really enjoy reading your comments and appreciate the feedback.

And, for those of you waiting for Heather and Gerald's story (secondary characters in *After Hours*)—fear not! For its publication date, tentatively scheduled for June 1998, is around the corner. Look for it. I think you'll enjoy it!

Sincerely,

Anna Larence

Anna Larence
Post Office Box 17875
Dallas, Texas 75217-0875

About the Author

Anna began writing professionally in 1990 and since then has published two novels. *After Hours,* her first book, was highly successful, entering its second printing mere months after its initial release. She credits her writing accomplishments to faith in God Almighty, to family, and to various writing organizations. She makes her home in Dallas, Texas.

Look for these upcoming Arabesque titles:

SENSUAL AND HEARTWARMING
ARABESQUE ROMANCES FEATURE
AFRICAN-AMERICAN CHARACTERS!

BEGUILED   (0046, $4.99)
by Eboni Snoe
After Raquel agrees to impersonate a missing heiress for just one night,
a daring abduction makes her the captive of seductive Nate Bowman.
Across the exotic Caribbean seas to the perilous wilds of Central America . . . and into the savage heart of desire, Nate and Raquel play a
dangerous game. But soon the masquerade will be over. And will they
then lose the one thing that matters most . . . their love?

WHISPERS OF LOVE   (0055, $4.99)
by Shirley Hailstock
Robyn Richards had to fake her own death, change her identity, and
forever forsake her husband, Grant, after testifying against a crime syndicate. But, five years later, the daughter born after her disappearance
is in need of help only Grant can give. Can Robyn maintain her disguise
from the ever present threat of the syndicate—and can she keep herself
from falling in love all over again?

HAPPILY EVER AFTER   (0064, $4.99)
by Rochelle Alers
In a week's time, Lauren Taylor fell madly in love with famed author
Cal Samuels and impulsively agreed to be his wife. But when she
abruptly left him, it was for reasons she dared not express. Five years
later, Cal is back, and the flames of desire are as hot as ever, but, can
they start over again and make it work this time?

ROMANCES ABOUT AFRICAN-AMERICANS!
YOU'LL FALL IN LOVE
WITH ARABESQUE BOOKS FROM PINNACLE

SERENADE   (0024, $4.99)
by Sandra Kitt

Alexandra Morrow was too young and naive when she first fell
in love with musician, Parker Harrison—and vowed never to be
so vulnerable again. Now Parker is back and although she tries
to resist him, he strolls back into her life as smoothly as the jazz
rhapsodies for which he is known. Though not the dreamy innocent she was before, Alexndra finds her defenses quickly crum-
bling and her mind, body and soul slowly opening up to her one
and only love, who shows her that dreams do come true.

FOREVER YOURS   (0025, $4.50)
by Francis Ray

Victoria Chandler must find a husband quickly or her grandparents will call in the loans that support her chain of lingerie bou-
tiques. She arranges a mock marriage to tall, dark and handsome
ranch owner Kane Taggart. The marriage will only last one year,
and her business will be secure, and Kane will be able to walk
away with no strings attached. The only problem is that Kane
has other plans for Victoria. He'll cast a spell that will make her
his forever after.

A SWEET REFRAIN   (0041, $4.99)
by Margie Walker

Fifteen years before, jazz musician Nathaniel Padell walked out
on Jenine to seek fame and fortune in New York City. But now
the handsome widower is back with a baby girl in tow. Jenine is
still irresistibly attracted to Nat and enchanted by his daughter.
Yet even as love is rekindled, an unexpected danger threatens
Nat's child. Now, Jenine must fight for Nat before someone stops
the music forever!

*Available wherever paperbacks are sold, or order direct from the
Publisher. Send cover price plus 50¢ per copy for mailing and
handling to Penguin USA, P.O. Box 999, c/o Dept. 17109,
Bergenfield, NJ 07621. Residents of New York and Tennessee
must include sales tax. DO NOT SEND CASH.*

TIMELESS LOVE

Look for these historical romances in the Arabesque line:

BLACK PEARL by Francine Craft (0236-0, $4.99)

CLARA'S PROMISE by Shirley Hailstock (0147-X, $4.99)

MIDNIGHT MOON by Mildred Riley (0200-X; $4.99)

SUNSHINE AND SHADOWS by Roberta Gayle (0136-4, $4.99)